Dead Money

A Jack Mowgley Crime Thriller

George East

A La Puce Publication
www.la-puce.co.uk

Dead Money

Published by La Puce Publications

website: www.la-puce.co.uk

© George East 2014

First printed in paperback 2018
Typesetting and design by Francesca Brooks

The author asserts the moral right to be identified as the author of this work.
All rights reserved. No part of this publication may be reproduced, stored in a retrieval system, or transmitted in any form or by any means, electronic, mechanical, photocopying, recording or otherwise, without the prior permission of the publisher

paperback ISBN: 9781908747266
mobi-kindle version ISBN 9781908747242

More about George East at www.george-east.net

Other Books by George East

The Mill of the Flea series

Home & Dry in France
René & Me
French Letters
French Flea Bites
French Cricket
French Kisses
French Lessons

French Impressions series

Brittany
The Loire Valley
The Dordogne River
Lower Normandy

also

150 Fabulous Foolproof French Regional Recipes
by Donella East

The Naked Truth series

How to write a bestseller
France and the French
The Truth About Women
The Truth About Dieting

Jack Mowgley Crime Thrillers

Death Duty
Deadly Tide
Death á la Carte

Other Titles

A Year Behind Bars

Home & Dry in Normandy
French Kisses
(compilations from Orion)

Detective Inspector Jack Mowgley's patch is a Continental ferry port on the south coast. Critics say he sees himself as sheriff of a frontier town in the Old West, maintaining order by applying his own form of sometimes rough justice. The hard man with a soft centre certainly sees himself as an old-fashioned policeman in a too-rapidly changing world.

Alarms sound when a pensioner on his way to a holiday in Spain collapses with a heart attack and is found to be wearing a money belt stuffed with cash. Inspector Mowgley decides to investigate, and the maverick policeman finds himself encountering a series of bizarre and grisly deaths…

What readers say about Jack Mowgley:

"Deliciously non-PC."

"Jack's the Lad for me."

"Deceptively clever, funny and eminently readable."

"At last, a hero for our times - if you're fed up with political correctness gone mad."

'As an ex-CID officer, what I really like is the way the author gets the right 'feel' for the main characters. Even nowadays, policemen (and women) do make politically incorrect remarks and cut corners for the sake of a result. It was much more common in the times Mr East is writing about. I also like the way he does not neatly tie up all the loose ends in the final chapter. As one of the fictional detectives says (and I know to be true), crime usually leaves more questions than answers.'

Main Characters
(roughly in order of appearance)

Detective Inspector Jack Mowgley:
Officer in charge of police affairs and interests at the City's continental ferry port.

Det. Sgt. Catherine McCarthy:
Mowgley's fierce defender, conscience, confidante and drinking companion.

Det. Constable Stephen Mundy:
Son of Mowgley's former boss and junior member of the Fun Factory crew.

Detective Inspector Dave Hopkirk:
Drug Squad officer and long-term friend of DI Mowgley.

Michael Finlayson:
Premier League drug trafficker aka Mickey Finn.

Sarah Wheatcroft:
Daughter of money-smuggling OAPs.

Andy Wheatcroft:
Brother of above.

Det. Superintendent Jane Stanton:
Very special Special Projects Unit Officer.

DS 'Dickie' Quayle:
Efficient but generally unloved member of Team Mowgley.

Detective Superintendent Brand:
Mowgley's new boss.

DS Karen Ross:
Drug Squad officer and lover of DI Hopkirk.

DCI Iain Gentley:
Internal Affairs Special Case Investigator.

Teniente Coronel Juan Romero:
Senior Spanish *Guardia Civil* officer.

Offender Profile

Name: John ('Jack') Mowgley.

Rank: Detective Inspector (just).

D.O.B. 31.1.50.

Height: 5ft 11 inches.

Weight: 16 –17 stones (depending).

Body shape: Lumpy.

Distinguishing features: 'ACAB' tattooed on fingers of left hand. Scar on right temple. Frequently broken nose. Right earlobe mislaid.

Eyes: Two.

Teeth: Mostly.

Hair: Dark, copious and untended.

Facial type: Lived-in (as if by squatters).

Favourite haunt: Any proper pub, but mostly his local, The Ship Leopard.

Favourite activity: Drinking in proper pubs like The Leo.

Favourite drink: Any cheap lager.

Favourite smoke: Any duty-free rolling tobacco.

Favourite food: Indian/fry-ups.

Favourite film star: Paul Newman in *Hombre* and *Cool Hand Luke*.

Favourite film/s: See above.

Favourite film themes: Amongst others, *'The Trap'* *'The Magnificent Seven'*, *'633 Squadron'* and *'The Great Escape'*.

Favourite music: Country & Western.

Favourite song: *'Ring of Fire'*.

Favourite singer: Johnny Cash.

Heroes: Father & mother, Winston Churchill, Margaret Thatcher, Dennis Skinner MP, Muhammad Ali.

Politics: Left, Right and Centre (depending).

Ideal woman: Modest, demure, caring and companionable, with really big tits.

Author's Notes

The usual thanks are due to editrix Sally Moore and designer Fran Brooks.
Special thanks are due to a number of Portsmouth CID's finest during the 1970s, 80s and 90s. Old and sometimes arresting friends include Dougie, Floodie, Hoppy, Nick-Nick, Bingabong, Ace, Jock, Trev... and most of all 'Mad–Eye' Big John Mosley. Mind how you go, lads.

Fact: Police officers with Special Branch accreditation are based at all UK continental ferry ports. Their brief is to investigate all criminal matters taking place within or affecting the port, and detain British and foreign criminals or suspected criminals passing through their domain.

Fiction: Although based in part on real people, places and events, the characters and events and places featuring in this story are all works of complete fiction.

Prologue

The man was slumped forward, head down and arms outstretched to either side at shoulder level. His hair was long and tangled and wet from the sea, and was crowned with a circle of barbed wire.

The grim tableau reminded Mowgley of the life-sized crucifixion scene above the altar at the church he attended every Sunday as a small boy. He had not attended regularly because he had been religious, but because there was a cream bun and cup of tea in the Vicarage after the service as a reward for a show of piety and attention. He had noticed that one or another of the prettier boys would be invited to stay behind afterwards, but had thought nothing of it until the Vicar had been arrested and charged with what was commonly known in those less concerned times as kiddie-fiddling. On later reflection he took being passed over for special attention as some compensation for being an ugly child.

More barbed wire secured the drowned man's arms to one of the barnacle-encrusted lateral struts stretching between the massive iron pillars on which the pier sat. His killer or killers had obviously chosen a strut which was of a height to ensure that their victim was just able to stand on tiptoe. This, Mowgley realised with a wince, was not to allow him to take the strain off his arms, but to ensure he would remain conscious for the maximum time it took the incoming tide to reach his mouth and nose.

'I suppose, what with it being February,' Mowgley observed, 'they weren't too worried about any courting couples hearing him shout for help.'

'Not much danger of that, mate' his colleague said dryly, 'they cut his tongue out before they left him to wait for the tide.'

one

She found him at breakfast in Ginger's Caff.

Detective Inspector Mowgley was in his favourite seat at a window facing the car park. Had he chosen another table he could have looked out over the Solent waters and the entrance to Portsmouth harbour. Nelson had sailed from here on HMS Victory; nowadays there was a constant movement of less striking but pleasingly varied vessels.

Detective Sergeant McCarthy had once asked him why he chose to look over at a car park rather than the swirling green waters and the craft which passed over them. Mowgley had replied that looking at the passing ships made him think of all the exotic places he would rather be. It was not for nothing, he reminded her, that American sailors liked to call Portsmouth The Shitty City.

After death-raying one of a pair of beefy draymen who had made the potentially dangerous error of winking at her as she passed, DS McCarthy arrived at Mowgley's table. She saw he was studying a copy of the *Daily Mail*, and that the page he was reading had suffered collateral damage from the sauce dribbling out of a large plastic tomato. The squeezee dispensers were dated even in comparison with the general vintage of the fixtures and fittings, but, as Mowgley said, Ginger was nothing if not a traditionalist.

Alongside the plate containing the remains of the All Day Bumper Breakfast was an ashtray overflowing with roll-up butts and a pint mug. The mug had *Always on the Job* printed on its side, and had been presented to Inspector Mowgley by the proprietor. It had been a token of appreciation for his assistance in the matter of convincing a posse of would-be gangsters that Ginger's caff would not be joining their proposed protection scheme. Two of the gang members were still receiving Out-Patient treatment.

DS McCarthy took a seat and they regarded each other in silence for a moment. Then he said: 'Hello, you. I suppose I'd better ask what you're doing here.'

She waved a piece of paper with a number scrawled on it. 'I've just ordered a bacon sandwich.'

'Good for you. Just make sure you put brown sauce on it.'

'Why?'

'Because as you well know, it is The Law. Red sauce and mustard on hot dogs. Brown sauce on bacon sarnies. You have free rein with sausages, but purists go for brown. If Ginger catches you breaking the house rules you could get us barred.'

She shook her head in tolerant exasperation as Mowgley emptied his mug and reached for his baccy pouch. 'Okay,' he sighed. 'I surrender. You want to talk about work, don't you?'

'Not particularly, but I think we should. Something's come up at work and everyone's been trying to get hold of you. As you only have one set of jacket and trousers and are wearing them, I must assume you left your mobile at the Midnight Tindaloo, pawned it or lost it in a game of chance at the pub again?'

Mowgley pantomimed a search of his pockets, then shrugged unconvincingly: 'I'm sure I had it when I left home. I probably left it in the car.'

'You don't have a car.'

'Then it can't be there. I seem to remember a little wager with Pompey Fats on a game of pool at The Leo last night. I was out of funds so left it as collateral. A good excuse to drop in at lunchtime, and pay our debts and get my phone back, actually.'

'Our debts?'

He pantomimed a look of deep hurt. 'I thought we were partners, Sergeant. Anyway, you know I can't get on with the bloody handset. All this newfangled technology stuff gets in the way of good policing.'

'We've been using mobile phones since 1995. You've had nearly a decade to get used to using one.'

He grimaced. 'Yes, but in the early days they were a sensible size and you couldn't lose something the size of a car battery very easily. Anyway, I've had more than a year to get used to the idea of having a double-barrelled fast-track middle-class university-educated woman as my boss, and that hasn't worked.'

'Better get used to it. It's the shape of things to come.'

'I suppose so. Your lot are taking over everywhere, aren't they? Bit too late for you at your age, but your daughter could do well. If you had one.'

Mowgley looked into the future and shuddered, then paused as his sergeant's bacon sandwich and his refill arrived. 'So what have you come to get me for? An overboard, bits of a body in a cabin, or someone passing out whilst having a bunk-up in a bunk on the overnight crossing from Cherbourg?'

'None of the above. An elderly man collapsed before boarding the early morning boat to Santander.'

'What, when he saw what they were asking for a pint in the terminal bar?'

'Nope. He was pulled over for a random check by Customs, and collapsed with what looks like a stroke.'

'Ah. Not a nice way to start your holiday. I believe the boys can be a bit intimidating and surly on an early shift. But why is it our business?'

She cleared her mouth of bacon and bread, then said: 'When the paramedics arrived, they found he was wearing a money belt.'

Mowgley took a long swig of tea and pointed to a spot of brown sauce on her cheek. 'So what's the problem? Some older folk feel a bit nervous about taking a bit of ready cash to a foreign land.'

DS McCarthy dabbed at the spot with a paper serviette, then put her sandwich on the plate. 'He was understandably nervous. At a guestimate, my mate in Customs reckons the belt's got the thick end of fifty thousand pounds in it.'

Mowgley started to show interest. 'Blimey, matey must have been planning quite a holiday. So what's to do now?'

'Stephen's gone to the hospital with the old man and his wife. They've got the belt at the Customs shed. I thought you might want to, as we are supposed to say, look into it.'

'Too right. And we need to get there before those Revenue boys start helping themselves.'

*

In spite of dwindling numbers of ships and men to crew them, Portsmouth is still best known as the home of the Royal Navy. Its dockyard dates back to the thirteenth century. Visitors can inspect the remains of Henry VIII's doomed flagship the Mary Rose, or stumble over the raised plaque marking the spot where the Lord Admiral Nelson fell on the quarterdeck of HMS Victory.

As ruling the waves became less of a factor in the country's post-war Defence strategy, the role of the senior service diminished ever more rapidly. Consequently, the importance to the City of commercial traffic and making the use of its location increased.

The Continental Ferry Port was established in 1976, built on four acres reclaimed from Portsmouth Harbour. By the start of the new Millennium the ferry port had expanded in size tenfold, with approaching a million vehicles and three million people passing through its gates each year. The vehicles were a mixture of freight lorries, coaches and cars. The people were a mixture of business and leisure travellers and miscreants. Smugglers of contraband in all its forms, criminals on the run and the odd domestic murderer or international terrorist regularly attempted entry or exit through the port. A number of local opportunists - or duckers and divers as they are known in the trade – also make an illicit living off the port.

All these people and their activities came technically within the remit of Detective Inspector Jack Mowgley and his handful of officers and support staff.

In conjunction with their colleagues in HM Revenue & Customs, it was down to the members of Team Mowgley to take an interest in all those who arrived at the gates of the port from either direction bearing criminal intent or having been up to no good. It was also the team's job to follow up intelligence leads, investigate any relevant criminal activity connected with the ferry port, and, as Mowgley would say, generally to keep the lid on.

Every Continental ferry port in the United Kingdom would have its own Special Branch accredited Mowgley. It was generally agreed by those who knew him that there could be few with his singular approach to the requirements of the job.

As with many a senior officer of what had become known as the Old School, Mowgley had long since learned the benefits of taking a pragmatic approach to his role. To him, keeping things on a fairly even keel was the main objective. It was the intent rather than the letter of the law which should be observed. And he was certainly not going to go without his supply of duty-free tobacco and alcohol.

In a disorderly and unjust world, he tried to bring at least a degree of order and justice to his small area of responsibility. Sometimes and if there were no other way, his justice could fairly be called rough.

*

Come August and hundreds of vehicles would be shuffling past the check-in kiosks and into the appropriate lines marked out in the giant marshalling yard. Somehow, all those cars and lorries would be guided more or less intact across the link spans connecting the mainland to the insides of hopefully the right ferry boat.

As it was February, there was an air of almost quietude as DS McCarthy drove Mowgley down the road alongside the single-storey terminal building. As those who worked in it often observed, the terminal building was in a terminal condition.

Designed to match the tastes and needs of an earlier generation and provide services for a much smaller headcount of passengers, the squat, ugly building reminded Mowgley of one of those rickety clapboard airports seen in television news items reporting on another civil war in Africa.

Beyond the terminal, DS McCarthy found a parking spot near where the non-commercial vehicles were queuing to move from the marshalling yard into the port proper. Their drivers and passengers sat obediently watching the high-visibility-jacketed stewards for the signal to proceed. Mowgley enjoyed watching these ushers in action from his vantage point in the Fun Factory, and would often mark them for style and general performance.

Some were natural performers and would give over-exaggerated gestures and facial expressions as they mouthed silently at the drivers. The real artistes would twist round in a balletic manner as if he could propel the vehicles in the right direction by the sheer force of his bodily movements.

Other misanthropic types would point accusingly at the driver, then use the same finger to indicate the obvious direction he or she must follow. Some were clearly fans of a minimalistic approach, and would do no more than nod in the general direction of the gateway to the rest of Europe.

In France, their opposite numbers generally lived up to national stereotyping. Some clearly relished the opportunity to wave their arms with Gallic abandon. Like many French civil servants, some seemed to take pleasure in obfuscation, pointing at different cars and in different directions during the same action.

As the cars, campers, vans and motor cycles moved slowly forward from the Portsmouth marshalling yard they would come under the eye of a number of uniformed officials representing her Majesty's Revenue and Customs Service. This was a nervous time, for seasoned passengers, as they knew they might be pulled peremptorily out of the line like predators snatching fishes from a shoal.

Mowgley had never quite understood the logic of the apparently random stopping of travellers at this point. He knew that sometimes Customs would be acting on a tip-off or watching for a known face or licence number, but it seemed odd to choose to delay a carful of middle-aged and middle class people and ask them where they were going and why. Strangely, it seemed to him that those guarding the kingdom's borders often showed more interest in travellers leaving the country than those entering it.

This seemed a strange preoccupation, as a significant part of the job description of Customs was to help prevent the importation into the UK of dangerous goods. These would include firearms, drugs, endangered species of animals and excessive amounts of tobacco and alcohol on which the proper and full UK duty had not been paid.

In the environs of the ferry port, the stop-and-search powers of Customs officers were virtually limitless. Officers could lay hands on and investigate any vehicle or person (including orifices) without having to justify their actions. Mowgley had once tried to find out what the hit and success rate was, but had been refused access to records. Logic dictated there had to be statistics detailing the number of successful actions by the Revenue and what was discovered. Equally obviously, there could be no record of the quantity of illegal goods and humans who made it through the ferry and air ports each year.

Across the Channel it was generally agreed by seasoned cross-Channel smugglers that the best time to attempt to enter or leave a French port was when it rained, or during the sacred Gallic lunch hours. On the UK side, there were no such helpful pointers. According to the lore of the ferry port, apart from tip-offs, the officers worked mostly on intuition. As Mowgley knew from a Customs drinking companion, boredom, the nearness of an end of shift or simple bloody-mindedness would often be the spur.

*

According to the senior officer on the shift, the pulling over of the small camper carrying an elderly couple en route to northern Spain was a random action. The vehicle had been ushered into an inspection bay with the intention of no more than a cursory enquiry before speeding the driver and his companion on their way. But, the officer had said, there had been something not quite kosher about the driver's response.

Inspector Mowgley and his sergeant were sitting at a desk occupying most of the limited space in a cubicle in one corner of the largest inspection bay. At one end stood a camper which appeared to be a small delivery van on top of which a box had been welded.

Two metal-topped tables stretched for most of the bay's length, and the barn-like structure was illuminated by a series of neon tubes. On one of the tables lay a large suitcase of a traditional design. It was open, and alongside it was a matching valise, the zip undone to its full extent.

The man in charge of the shift was Geoffrey Thompson, a Senior Preventative Officer who was hoping soon to be an Assistant Chief Preventative Officer. He was one of the few people at the ferry port who Mowgley had found impossible to even rub along with. If asked, most of the thirty seven people employed in a fairly senior official capacity at the port would probably say they thought Inspector Mowgley was not the sort of officer they would have chosen or expected to be in his position. But as long as he kept out of their spheres of influence and his actions did not impact upon their business, his ramshackle appearance and reputation might even enhance their reputations for effectiveness and efficiency.

There were, however, exceptions to this general rule, and the duty chief officer was one of them. He did not like Mowgley, and seemed actually offended by his presence. This was not a problem for the detective inspector, but clearly nettled his sergeant.

In the cubicle and on the desk between the two police officers and the Revenue official was what looked like a cross between an ammunition belt and the sort of support worn by men who like to lift weighty objects for a hobby. The belt was khaki in colour and made of some form of webbing material. Apart from a couple of pouches, the main length of the belt was occupied by a zip fastener, and the whole thing bulged like a recently fed African rock python.

'What do you mean, 'not quite kosher'?'

The SPO looked at Mowgley as if he were a suspicious package, then sat back in his chair and smoothed his tie: 'He was clearly more nervous than an innocent traveller need be. And he started sweating noticeably when asked about where he was going and why.'

DS McCarthy held a hand up. 'Isn't breaking into a sweat one of the observable symptoms of an impending heart attack?'

'I wouldn't know,' said the officer coldly, transferring his disapproving look to her. 'It's certainly an observable symptom of someone who is feeling uneasy that they have been stopped.'

'I bet.' Mowgley nodded at the swollen belt: 'So when did you find that - when you frisked him?'

The Customs officer looked even more irritated, then said: 'We didn't get as far as 'frisking' him. He and his wife were asked to bring their baggage into the inspection bay. While their luggage was being inspected and someone was looking at the vehicle, Mr Wheatcroft clearly suffered some sort of seizure and collapsed. We immediately called for an ambulance and went through the standard resuscitation process.'

Mowgley nodded in what he hoped might be an approving

manner. 'So when did the money belt come to light?'

'When the paramedics arrived, one of them removed Mr Wheatcroft's coat and jacket and unbuttoned his shirt. That's when it showed. The medic said he first thought it was some sort of truss, but my officer realised it was a money belt.'

Mowgley nodded in solemn approval: 'What happened next?'

'The paramedics took Mr Wheatcroft to hospital and his wife went with him in the ambulance. As standing orders require, we then called you to notify you of the event. Or rather we tried to call you.'

'So I believe,' said Mowgley, 'I was out of range.'

'Your mobile was out of range?'

'It's a long story. So how much is in the belt?'

The officer looked pointedly at his watch and stood up. 'We haven't counted it yet. Now, if there's nothing else...'

McCarthy looked at Mowgley, who shook his head imperceptibly and stood up. Then he looked down at the belt. 'No, nothing more at the moment... Charlie. I suppose we should take the belt and its contents into safe custody.'

The officer gave the thin-lipped smile of a man unused to showing amusement. 'It will be quite safe in our custody, inspector. And anyway, we would need to count it and make note of the amount before handing it over.'

'Of course.' Mowgley took a last look at the belt, resisted the temptation to say he would send an officer to be present for the counting, and was turning away when the door to the cubicle opened.

'Sorry sir, I thought you'd want to know. I just spoke to the hospital.'

The messenger was Detective Constable Stephen Mundy. He was a tall, slim young man with a prematurely receding hairline, a beaky nose and large, round eyes. With his stoop and general air of uncertainty, when they had first met he had reminded Mowgley of a new-born eaglet fallen from its nest.

Over the three years they had worked together, DC Mundy had proved to be a diligent and intelligent officer with a flair for the job and an unwavering loyalty to Mowgley. This was more than could be said for his father. Before the first-ever female senior officer in the city had taken over, the post had been held by Chief Superintendant Cyril Mundy, who was not a fan of

Mowgley's unusual and independent attitudes to police work. It was thought in some quarters that Mundy Senior had had his son seconded to Team Mowgley to act as a fifth columnist. In fact, Mundy the Younger had applied for the post without reference to his father.

Now, Mundy senior had retired and passed on to his Heavenly reward and his place as top police dog in the city been awarded to a very representative, representative of modern policing, Detective Chief Superintendent Cressida Hartley-Whitley. When Mundy Maximus had left the Force, Mowgley had thought the world was turning in his favour. When he met his new superior officer, the words 'frying pan' and 'fire' came unbidden to mind.

'Ah, Young Stephen. What news from the infirmary, lad? Is our sweating man sitting up and taking nourishment and enquiring as to the whereabouts of his money belt?'

Mundy looked awkwardly at the DS as if seeking help in delivering the news, then said: 'I'm afraid not, sir. Mr Wheatcroft was pronounced dead on arrival at the hospital.'

two

'Pan fried? Pan bloody fried? Can you tell me how else you can fry something but in a bloody frying pan? In a sock, or a hot water bottle or a copy of A Tale of Two Cities?'

'Sorry pardon?' DS McCarthy looked momentarily up from her crossword. 'Was that a private rant or did you wish to share it?'

Mowgley tossed the recipe book on to his desk. 'It's all such bullshit now.'

His sergeant returned her attention to 12 across. 'Mmmm? What is?'

'Cooking in particular and everything in general. In the old days it was all so simple. Fanny and Johnny and Delia just telling you how to make a nice stew. Now it's confit of sparrow's leg covered with gravy pronounced "jew".'

She sighed and put her pen down. 'Since when were you interested in cooking? Your idea of a varied cuisine is curry and chips or pasty and chips or chips and chips.'

'That's not the point. I'm just really fed up with people being so...pretentious. Why can't they be ordinary?'

'What do you mean, "ordinary"? '

'Well, like me...and you.'

'You mean you reckon you and me are alike?'

'Well, we are, in a lot of ways.'

'Thanks,' said McCarthy dryly. 'Anyway, why were you looking at that cookbook?'

Mowgley made the face of a petulant child. 'I'm bored.

Can't we go down the pub?'

'Not until Stephen gets here.' She pointed at the stack of paper piled on her boss's desk. 'If you want something to do, you could make a start on that lot...'

Mowgley snorted, got up and walked to the window, looking morosely down at the car park and the ferry port beyond. 'Don't be silly.' Then his expression brightened. 'Ah, saved by the bell.'

'What, has the wonky fire alarm gone off again?'

'No. Mundy Minor is here. That's a thought.'

'What is?'

'If his dad had been called Morris, he would have been Morris Minor.'

*

'So, Mr Wheatcroft is or was not the sort of person you would expect to have a few grand in readies about his person when going on holiday?'

'No sir.' DC Mundy was standing in front of Mowgley's desk, his note book in his right hand, his other fiddling with the knot of his tie. Mowgley had his feet up and was folding a piece of paper; Sergeant McCarthy was perched on her usual corner of the desk.

'Carry on then, son.' Mowgley smiled encouragingly. 'Tell us what your enquiries have revealed.'

Mundy cleared his throat, smoothed back an errant strand of hair and continued his report.

As he explained, Frank Wheatcroft came from a long-established Portsmouth family and had been 74 at the time of his collapse at the ferry port. He had lived with his wife Peggy in the same terraced, two-bedroom house in the north of the city since they had married in 1951. They had rented the property for twenty years, then taken advantage of a scheme allowing them to buy it. Mr Wheatcroft had worked for more than fifty years as a slinger in the dockyard. Mrs Wheatcroft had retired from her part time job in the local Co-op about a year ago.

'And what might a slinger be?' interrupted Mowgley. 'Is that where the expression to sling your hook comes from?'

'Possibly sir. I think a slinger is the man who puts the straps or slings around things to connect them to the hook of the crane.'

'Not a demanding or particularly well-paid post, then?'

'I should think not, sir.'

'Certainly not the sort of job that would have enabled the Wheatcrofts to prance around Spain with a belt stuffed with dosh, I would have said.'

'No sir.'

'Anything else, Stephen?' DS McCarthy asked. 'What about the neighbours?'

'On one side there's a family from Bangladesh who don't speak much English and didn't know their neighbours, Sergeant. But the couple on the other side have been there almost as long as the Wheatcrofts.'

'And were they more forthcoming?' asked Mowgley.

'They were quite happy to talk to me, sir. They said that Mr and Mrs Wheatcroft had always lived very modestly, and as far as they knew had no more coming in to the house than the state pension and a small one from the dockyard.'

Mowgley launched the paper plane. It missed the open window, hit the frame and fluttered to the floor. He frowned and then reached for his tobacco pouch. 'So where did the dosh for this diddy little van thing come from - and the trip to Spain, let alone the corset stuffed with readies?'

'According to the neighbours, they bought the Bedford Bambi at about the same time as they started to visit their holiday home in southern Spain.'

Mowgley and his sergeant sat up straighter and exchanged glances, then spoke as one: 'Holiday home?'

The young DC looked momentarily worried, as if their reaction implied a criticism of his work. 'Yes, sir...sergeant. Mrs and Mrs Wilson - the neighbours - said their daughter bought it for her parents as a fiftieth anniversary present. The Wheatcrofts had been to Spain on package holidays several times when younger, and it had been their dream to own a holiday home there.'

'So who is this daughter?' DS McCarthy asked. 'She must have a nice few bob or a very good job to buy her aged parents a place in the sun.'

'Mrs Wilson said that Sarah Wheatcroft did very well at school, then went to university and got a degree in chemistry.

They believe she works for a big pharmaceutical company and is based in London. Mrs Wilson said the house is somewhere in some mountains in the south of Spain and she's seen pictures of the town but could not remember what it's called.'

'Thank the Lord for nosy neighbours,' said Mowgley.

'I don't think the Wilsons are particularly nosey, sir. They were just passing on what they had been told.'

'Well said, Stephen.' The sergeant took Mowgley's tobacco pouch and began to roll herself a slim cigarette. 'And do we know how to get in touch with the daughter?'

Mundy glanced down at his notebook. 'The Wilsons said she is down from London, consoling her mother, sergeant.'

'Okay. And are there any other children?'

Mundy consulted his notebook again. 'There's a son - Andrew. The Wilsons say he was a late child and came along some years after his sister. They think he's in his early 30s.'

'Anything known?'

The young detective looked disconcerted. 'I didn't think to look him up as yet, sir- '

Mowgley held up a reassuring hand. 'Don't mither yourself son. I meant is there any info on him from the neighbours, not from the C.R.O?'

Mundy looked relieved, then referred again to his pad: 'The Wilsons said he was a bit of what they called a tearaway as a youngster, sir. The parents persuaded him to join the army a decade ago. They don't know which branch or regiment, but say he often has a suntan when he comes home to see his parents.'

'And do they know where he is at the moment?'

'They said he is at the family home on compassionate leave, sir.'

'With or without a suntan?'

Mundy again looked flustered. 'They didn't say and I didn't ask, sir...'

'I was only being facetious, lad. And finally finally, did you get any idea of how the old lady is?'

'Erm, obviously very upset sir. As you instructed, I did not try and contact her, but I left a message with the Wilsons that you would need to speak to her in the near future.'

'Good work, my son,' said Mowgley. 'Go and get your coat and you can take us down the pub for lunch.'

As Mundy put his notebook away and exited the office, Mowgley stood up, reached for his overcoat and began to struggle into it. 'Do you know,' he said, 'this allegedly rain

-proof smother has shrunk in the rain.'

McCarthy was unfolding the paper aeroplane she had retrieved from the floor. 'It may be that it's just you getting even fatter,' then: 'Hello Hello.'

Mowgley looked hurt, then patted his paunch and said: 'That's what all you coppers say.'

'What, that you're getting fatter?'

'No, 'Hello Hello.' Did you know that 'hello' was originally an expression of surprise and only became a greeting after people started saying it when they picked a phone up and heard someone talking at the other end of the line?'

'So I used it in the right context then.'

'Why? Did my paper-folding skills surprise you?'

'No, this is my expenses sheet from last month. It could have gone out of the window.'

Mowgley shrugged as best he could while encumbered by the overcoat. 'It could have been worse.'

'How so?'

'It could have been my expenses sheet...'

As his sergeant was about to point out that Mowgley had not made out an expenses claim since she had known him, the desk phone rang. She spoke briefly with the caller and then hung up.

'That was someone you do not like, wasn't it?' Mowgley observed.'

'What makes you think that?'

'Elementary, my dear sergeant. It was the way you looked as if someone had just farted in your face. So who was it?'

'Your mate on the drug squad.'

'Hoppy? What did he want?'

'He wanted to know if you were free for lunch.'

Mowgley grunted. 'He's only after an official introduction to Twiggy the barmaid at the Ship.'

DS McCarthy shook her head. 'He wants you to meet him at the pier. He said there's something nasty underneath it you might want to see.'

'What, a dead cuttlefish or the all-year round nudist swimming society?'

'No. He said it's a body...

three

Although found elsewhere on the planet, it is generally agreed (at least amongst the English) that there is something quintessentially English about the seaside pleasure pier.

Portsmouth's South Parade Pier was built in 1875 and has so far survived several Storms of the Century, two major fires and the visits of the Luftwaffe during World War II. It suffered major damage during a visit from film director Ken Russell in 1974 when he was in the city for the making of the rock musical Tommy. A major conflagration broke out during filming, and the director had ordered the cameras to keep turning.

In its mid 20th-century heyday, the pier was a popular venue for locals and visitors of all ages. Punch and Judy would put in daily appearances, and there would be tea dances, beauty contests, variety shows and a once-a-week rock 'n' roll hop, culminating officially in a firework display featuring at least one rocket. Unofficially the dance invariably culminated in a punch-up between rival gangs of Teddy Boys.

Nowadays, the pier was, depending on your age and viewpoint, a rather poignant or rather sad reminder of simpler times and pleasures. The same man who had run the original tea dances still oversaw the weekly gathering of pensioners who had once been the teenage patrons of the rock 'n' roll nights. There was the inevitable arcade which had long since lost any claim to justify the prefix 'amusement', and a cafe which served what was said to be the worst cup of coffee in the city.

Today, however, there were more people on and around the pier than would be found in its vicinity in mid-August.

Arriving with his sergeant, Mowgley saw a marked police car with its light flashing was drawn up at an angle in front of the steps leading up from the road to the entrance to the pier. Alongside were three unmarked cars and the panel van used to carry the duty scenes of crime officers and their kit. All the vehicles were parked on yellow lines, and a traffic warden was standing by the van looking vaguely frustrated.

Although the pier appeared to be open for business, all the interest of the not inconsiderable crowd was focused on the beach directly to one side of the Victorian structure. A plastic tape stretched from the promenade, parallel with and close to the massive legs, and reached down to the water's edge. The tape was supported at intervals by red plastic cones, and three uniformed officers were keeping the spectators at bay. The tide, Mowgley noted, appeared to be on the turn.

*

The man was slumped forward, head down and arms outstretched to either side at shoulder level. His hair was long and tangled and wet from the sea, and was crowned with a circle of barbed wire. The grim tableau reminded Mowgley of the life-sized crucifixion scene above the altar at the church he attended every Sunday as a small boy. Not because he had been religious, but because there was a cream bun and cup of tea in the Vicarage after the service as a reward for a show of piety and attention. He had noticed that one or another of the prettier boys would be invited to stay behind afterwards, but had thought nothing of it until the Vicar had been arrested and charged with what was commonly known in those less concerned times as kiddy-fiddling. On later reflection he took being passed over for special attention as some compensation for being an ugly child.

Barbed wire secured the drowned man's arms to one of the barnacle-encrusted lateral struts stretching between the massive iron pillars on which the pier sat. His killer or killers had obviously chosen a strut which was of a height to ensure that their victim was just able to stand on his tiptoes. This, Mowgley realised with a wince, was not to allow him to take the strain off his arms, but to ensure he would remain conscious for the maximum time it took the incoming tide to reach his mouth and nose.

'I suppose, what with it being February,' Mowgley observed, 'they weren't too worried about any courting couples hearing him shout for help.'

'Not much danger of that, mate' his colleague said dryly, 'they cut his tongue out before they left him to wait for the tide.'

*

When Britain boasted the largest and most powerful fleet in the world, its premier port was said to have more public houses than lamp-posts. The Blitz, dwindling numbers of Naval personnel, road and housing development and changing tastes had since put paid to hundreds of ornate and overblown Victorian gin palaces, seafront bars and corner locals. Mowgley mourned the loss of each one. Once upon a time and when they were run by real characters, Pompey pubs were known by their landlords' names. It would be Johnny Duthwaite's rather than The Cambridge and Snowy's gaff rather than The Admiral Nelson. Now their character hosts had long gone, along with the pubs which had been their little empires.

Mowgley and his friend and fellow officer were sitting in one of the pubs which had survived. It had done so by adapting to changing times and tastes.

Overlooking a corner of the docks where the remains of Portsmouth's fishing fleet tied up, the Bridge Tavern dated back to the 17th Century and was the last of the eight hostelries, gambling dens and bawdy houses which had served the passing and local trade. The swing bridge from which it got its name had also disappeared and the Tavern would be unrecognisable to most of the people who had made their living from the docks or the water surrounding them in not so far-off days. Until relatively recently, The Bridge had been in the hands of one of the City's true eccentrics.

Mad Maxie was renowned for putting liberty before licence, and had opened and closed his pub when it suited him and not the brewery or the Licensing Justices. He also only admitted people he chose to serve and whose company he could bear. This was not a large number. It was said that the more Maxie liked a customer, the ruder he would be to him. From the way he spoke to him he clearly liked Mowgley, and had once called him a pouffe and threatened to bar him for life for asking for a lump of ice to be put in his girlfriend's glass.

Time passed and the popularity of Maxie's honest boozer and his style of stewardship diminished until the old man rarely opened the doors. He did not get out of bed one morning, and Mowgley had been one of the three mourners at his funeral.

Now, the pub was twice as big and very much cleaner than when Maxie had been in charge. Given the option Mowgley would have liked it to have stayed as unchanging as the near-fossilised jar of pickled eggs which had been the establishment's only gesture to catering.

'I bet you're thinking about when Maxie was here.'

Mowgley nodded. 'You're right, Hoppy.'

'And any minute you're going to say they don't make them like that again.'

'Well, I was, but I won't give you the pleasure.'

Mowgley rolled his third cigarette of the session and raised his glass to propose a toast to their former landlord. His friend endorsed the toast and frowned in distaste at Mowgley's baccy pouch.

Detective Inspector Dave Hopkirk had gone to school with Mowgley, and been a fellow traveller around the pubs and seedy clubs of the city. He had applied to and been admitted to the drug squad early on in his career, and it was said in some circles that he was just the man for the job as he had been an enthusiastic member of the city's drug community throughout the latter half of the 1960s. The apprenticeship had in fact proved useful, as the detective knew the key people on the City scene and where to find them.

Like Mowgley, DI Hopkirk believed in making and following his own rules, and also like his colleague, administering his own form of punishment and reward. But now, like Mowgley, he was approaching retirement age and seen by many of his younger colleagues as an interesting reminder of a past age.

His style of clothing did nothing to alter that view. He was as fastidious about his appearance as Mowgley was unconcerned, and his short, razor-cut and neatly parted hair and penchant for button-down shirts, Sta-Prest trousers and Ben Sherman moccasin loafers indicated his age and favourite era.

Putting his glass down and leaning forward, Mowgley nodded towards his friend's footwear. 'You must be getting old, my Mod mate. You got your feet wet.'

His friend nodded and looked ruefully at his shoes. 'Not like me, is it? They cost nearly a ton and they're ruined now. And I don't suppose I'll be able to claim for 'em.' He took a reflective sip of premium lager, then said: 'To tell you the truth, I got such a shock looking at the body that I stepped back and went in up to my ankles.'

'Not a pretty sight, eh?'

'It wasn't so much that, but that I knew him.'

Mowgley made no comment and watched and waited as Hopkirk moved his glass in small circles on the table top. Then he said: 'He was one of mine.'

Mowgley raised an eyebrow. 'Yeah?'

DI Hopkirk nodded. 'Yeah. One Colin Chapman, a born and bred Pompey bad lad. I nicked him over twenty years ago when he was just a boy, knocking out spliffs round the artier boozers in Southsea. The punters thought they were getting whacky baccy, but it was really just Digger Shag pipe tobacco with an aspirin crumbled up in the roll-up. It's amazing how clean Pompey was then and how little the youngsters knew about drugs.'

Mowgley lifted the other eyebrow. 'Surely they didn't fall for it, even in those days?'

'Oh yeah. My boy picked his customers carefully, and the power of suggestion is a wonderful thing. As long as they thought it was some sort of hooky substance they were happy, and liked to look big in front of the ladies. He told me he even had regular punters. Anyway, I couldn't really do him for not selling proscribed substances, and he couldn't be done for false pretences as I doubt the customers would have admitted they thought they were buying joints.'

'Quite.'

'Besides, I sort of admired his initiative, and followed his career as he started doing a bit of dealing with the real stuff.

He was only a minor player, so I let him do a bit of trading as long as he kept me up to snuff with who was doing what on the scene. Then, about three years ago, he made a jump into the big league and joined the top team in the city.'

'Would that be Mr Finlayson and his cohorts?'

The DI nodded. 'I'm glad to see you've been keeping up on the league tables.' He held out a hand for Mowgley's glass and stood up. 'My turn, then.'

Mowgley watched his former school friend walk to the bar, then found his mobile and punched in a number.

After trying and failing to impress the young barmaid, DI Hopkirk returned and set the glasses down on their table. 'Anyone I know?'

Mowgley looked around the bar. 'Where?'

Hopkirk gave a tired smile. 'I meant on the blower. I thought you didn't know how to use a mobile.'

'I like to keep up with the times. I was just making arrangement with my sergeant to meet at The Ship tonight.'

'Ah.' Hopkirk sat down and reached for his pint. 'The Ship. Is that lady with the giant jugs still the main attraction?'

'Depends where your tastes lie,' said Mowgley. 'You get all sorts at the Ship. I use the place for the sophisticated ambience. And the fine cuisine, of course.'

'Of course.' DI Hopkirk looked thoughtfully at his friend. 'You are a funny bloke, Jack.'

Mowgley bowed gravely. 'I do my best.'

'No, I mean funny strange. No car, no house, no bird and dressing like a tramp. It's not even as if you're undercover...'

'Bloody cheek. A bloke who pays a fortune for clobber that's thirty-odd years out of date and pays to have his nails filed, and you call me strange. And what about that motor you brought us here in? It must have cost more than I spend in a decade on beer and fags.'

Hopkirk shrugged: 'Nothing wrong with wanting to be well turned-out, is there? And I'm on my own - and don't have an ex-missus keeping me skint.' He started moving his glass on the table top again. 'Anyway, back to business.'

'Fair do's. So your nark got himself invited to join the big time, then?'

'Not so much invited as made an offer he would be very silly to refuse. Chapman was starting to be a bit of a player, and so Finlayson hoovered him up. I was quite chuffed with the situation as it meant I had a snout in the top team. Especially the way the business was going.'

Mowgley nodded. He knew that the drug scene in Portsmouth had expanded dramatically in recent years. More than 100,000 people were crammed into the twelve square miles of the UK's only island city. If the statistics were anywhere near correct, one in every hundred Portmuthians was a regular consumer of heroin or crack cocaine.

The general rule for most commodities is that scarcity increases its price, while adequate supplies and stiff competition can reduce it. In spite of the continuing rise of users, the price of hard drugs on the street had actually fallen sharply in recent years. This was because of the increasingly savage battle for control of the market.

Unlike competing supermarkets, the main players had begun cutting faces and even throats as well as prices. Thirty years before there had been a mixture of semi-professional and full-time dealers plying their trade in Portsmouth. As the business became more organised, the number of suppliers grew smaller. Competing groups had either been put out of business by undercutting or threats or real violence. Nowadays, the acknowledged main dealership in Portsmouth was held and fiercely protected by one man.

Michael Finlayson was a prime example of how driving ambition, focus and a complete lack of scruples or fear can be the key to success in any activity. It was just that he had chosen criminal activity as the best short cut to success and the things it could buy.

Much to the relief of his teachers, Finlayson had left school at fourteen and immediately taken up an apprenticeship in petty crime. He had soon graduated from being a look-out and runner and gone into business on his own account. Before he was out of his teenage years he was the head of a small team of freelance night club bouncers. As well as keeping the patrons in order, his men would supply them with the noxious substances for which they were supposed to be frisking them. As he liked to be known at that stage of his career, Mickey Finn also found a niche as a debt-collector, enforcer and dispute settler.

Within a couple of years he had no need to do the dirty work himself, but liked to keep his hand in. From a tower block in one of the roughest areas of the City, he had moved literally up in the world to the top of Portsdown Hill. Here, he could look down from his rambling neo-Georgian house with its covered swimming pool and unused tennis court on to the streets where his troops were permanently in action. Together with his small army of bouncers, buyers and sharp-end dealers, the big house on the hill also served as an advertisement for his official income-bringing activities. According to his website, he and his associate companies ran a small but burgeoning property, business and security consultancy empire. To his neighbours and fellow club members, Michael Finlayson was the hugely successful proprietor of, amongst a number of thriving concerns, Manor Securities. To the city drug squad and his hundred or so employees and business associates on the street, he was still Mickey Finn, main man on the Portsmouth drug scene.

Nowadays, though and as Mowgley knew from Dave Hopkirk and his other sources, Mike Finlayson was not having it all his own way on the streets of the city. Previously, he only had to contend with would-be rivals in the shape of bold but unwise newcomers and the odd organised gang from other major cities. Of late, he was having to take on some very determined and battle-hardened competitors from eastern Europe.

In recent times and as events had shown, the expansion of what had been called the Common Market and the dramatic upheaval in Soviet Russia following the apparently desirable perestroika and glasnost initiatives had brought unofficial and unwelcome business organisations to Britain.

A number of the loosely affiliated Russian mafia groups had shown an interest in the lucrative and growing trading opportunities in the United Kingdom. As Mowgley had seen, the groups found his ferry port a very convenient entry point. They also found the city it was attached to a promising trading area. The smaller independent dealers holding a franchise agreement with Mike Finlayson had been persuaded to cease trading. Now, as DI Hopkirk explained, it seemed the Russians were moving on to question the power and authority of the city's main Class 'A' provider.

'I know it's early days, mate,' said Mowgley, 'but any ideas who strung your man up under the pier?'

Hopkirk looked across to where the barmaid had joined in a burst of amusement from a group of suits, then raised his hands in a don't-know gesture. 'Not a clue at this stage. It could be the Russians trying to put the frighteners on Finlayson

- it's their sort of style. One thing's worth a bet: suicide is very unlikely to be the Coroner's verdict.'

Mowgley looked directly at his friend, then said: 'Of course, you'll have considered that it might be Finlayson who done the deed, letting it be known that he found out about your arrangement with Mr Chapman.'

DI Hopkirk dropped his eyes and started making circles with his glass again. 'Yes, I had thought of that and thanks for reminding me, mate. I thought I'd done enough to keep him safe. Perhaps I didn't...'

four

'Come on then, spill the beans.'
Inspector Mowgley frowned. 'I wonder why we say that?'
'What?'
'Spill the beans. Why would spilling beans have come to mean letting someone into a secret?'
DS McCarthy shrugged. 'Dunno. But if there are beans to be spilled, proceed to spill them. I still haven't forgiven you for going off to the pub with your mate and not letting me come.'
'I thought you didn't like Hoppy?'
'I don't, as it happens. I think he's creepy with all that Mod gear and he obviously fancies himself, but that's not the point.'
'Oh, Hoppy's alright. He's just stuck in the late '60s. He always had to pull the best-looking bird when we went out, and spent fortunes on his clobber.'
'He's still spending fortunes on his car.'
Mowgley nodded. 'You checked it out, then?'
'Yep. Amazingly, you got part of the registration wrong, but from all the evidence that 'big shiny grey car' as you described it is a Lexus RX300.'
'Is that good?'
She shrugged. 'He bought it brand spanking new last year; with all the trims it would have set your chum back more than he's earned since then.'
'You mean he bought it cash? That would be a bit interesting.'
'Well, no. He had a big loan on it as it happens.'
It was Mowgley's turn to shrug: 'So, what are you saying? He's not allowed to have a flash motor? He's single and lives in a little flat. Some people just like to spend their money on cars. Besides, Hoppy's no mug. Do you really think he'd

tool about in an expensive car if he was on the take?'

'I didn't say that. But you must have wondered or why did you get me to run his licence plate?'

'Just curious.'

DS McCarthy pulled a face. 'Sure you are.'

She lifted a hand from the steering wheel and pointed through the windscreen. 'On the subject of curious colloquialisms, why do they say 'nark', do you think?'

Mowgley thought about issuing a warning about the man on the bicycle about to pedal out of a side street a hundred yards ahead. Instead, he asked: 'Who?'

DS McCarthy sounded her horn sharply: 'It's alright, calm yourself - I saw him.' Then she pointed again to the high grey wall topped with spiked railings and said: 'People in there.'

They were on their way to see the widow of the man with the over-stuffed money belt. At the right time of a sunny day, the Wheatcroft home could literally be described as being in the shadow of Portsmouth's only prison.

Built in the year Queen Victoria was pronounced Empress of India, Kingston had had a varied career. Apart from a general place of incarceration, it had served as a borstal for young and persistent male offenders, and as a very large police station during the Second World War. Come the abolition of capital punishment in 1965, and it became a home solely for men serving life sentences for murder. There had been a furore at the time, when some Portmuthians made a fuss about their city becoming a dumping ground for killers. This abated when it was learned that all the murders were domestic, or had only involved the killing of wives. Kingston would also become the only prison in England and Wales to house a unit exclusively for elderly male murderers. As the Home Office pointed out, men who have killed their loved ones are not likely to move on to slaughter members of the general public, especially when too old to make much of an effort to get over the wall and find fresh victims.

*

The door to number 22, Olinda Street looked as if it were of the same age as the mid-Victorian terrace. This row of what were nowadays being referred to as 'town cottages' had been built to house workers on the railway line which ran directly behind the tiny back yards.

After a moment, the door was opened by a woman who Mowgley took to be Sarah Wheatcroft. His deduction proved correct, and he and his sergeant were invited in.

Their host spoke with a well-modulated, accent-less voice and was, Mowgley estimated, in her late forties but looked younger. Of above average height, she was wearing what he thought was an unfussy but probably expensive knee-length, red wine-coloured dress which closely followed the pleasantly varying contours of her body.

He also noted she was wearing a pair of low-heeled shoes of similar colour to the dress and which appeared to be of similar pedigree as to quality. Her short brown hair was kept in an equally simple manner, and she wore little or no make-up that he could detect. Bodily ornaments seemed restricted to a small, plain watch on her right wrist, a thin gold necklace, and a pair of earrings of the same material. Her features were small and even, and he thought he saw a flicker of instant analysis and conclusion when she opened the door.

She moved ahead of them with a confident and easy carriage which was pleasing to Mowgley's eye. She was clearly a sophisticated and self-possessed woman, and Sergeant Quayle would probably have assessed her as posh totty.

In the small living room, she asked if they would like a drink, apologising for having no alcohol in the house. Mowgley asked for coffee and said he preferred it black with sugar, and DS McCarthy said she would like the same.

If Sarah Wheatcroft was not the sort of person one would expect to find in this sort of house and area of the city, the sitting room conformed exactly with Mowgley's expectations of a place furnished to suit an elderly working-class couple.

A jarringly sleek, wide and flat-screened television dominated one corner, and facing it were two comfortable-looking armchairs. One had a floral cover and a couple of embroidered cushions placed where the sitter's lower back could make most use of them. A wooden walking stick hung off one arm. The other chair was of the variety in which the back and footrest can be adjusted to any combination of angles. It looked new, Mowgley surmised, and probably cost more than the giant television.

Alongside the adjustable chair was a freestanding ashtray of much older vintage, with the bowl held up to the height of the armrest by an ornamental pillar. The brass workings vaguely evoked an Ancient Egyptian theme, and the pillar stood on three supports shaped like the front paws of the inscrutable Sphinx at Giza.

The wallpaper was less exotic in theme, and the pattern was of vertical pink stripes intertwined with healthily blooming roses. As the fireplace had been boarded over and there was no sign of radiators, it appeared the sole source of heating was a triple-barred electric fire, with a coal-effect base. Heavy curtains hung over what Mowgley thought must be one of the few remaining original sash windows in this part of the city. Another drape hung from a brass rail on the back of the door, and a draught excluder of the same material lay along the skirting board nearby. It had at some time been augmented with a pair of ears and whiskers to give the appearance of an amiably grinning sausage dog.

Mowgley turned his attention to the bathroom-tiled mantelpiece, which held a row of photographs. He noticed that the era in which they appeared to have been taken roughly tallied with the age and style of the frames which contained them. At the left hand end, a varnished wooden base with two slotted uprights held two pieces of glass sandwiching an old black and white photograph. It was surprisingly sharp, and showed a couple standing halfway up a flight of stone steps which led to an impressively arched doorway. Mowgley recognised it as the entrance to the city registry office, where he had started his married life probably twenty years after the couple in the photograph. Unlike them, his had ended a decade ago.

The couple were either caught before going in or on their way from the registry office. There was no confetti or sign of guests, and they stood close together and somehow uncertainly on the steps. As people did in those days, they were smiling obediently but not enthusiastically for the camera.

He had not seen either Mr or Mrs Wheatcroft as they looked now, but they made a handsome couple in 1951. She was wearing a two-piece costume with what he thought had been called a pencil skirt, and to one side of her head and set an angle was a small pill-box hat of the type hotel bell-boys wore in old American movies.

The man was wearing what looked like a demob suit, and both he and his partner had sprays wrapped in silver paper pinned to their lapels. She had middle-length hair curled inwards and upwards at the bottom. His hair was cut short at the sides and parted in the middle, with shiny evidence that Brylcreem had been lavishly applied after his morning toilet.

Mowgley lingered over the photo and thought about the couple and all the trials and small triumphs of half a century they would have shared, and how it had come to a sudden and undignified end a couple of days before on the concrete floor of the Customs shed.

The next photograph on the mantelpiece was held in a cheap tin frame of 1950s art-deco revival style, and featured the woman in the wedding photograph. She was holding a baby and smiling with obviously genuine pleasure at the camera. The child was wrapped in a lace shawl and Mowgley assumed it was a newly-born Sarah Wheatcroft.

The next frame in the line was of plain plastic and showed a girl in her teens, holding the hand of a little boy. The next photograph was in a modern embossed metal frame, and showed a young man standing stiffly at attention. He was wearing dress military uniform, and there were corporal's stripes on his sleeve. He was stern-faced, and Mowgley thought he was probably the sort of person who did not smile easily, especially if someone holding a camera told him to.

The final photograph in the line-up was held in a similar frame to the previous one. It was a distance shot and showed a cluster of white houses, sitting on a steeply sloping hill or mountainside. Looking down on the huddle of dwellings was a church with an ornate bell tower, and alongside it an impressive and clearly ancient castle. It was clearly somewhere foreign.

'Apart from the television and chair, not much sign of conspicuous over-consumption here, then.'

Mowgley turned away from the small gallery to where his sergeant was standing by the closed door.

He was about to reply, when the handle turned and Sarah Wheatcroft entered. She was carrying a plastic tray on which were arranged two cups and saucers, a matching bowl of granulated sugar and a plate bearing a handful of rich tea biscuits.

'I'm afraid there's only instant,' she said.

'Just how I like it,' said Mowgley reassuringly. 'Anything else is wasted on me.'

He took one of the cups and obeyed her invitation to take a seat in the adjustable armchair. DS McCarthy took the other cup and moved round to stand behind Mowgley. He knew she was doing it to forestall an invitation to take the other chair, and then have to look up at their hostess.

After offering the sugar bowl and plate of biscuits, the woman walked over and put the tray on a sideboard on the other side of the chimney breast to the television set. As she did so, Mowgley patted his overcoat breast pocket but stopped after a warning glare from his colleague.

'It's fine to smoke if you want,' the woman said. 'I once worked out that Dad must have got through a quarter of a million cigarettes in this room. I don't think another one will make any difference.'

Mowgley smiled his gratitude, but kept his pouch in his pocket. There was an awkward moment as Mowgley and McCarthy sipped at their coffees, then the woman said: 'When your office rang to make an appointment, they wouldn't say what you wanted to talk to me about.'

Mowgley sat back in the chair, inwardly relieved. She was obviously setting up the ground for what she knew was coming, and not putting him through the awkwardness of pussyfooting around. He looked at his cup and saucer for a moment, then said: 'Yes, of course you must be wondering why we're here.' He took another sip and continued. 'As you may know, I'm the senior police officer at the ferry port. It's my job to follow up on any major... incident. We wanted to come and say how sorry we are for your loss - and to ask your mother a few formal questions and find out if there's anything you would like to ask us.'

'Thank you. I'm afraid my mother is not in a state to speak to anyone yet. She's upstairs and quite heavily sedated.' Sarah Wheatcroft stepped to the empty armchair and sat down, perching on its edge and cupping her hands on her lap. 'This is a first for me, so I have no idea what happens next. I don't even know what will happen with my father's...body and what I need to do.'

Mowgley nodded, then looked at his sergeant. She asked:

'Do you know if your father had seen a doctor in the last month?'

The woman shook her head. 'I don't know - mum will know, but...'

DS McCarthy lifted a hand slightly from the back of the chair in which Mowgley was sitting. 'I only ask because a doctor can't sign the death certificate unless there has been contact in the previous 28 days. If not, a coroner needs to be consulted and he or she can approve the signing if the cause of death is obvious and not in any way unusual or suspicious.' McCarthy paused to see that Sarah Wheatcroft was absorbing the detail, then continued: 'Whatever happens, we will make sure that you are kept informed of what is happening. If you like, I can also help you through the process. I'll give you my number before we leave.'

The woman nodded her appreciation, then asked: 'And did you say you wanted to ask some questions? I expect I can answer for mum.'

I wonder if you can, thought Mowgley. Aloud, he said 'If that's okay with you. Though of course we will need to speak to your mother at some time in the future.'

Sarah Wheatcroft nodded again, and Mowgley leant over the arm of the chair and set his empty cup on the floor. He looked at his colleague to signal he would take over, and said: 'At this stage I'd like to keep it informal. To start with, can you tell us about where your mother and father were going, and why?'

He noticed she shot a glance towards the mantelpiece before replying. 'They were on their way to Spain. To southern Spain.'

Mowgley lifted his eyebrows to show enlightenment, although she would obviously know that he would know where the Wheatcrofts had been bound for. Then he said: 'I believe they had a small campervan. Did they travel much in Spain?'

'Not really. They always went to the same place, but they liked to take their time and spend a couple of nights in the Bambi.'

'So where exactly did they go – and how often?'

'I suppose once a month in the past year since they bought

the little campervan. They were going to Olvera. It's what they call a Pueblo Blanco, or white village. It's in Andalucía, inland from the Costa del Sol.'

Mowgley nodded and paused, and as if anticipating his next question, she said: 'They have a small property there.'

The detective tried to look a little surprised. 'A holiday home, then?'

Sarah Wheatcroft smiled. 'Not so much a holiday home as a holiday ruin. It's a tiny cottage at the top end of the town. It's uninhabitable and held up on each side by the adjoining properties.' She smiled again at a fond memory. 'Mum and dad first went to Spain when package holidays came in during the Sixties. It was quite a big thing in those days. They visited and stayed in Olvera, and it was always dad's dream to buy a home and spend the English winters there. It was never going to happen, but I took a look at prices, and bought the pequena casa - it means the tiny house - as a surprise present for their fiftieth wedding anniversary.'

Again she seemed to anticipate his response, and said: 'It was slightly less than the equivalent of £4000. I know it sounds like a grand gesture, but I had just got a good promotion at work, and a settlement from my ex-husband. He kept the house and paid me half the market value.' She smiled ruefully and continued as if she wanted to emphasise how buying a ruin in Spain for her parents was no great extravagance. 'Or at least, it was his idea of the market value. But it was in London and had soared in price since we bought it, so I had no real complaints. Of course I knew dad would never get round to restoring the place, but that was part of the fun. They would go over in the Bambi every month or so, and dad would sit in their local bar and make sketches of all the things he was not going to have done to the building.' She looked down at her hands as she pressed them together. 'I think it made him very happy and that makes me glad I did it. I couldn't know what was going to happen.'

'Of course not.' Sarah Wheatcroft looked up as DS McCarthy spoke. 'I think it's a wonderful story and a wonderful thing you did for your parents.'

There was a moment's silence as his sergeant looked at Mowgley to see when he was going to broach the subject of how the woman's father came to be wearing a money belt containing over fifty thousand pounds when he suffered a stroke at the ferry port.

Before she found out, there was a crash and the door swung violently open. As Mowgley began to rise from the chair, a young man burst into the room. He was tall and looked muscled and toned beneath his khaki tee-shirt; he was also clearly not in a good mood.

Moving close to the adjustable chair and looking down at Mowgley, he bunched his fists and stood with his feet apart and his arms slightly akimbo. His face was flushed and DS McCarthy saw that a small vein was pulsing on his brow.

'You've got a fucking nerve, haven't you? Get out of my dad's chair.'

Mowgley did so, and Sarah Wheatcroft rose at the same time, positioning herself between the man and the detective. When she spoke, it was with a sharp and authoritative voice.

'Andy, calm down! They've only come to tell us what's happening with dad... and what we need to do next.'

The young man contorted his mouth into a savage sneer and looked straight at Mowgley. 'You mean now they've killed him, they're going to help with the funeral arrangements?'

Mowgley spoke in soft tones, remaining half upright and keeping his hand still and by his side. 'As a matter of fact, Andy, we're the police. It was the Customs who stopped and searched your dad.'

'He's still just as dead. We can look after the arrangements. So why don't you fuck off before I throw you out on your arse...?'

five

'So what do you reckon?'

DS McCarthy and Inspector Mowgley were sitting on a bench on the promenade. Behind them was Southsea Castle. More than four centuries on, they had the same view as Henry VIII when he watched his flagship sink below the choppy waters of the Solent during an engagement with a French invasion fleet.

The Mary Rose went down with the loss of almost all the hundreds of her crew members and a host of officers and noble hangers-on along for the ride. Somehow making the event even more tragic, the warship was unscathed by enemy fire. She simply keeled over too far during a manoeuvre and sank very quickly when water flooded through the gun ports. Experts were still debating exactly how it happened. Mowgley's theory was that it was just another case of too many chiefs and not enough Indians.

'Not as good as when I was a kid,' he replied. 'Or perhaps it's true that things tasted better when you were young. Or we all have False Memory Syndrome about how good they tasted.'

'You must be joking.' She shuddered, made a face and turned her head away as he held out the pot of jellied eels. 'I can't believe anyone could put that in their mouths, drunk or sober.'

Mowgley chewed contentedly then spat a piece of spine into a cupped hand. 'You might be surprised at what people have put in their mouths on this promenade, drunk or sober,' he said reflectively. 'I remember a story about Pompey Lil and a chief stoker off the Ark Royal-'

'-I don't want to know about Pompey Lil and I wasn't talking about the bloody eels. I meant about our meeting earlier with Wheatcroft frère and soeur.'

'Ah. Well, in brief I liked her and not him.'

'I could see you liked her. Just your type, really, isn't she?'

'Yes, I suppose so. Obviously intelligent, sophisticated and with a lot of style.'

DS McCarthy nodded thoughtfully. 'Funny how opposites attract isn't it?'

Mowgley made no response, but paused with a plastic spoonful of jelly and eel to his mouth as an elderly couple shuffled by with an equally elderly and decrepit dog trailing behind. He sighed heavily as they passed, and said: 'If they're going to Clarence pier, it'll be tomorrow before they get there. Perhaps we should offer them a lift.'

'I think they're here because they want to walk.'

'Perhaps. Have you noticed how many really old people wear trainers? Comfortable and cheap, I suppose.'

Mowgley sucked his teeth, then threw the empty tub and spoon into the waste bin next to their bench. He watched the old couple for a moment, then said: 'Life's just a bloody joke isn't it? When you're young you think you know it all and you're never going to die. Then you realise you know bugger-all and you're going to die soon and there's nothing you can do about it. So you just spend the last years rotting away and waiting for oblivion. The really cruel joke is that we spend all that time learning things, then forget them.'

She shrugged. 'I suppose that's life, if you'll forgive the pun.'

'I think it's more of an aphorism in the way you've used it.'

'If you say so. Anyway, we all die, so we might as well make the most of what we've got left. Did you know that we're the only species that knows it's going to die?'

'Another bloody cruel trick of nature.'

'I don't know. At least we can prepare for the end.'

Mowgley made a gloomy face. 'Not if it comes unexpected. Like to Frank Wheatcroft.' He shuddered. 'Anyway, what did you make of Rambo?'

'I was pleased you went so lightly on him. We could have done him for threatening behaviour - at least.'

'I didn't let him get away with it just because his dad's just died. Did you see how fit he was?'

'Yes, in more ways than one.'

The detective wagged a reproving finger at his sergeant. 'Now, then. He's far too young for you. And he'd wear you out with all those press-ups.'

'Bloody cheek. But he was in tip-top condition. Do you think he's a physical training instructor or something like that?'

'Dunno, but he looks a bit special to me. Then there's the neighbours saying he comes home with a suntan. Best to have a look at him.'

DS McCarthy raised one eyebrow. 'Why would we want to know more about him? You don't think he's involved in any way with the money belt business?'

'Could be.' Mowgley waved at a long, narrow boat which was being propelled along close to the shore at a high speed. The four rowers were sporting brightly coloured Spandex tops, and all were wearing sunglasses. They all ignored his wave and bent over their oars, upping the stroke rate as if trying to escape.

'Why do they do that?'

She followed his gaze towards the boat as it rounded the point. 'Believe it or not, a lot of people like to stay in shape through exercise. It makes them feel as well as look good. I was reading somewhere that Olympic rowers need to eat eight thousand calories a day to keep their weight up. Imagine that, pigging out on everything you like without having to worry about your weight.'

Mowgley grunted. 'I do that anyway. What I was talking about was them wearing sunglasses in February.'

His sergeant shrugged. 'It's part of the outfit, isn't it. I know you don't follow fashion, but people like to look cool. Moving on, what do you reckon to the situation? When are we going to talk to Mrs Wheatcroft? Do you want me to put Stephen or Dickie Quayle on having a look at the son and daughter?'

'Put Mundy Minor on it. He's good at digging and doesn't offend anyone. I've got something else in mind for Quayle.'

'Okay.' She opened her handbag and took out cigarettes and lighter. In response, Mowgley reached for his baccy pouch. She lit her own cigarette, then took a long drag and watched the smoke tumbling away in the breeze. 'So, what do you think the Wheatcrofts were up to? And where did all that money come from? Surely not the proceeds from a bank job?

I bet you asked your drug squad oppo about it.'

Mowgley took a light, drew deeply on his cigarette and looked reflectively at the glowing tip. 'I did. And I got Stephen to go and be nice to lairy bollocks in the Customs Shed.'

'And?'

'Like I told him to, Young Mundy was nice to the tight-arsed anal fart...'

'Isn't that a tautology-?'

'Where?' Mowgley shaded his hands and looked out to sea. 'I thought it was the Isle of Wight ferry.'

'You know what I mean. Surely by definition, a fart must be anal. But carry on.'

'Thank you, Sergeant. As I predicted, Thompson jumped at the chance of impressing the lad. As a matter of fact, he invited him to lunch at The Intrepid Olive so they would not be interrupted.'

'Blimey. I always thought Thompson was a bit clean around the fingernails. Did Stephen go?'

'Of course not. Anyway, our Assistant Preventative Officer gave Mundy the full SP on the latest stats and information from all ports and even the Home Office and HM Prisons on the growing use and subsequent incarceration of Grey Mules.'

Sergeant McCarthy groaned. 'Why do they have to give everything a silly name?'

'Because they can. The point is that there's been a rapid and big increase in the number of pensioners caught trying to smuggle hooky gear, Class 'A' stuff and money while apparently going on a nice outing or break across the Channel.'

'Getaway.'

'No, honestly. Somebody noticed that the average age of people caught trying to get bent stuff in or out of the country had shot up. They also did a crunch and found out there was a fast-growing number of pensioners doing porridge.'

DS McCarthy stubbed her cigarette out on the arm of the bench and leaned over Mowgley to drop it in the waste bin. 'I still don't get it.'

'Apparently, 70 is the new 50, and today's wrinklies want to make the most of what time they've got left. What with better health and diet, more money to spend than the previous generation and all those cheap package holidays, it's party time. Since Viagra came out, they've been at it like rabbits.'

'There's hope for you yet, then.'

'Absolutely. Anyway, all sorts of villains picked up on what was happening, and realised that retirees Sid and Doris Bonkers were much less likely to be stopped and searched on their way to a week in Benidorm than a dodgy geezer in a flash motor. Get the picture?'

'Absolutely.'

'So the smugglers and bad boys started bunging suitable oldie couples a nice few bob for taking stuff in and out of the country. It was a simple and successful wheeze and probably still is, but OAPs no longer get waved through as a matter of course.'

'And that's why the Wheatcrofts were stopped?'

'Not really. Just bad luck. Someone with Thompson's type of personality noticed that the Bambi was going through every month. Instead of assuming that they liked to toodle round Spain at regular intervals, he flagged the licence plate, so they were pulled over. I reckon nobody was more surprised than Thompson when poor old Frankie dropped and they found the belt.'

'And do Customs have any idea whose ill-gotten it was?'

'If they have, Thompson didn't pass it on to Stephen.'

'So it could be the proceeds of a blag, or a month's takings by a drug ring?'

'Exactly. But if it is drug money, it could be no more than a good week's profits. Some of these guys earn more than a First Division soccer player.'

Sergeant McCarthy shook her head. 'Blimey again. I knew about laundering funny money abroad but not that OAP's were being used as mules. What did your mate DI Hopkirk say?'

'He said he'd not heard of any drug money going out of the city with oldie couriers. In fact, he didn't seem to think there was any drug money going out of Pompey.'

'That's a bit sweeping, isn't it?'

Mowgley pulled at his chin and looked thoughtfully out to sea. 'That's what I thought.'

He turned the collar of his overcoat up and shivered. 'Come on then. I'm beginning to feel the cold. Time you bought me a hot toddy or at least a hot pasty at the Leo.'

After throwing the dog-end of his roll-up at the sea and

ducking as the onshore breeze blew it back towards him, Mowgley stood up. Then he leaned forward to look at the brass plate screwed to the top strut on the bench and groaned. 'Oh shit.'

Catherine McCarthy looked at him and then the plate. 'Someone you knew?'

Her boss nodded glumly. 'Yeah.'

'I'm sorry to hear that.'

'Not as sorry as me. He owed me money...'

six

The battered taxi scrunched to a stop in the gravelled car park. Mowgley got out, reached into his pocket, then carefully counted the exact fare into the driver's cupped hand.

He turned away, then hesitated and smiled at the bulky, slab-faced man: 'Sorry, I forgot to give you a tip.' He stepped closer to the driver's open window, bent down and said sotto voce: 'Try driving a bit less like a fucking lunatic in future.'

The man looked at his hand and then back up at Mowgley. For a moment it seemed he was about to say or do something, but after glaring at the detective he threw the car into gear and screeched off, one hand out of the window and making a you're-a-wanker sign.

Mowgley waved amiably in reply and walked quickly through the rain, across the bridge over the dry moat and through an arched entry in the thick flint walls to the castle grounds.

A few miles westward along the coast from Portsmouth and alongside acres of mudflats lining the main channel into the harbour, Portchester Castle had started life as a 3rd-century Roman fort. It had been built to deter pirates and any other unwelcome visitors, and show the locals who was now in charge. In the Middle Ages, a castle had been constructed within the shell of the fort. In its time, it had played host to several kings and any number of foreign prisoners from countries whose navies had fallen out with England.

Now it was a popular place for dog-walkers and bird watchers, fishermen and courting couples. During public holidays, otherwise sensible men and women would dress up in silly clothing and re-enact battles which had never been fought in or around the castle.

The woman was standing by the lych-gate leading to a Norman church sitting in the lee of one of the lofty castle walls.

'So we meet again.'

She turned, gave a small, controlled smile and nodded. 'Hello Jack. How's the shoulder?'

'Okay. It only hurts when I laugh.'

'It doesn't bother you much, then.'

'No, Ma'am. That is if I still need to call you 'ma'am'?'

She smiled the same small smile again: 'Fraid so. I'm still on the job. In fact it's Superintendent Stanton now if you want to keep things official.'

He did not respond, and after a moment, she said: 'Thanks for coming. There's a pub just down the road a bit, or I see they do coffee in there.' She nodded towards the church and raised a quizzical eyebrow.

'Better make it a coffee,' Mowgley said, 'I think it best I keep a clear head.'

She looked at him and winced: 'Ouch.'

The heavy oak gate gave a satisfyingly ancient creak as she pushed it open, and he followed her down the flagstone path, past rows of variously weathered headstones and towards a modern annexe welded incongruously to the side of the 12th-century church.

Inside, they followed the arrow on the hand-made sign announcing that the coffee shop was open.

Beyond a door they found an elderly, tweedy woman fussing with a stack of cups and saucers alongside an old-fashioned tea urn. It was sitting on a counter which took up one corner of the low-ceilinged room. One wall was lined with tall windows overlooking the graveyard.

The woman stopped re-organising the crockery, looked up and smiled. 'Awful, isn't it? But at least it's dry in here. If you'd like to find a table I'll come and take your order.'

As the room was otherwise empty, the couple had no problem finding a place to sit. While Mowgley started to take his wet overcoat off, Jane Stanton asked where the toilet was and left him to order.

When the waitress arrived, Mowgley looked quickly at the hand-written menu and asked for a pot of coffee.

'And would you like something to eat?' the woman asked

as she carefully wrote down his order. 'The scones are fresh this morning and rather good, if I say so myself.'

She looked almost anxious, so he added four cakes to his order and, after laboriously writing on her pad, she returned to the counter and disappeared through a doorway disguised with a hanging curtain.

Mowgley sat down, shook water from his hair, wiped his face with his hand and took out his tobacco pouch. As he started to roll a cigarette, he was surprised and embarrassed to see that his hands were shaking slightly.

'Having a problem?'

He looked up, then shook his head. 'My fingers are cold and wet. Or I suppose it could be that I'm a bit nervous because the last time we met you shot me.'

'Ouch again.'

She pulled out a chair and sat down opposite him. 'You do believe it was an accident, don't you?'

'That's what the report said you said. And I know they believed you.' He put the damp cigarette in his mouth and made several attempts to light it. 'If it was an accident, you should put some more time in on the range.'

Jane Stanton made no reply, probably because the elderly woman was making her way to their table.

'I'm awfully sorry,' she said as if she meant it, 'but you're not allowed to smoke in here.'

'Oh, right. Sorry.' Mowgley took the cigarette out of his mouth and pinched the end between his fingers. He noticed that, like his, the woman's hands were shaking, causing the cup to jiggle in the saucer as she put it in front of him.

He laid the damp roll-up on the table: 'I'll save it for later.'

'I may join you,' said the old lady conspiratorially, 'I'm dying for one.'

She put the bill beside his cup, and before leaving said: 'I do hope you enjoy the scones. I've brought some butter and strawberry jam as well.'

'I bet that's home-made as well,' said Mowgley.

The woman smiled almost coquettishly. 'The jam is, but not the butter, I'm afraid. I used to make our own butter occasionally when we lived in the countryside, but now I'm in the town flat...' Her words trailed off as she looked over Mowgley's head and into a happier past. Then she smiled at him again, picked up the tray and walked slowly back to her post.

Stanton nodded towards her. 'I see you haven't lost your touch.'

Mowgley made no response as she picked up the coffee jug. 'I seem to remember you take it black.'

He nodded, still not speaking. She filled his cup, then hers, and picked up the milk jug. Then she put it down, sighed, looked at him levelly for a moment, then said: 'Look, I know I'm not going to win you over. This is not about apologising. I just wanted to let you know I was back on your patch.'

Mowgley returned her gaze, then said: 'I might have felt a bit better about it if you'd apologised at the time.' He smiled bitterly. 'Or at least sent me a card and some grapes in hospital.'

She shrugged. 'My boss thought it best for me to stay clear. I did call you a couple of times, but your phone wasn't working.'

Mowgley grunted and looked at her sceptically. It was coming up for two years since he had met the then Detective Chief Inspector Jane Stanton. She was a member of the elite Special Projects Unit, a small and select team attached to the Met. The S.P.U. were tasked with a number of unusual and very specific projects. On and off the record these tasks included stopping assassins carrying out their contracts, and harassing and arresting or sometimes - it was rumoured - eliminating major drug traffickers who wished to set up shop in the United Kingdom.

They had been at a warehouse in Sussex belonging to a Russian drugs cartel when a man with an AK 47 had come out of the building and surprised Mowgley. Jane Stanton had appeared as the man lifted his weapon, and had opened fire with her handgun. The man had been killed, but Mowgley had been in the direct line of fire and took the first bullet in the left shoulder.

He raised his coffee cup in mock salutation. 'So what are you doing down here now,' he asked, 'looking for some target practice?'

She shook her head and smiled a smile with no warmth in it. 'Okay, I understand you're not going to put me back on your Christmas card list. I set up this meeting because I wanted you to know I was going to be down here for a while.'

'So why the cloak and dagger stuff? My boss Madame double-barrelled could have told me you were going to be around.'

Jane Stanton opened her mouth, then paused as the door from the nave of the church opened and a middle-aged man wearing a cassock walked in. He looked across at them and smiled and nodded, then turned his attention to the elderly waitress.

Stanton leaned forward: 'I didn't think you would want to hear from her and anyway she'd probably not have told you. She doesn't know anything except that I'm down here on business...and I wanted to see you and tell you myself.'

'I'm flattered. But what about Dave Hopkirk? Didn't you give him a courtesy call as well?'

'No, and I'd ask you not to tell him.'

'Any special reason?'

She hesitated, then shook her head. 'To be honest, it's only my boss and me who know I'm here.'

'Sounds like you reckon someone's joined the other side?'

She made no response, then said briskly in the manner of someone concluding a business meeting: 'Anyway, whether you believe me or not, I wanted to tell you I was here.' Her voice softened as she continued: 'And I'm truly sorry for what happened.' She stood up and looked down at the piece of paper by Mowgley's cup. 'Shall I get that?'

He shook his head. 'That's alright. I won't mention you in the expenses claim.' He stood and fumbled in his trouser pocket before pulling out a five pound note and a handful of change. After looking at the bill, he put all the money on the table. Then he picked up the scones and the small jar of jam and put them in his overcoat pocket.

Stanton frowned. 'Is that for later? Can't see you as a home-made scone man, somehow.'

'No. I just didn't want to hurt the old lady's feelings. You know how it is.'

She followed him out of the church, along the path and through the lych-gate. They stood looking at each other as rain ran down their faces. Finally, she said 'I don't suppose you fancy one at the pub?'

Mowgley shook his head, which set off a small shower of

droplets. 'No thanks, I've got someone picking me up.'

'Ah, your loyal bag carrier? Is she the only woman you trust?'

He shrugged, 'There was my mum, and a few others.'

'You see the worst in everyone, don't you?'

'That's because there is a worst in everyone, isn't there?'

She repeated the small, tight smile. 'I reckon so. Anyway, remember not to tell her or anyone else I'm here. I'll keep in touch.'

Jane Stanton turned away, then looked back. 'Perhaps we'll get that drink in sometime.'

He did not respond beyond a slight shrug of his shoulders. An irritated look crossed her face as if she had lost points in a contest, then she turned and walked quickly away.

seven

According to the publicity handout, Gunwharf Quays was a premium retail destination with 'an unrivalled mix of outlets, restaurants, bars and cafés, all situated in a spectacular harbourside location.'

This was a significant change of role for this corner of the Naval Dockyard. Where once ships of the line would be repaired after battle, visitors could now browse in designer clothing and accessory shops, eat designer food and drink designer drinks as they pretended not to be who they were.

If the Council were to be trusted, the premier retail destination would soon be further distinguished by a landmark which would make it the envy of all other coastal cities.

The 170 metre-high tower would be of a design which would evoke giant sails billowing in the wind, and the view from the observation platform at the top would be breathtaking. The tower had been planned to mark the beginning of a new millennium, but technical problems and shortfalls in budget had delayed the process. To save face, the Millennium Tower-to-be had been re-named the Spinnaker Tower, and it was claimed with apparent confidence that it would be open for business within a couple of years. Local cynics said it was unlikely to be opened before the next millennium.

It was now two years since Gunwharf Quays had been unveiled, and after a guarded welcome it had become a popular attraction for locals and visitors from far afield. At first it had been a haunt for young mums with pushchairs who would normally visit the pedestrian precinct in the centre of the city. Now, people understood what and who the multi-million pound complex was for, and what was expected of those who used it. It was Catherine McCarthy's first visit, but she knew it was a regular haunt of the colleague she was meeting.

Dickie Quayle was leaning on the counter and eating nuts from a bowl on the counter as she pushed her way through the door of one of the bars overlooking the harbour entrance. He was not a short man, but the tops of the designer beer pumps reached above his head. Everywhere was chrome and stainless steel and glass, and it was all spotlessly clean. The lofty ceilings, picture windows and array of minimalistic tables and chairs put her in mind of the reception area of a newly-opened NHS hospital. At this time of day, it had a similar atmosphere.

She knew that DS Quayle knew she had arrived, because she had seen him looking at her through one of the giant windows while she crossed the waterside walkway. As she pushed open the big plate glass door, she noted that he had actually turned his back slightly so as to have an excuse not to greet her as she approached.

It was typical of his petty manoeuvring to score, as he saw it, points, and she chalked it up as another reason for disliking Quayle. The list was not long, but telling. None of the items on it would be considered heinous by an impartial judge; it was just that the sum of those items instilled in her a convinced dislike and distrust of DS Quayle.

He was, she had long ago decided, the most completely self-contained man she had known. It was not that he was shallow in a way that most self-centred people are; it was just that he did not care to have any depth.

To be fair, it could be that what she really disliked about Detective Sergeant Quayle was that he was so self-assured and at ease with who he was. She was deeply fond of Mowgley in an un-sisterly but completely asexual way; if she thought about why, she felt a good part of that protective affection probably because of his insecurities and uncertainties. She believed the inspector to be a good man, but inwardly unsure of the validity of his apparently simple philosophies on the human condition. He might like to appear to be a no-nonsense and very basic bloke, but she knew that to be a front.

Inspector Mowgley was constantly unsure about how to present himself to and how to deal with those who touched his life. Quayle, she knew, was totally untroubled by such thoughts.

'Morning.'

She strove to keep the irritation from her voice, as she knew he knew that she knew that he would not turn around or acknowledge her until she made the first gesture, and that would be another small victory.

Quayle stayed the hand which was transferring a roasted peanut from bowl to mouth and smiled his insincere smile. Looking up fleetingly at the giant Odeon-style clock above the bar, he said: 'I was beginning to think you might not make it. Have a problem with the car park? The bays are really tight, aren't they?'

He was clearly going to have his pound of flesh, and she tried not to let the anger show in her face and voice: 'I got a lift here from a friend'. She put a slight emphasis on the last word, and saw from his satisfied look that he had caught it. But, given who he was, rather than being wounded by the implied putdown, he would be pleased at the evidence that he had nettled her.

In a carefully neutral voice, she said 'Anyway, I thought you saw me through the window.'

Without missing a beat, he said: 'I didn't recognise you on your own.'

She did not respond. He could have his fun as long as she got what she wanted from the meeting. After studying her for a moment, he straightened up and appeared to be declaring a truce as he nodded at the pumps. 'What do you want? A beer?'

'No thanks,' she replied, 'coffee would be good.'

'Do you know what sort?' He looked at his watch, then continued: 'It could take half an hour to go through the list.' Another of his fleeting glances, this time at her hips, and then: 'What about a Skinny Latte?'

Clearly, the truce had not endured. Determined not to give him the satisfaction of showing she had not missed the jibe, she shook her head. 'Just black.'

Quayle made the order, then picked up his beer glass and led the way to a table in one corner of the cavernous bar.

They took opposite sides of the table and sat silently as she opened her bag and reached for her cigarettes. The anticipated dig about her giving up smoking did not come, but she saw that he was looking at her as if he were amused by her weakness.

The coffee arrived and Quayle told the waitress to add it to his bill.

She nodded her thanks to the young woman, took a drag of her cigarette and a sip of the coffee, then grimaced.

Quayle looked quizzical: 'Don't you like it? They reckon you get the best coffee in Portsmouth here.'

She looked at the menu in a chromium art deco-style stand on the table and said wryly: 'It should be at those prices. Anyway, how would anyone know what the coffee tastes like when it's drowned with milk and covered with grated chocolate and God knows what else?'

Quayle whistled and widened his eyes in an expression of mock horror. 'My God. It's true. You are turning into Mowgley. About time you asked for a transfer, maybe.'

She shrugged, then said 'So, any luck with your mate in the Drug Squad?'

Quayle moved his beer glass around on the table, then said 'Yes and no.'

'Yes and no?'

'Yes, most of the guys in the squad think Hopkirk's at it, but there's no real proof.'

'What about the flash new car - and all those retro designer clothes?'

He frowned, then smoothed one lapel of his immaculately-cut suit jacket: 'I wouldn't say his clothes were designer or retro. Just out-of-date. And the car's not that flash for a single bloke on a good screw.' Quayle took a sip of beer then put the glass back down carefully on the table. He was obviously enjoying being the possessor of information he knew she wanted. Then he said: 'But there's more. Quite a bit more.'

'Go on.'

'He moved into a new flat on the seafront in the middle of last year.'

DS McCarthy let out a spiral of smoke and watched it drift towards the lofty ceiling. 'As you said, he's a single bloke on a good wage. Is that it?'

'Nope. It looks as if he's also bought a flash holiday home.'

'What do you mean, "it looks like"?'

'I got it from a WPC whose mate had been having a thing

with him. He told her he had a place in Spain and invited her out there. He said for her not to tell anyone, or all his mates on the squad would be after a freebie.'

'He could have been stringing her along to impress her.'

Quayle shrugged. 'Maybe, but as I said, there's more.'

She sighed. He was enjoying himself. 'Go on, then.'

'My mate said the squad's been having a real bad run recently. Someone would get a tip-off from his snout about a big deal going down, but when they'd sorted out an action plan and turned up, there was nothing going on. They were just being fed crap bits of information, like the organisers were taking the piss. Or seemed to be.'

'What do you mean?'

Quayle smoothed his lapel again and fiddled with the perfectly tied knot of his tie. 'My mate said they got a lead while Hopkirk was on holiday last summer. He'd gone out of the country - perhaps to Spain - and the team got a last-minute tip-off. When they turned up, it was all happening just like the snout had said it would. When Hopkirk got back, he didn't seem best pleased. He said he was pissed off to have missed out on the action and credit, but...'

Quayle left the sentence unfinished as he swallowed the last of his beer.

She looked at the end of her cigarette and thought about what he had said. Then she made an effort and smiled at her colleague. 'Okay, is that it?'

'It's enough, isn't it?'

She raised her eyebrows. 'Maybe. Anyway thanks.'

He looked unconcerned. 'No big deal. Are you going to tell me why you wanted to know if Hopkirk was up to something? And are you going to pass it on to Himself?'

'I knew you had a mate in Drugs, and I didn't want it getting back to Jack that I'd been fishing around about his mate.'

Quayle stood up and adjusted his jacket. 'Well, just make sure that if you use it, you don't let him know you got it from me.'

'Of course not. Thanks again. I owe you one.'

He looked down at her. 'I reckon I can think of something you can do for me.'

After flashing a deliberately oily smile, he walked off towards the door. Melons sat watching him and finishing her cigarette. As she stubbed it out and prepared to leave, she noticed he had left the bill on the table for her to pay.

eight

'I wonder if it's true.'

DS McCarthy reached over and switched the radio off. Mowgley yawned and scratched his chin.

'What, that active sex only burns a hundred calories an hour? I suppose it depends how active it is. Missionary position with the socks on, or taking off from the top of the wardrobe?'

'Sorry, I wasn't listening. I was wondering if it's true we go to Heaven when we die, or it's just... nothingness?'

'The trouble is you only get to find out when you're dead, and if it's nothingness you wouldn't know anyway.' He scratched his chin again, then nodded through the windscreen towards where a man wearing a tail coat and striped trousers and holding his top hat in a peculiar way was walking in front of a slowly-moving hearse.

Mowgley wrinkled his eyes: 'I wonder if that's our man in there? The trouble is they all look the same. I bet a lot of people follow the wrong coffin in to the chapel.'

'Well,' responded Catherine McCarthy, that's certainly not Mr Wheatcroft's funeral party.'

Mowgley looked across at her: 'How do you know?'

'That big floral arrangement on the roof spelling out 'MUM' is a bit of a clue.'

'Well spotted, sergeant. Just testing to see if you'd picked it up.'

Their unmarked car was sitting in the overflow car park. It was higher up the slope of Portsdown Hill than the main buildings, so they had a good view.

The crematorium at Portchester had been built in 1958, and like churches of that era it looked functional but uninspiring.

But it was a sought-after venue. Cremation had become increasingly popular, and nearly three quarters of people or their surviving relatives chose this method of disposing of the earthly remains. Three thousand services took place at Portchester each year, and although there were two chapels, traffic jams threatened at peak times. Sometimes, it was rumoured, guests would be ushered in at the front entrance while the exit door was still closing.

They watched as the hearse pulled up under a sheltered porch-way and the bearers got out. Moving in respectful slow-motion. A small knot of mourners stood at a discreet distance, and from the number of elderly men and women present it was likely that the deceased had not died young.

The limousine behind the hearse eased to a stop, its doors opened by the waiting ushers. First to be helped out of the back of the car was a very old man. He was supported on either side while a walking frame was handed out, then guided gently on to it. As Mowgley opened his mouth, Catherine McCarthy held up an admonitory finger and said sharply: 'If you say 'No real point in him going home, is there?' I'll give you a slap.'

'As a matter of fact,' said Mowgley in an injured tone, 'I was going to say I wondered if it's true they take the handles and stuff off the coffins before they put it in the furnace and then sell them back to the undertaker.'

McCarthy chose not to give an opinion and reached for the cigarette packet on the dashboard. 'Remind me of why we're here? You don't think Portsmouth's premier drug purveyor will turn up to pay his respects and ask if he can have his money back, do you?'

Mowgley reached over, nipped the cigarette from her lips, waited for her to light it and then took a long draw. 'You never know. Haven't you seen all those films where the FBI stake out a cemetery when there's a funeral for a Mafia big shot? I just thought it might be a little insensitive to show up without an invitation, and I don't suppose Andy Wheatcroft would make us particularly welcome. I'm also interested to see who turns up… if anyone does except the neighbours.' He took another pull at the cigarette and made a face. 'I don't know how you can smoke these things. Besides, we don't know for sure if what Mr W had in his belt was drug money.'

His sergeant shook her head resignedly and reached again for the packet. 'I thought you said yesterday you were going to pack up smoking?'

'Only my own. I ran out this morning before I got up.'

'Of course. As to where Mr Wheatcroft's stash came from, I think Stephen's report makes it look very much as if it's drug money.'

'What report? Why didn't I get a copy?'

'You did. I put it on your desk first thing this morning.'

'Ah. So you did. I remember it now. I scheduled it for detailed study this afternoon, but as we're here killing time...'

Sgt McCarthy opened her window and waved the smoke out. 'Okay. Pay attention. To start with, Stephen did a really good job on Andy Wheatcroft. If you had read the report you would have seen the lad's got a bit of form from his early youth. A couple of assaults with Actual Bodily Harm and a Threatening Behaviour '

Mowgley looked unimpressed. 'We've all been there, haven't we? It's part of growing up.'

'Maybe for you. Anyway, that's not all. He also nearly went to jail for doing a spot of dealing when he was just seventeen.'

'Nearly went to jail?'

'His brief said his client wanted to join the army and they wouldn't have him if he'd been in clink. So he got a suspended.'

Mowgley shifted in his seat. 'A bit of youthful trading doesn't put him in the frame for being a big-time dealer.'

'No, but it helps when you add on his connections with Mr Finlayson.'

The DI sat up and showed considerably more interest. 'Do tell.'

'It seems the two go back a long way. They weren't schoolmates like you and Dave Hopkirk, but Wheatcroft was doing a bit of strong-arm stuff for Mickey Finn when he was still a teenager. Bouncing at clubs and pubs which were customers of Finlayson's agency, and collecting druggie debts and persuading trading rivals to find other localities.'

Mowgley nodded: 'Okay. But young Andy becoming a squaddie must have put an end to their working relationship?'

Sgt. McCarthy shook her head and reached for the dashboard, taking the last cigarette from the packet. She lit it and warded off Mowgley's hand. 'Not so, according to the inside info. It's said he used to do a regular bit of moonlighting for Finlayson when he was home on leave. I think Mr Mickey Finn admired Wheatcroft's talent for creating mayhem, and Wheatcroft liked getting paid for what he did best.'

She offered the cigarette. Mowgley took it, drew deeply then asked: 'So what does he do in the army? Given his mate's background and the opportunities for a bit of pilfering from the storeroom, the Medical Corps would have suited him a treat?'

'Officially, he's in Signals.'

'Officially?'

'Stephen didn't get far with his enquiries in that direction, but he thinks Wheatcroft might also be doing a regular bit for the boys in Hereford. Signals is unsurprisingly an important resource for any Special Service operation. They often bring in outside specialists, and make sure the ones they use are also good at helping out with killing people.'

Mowgley sat and digested this information with the remains of the cigarette, then said: 'Are you telling me that I managed to seriously upset someone from the S.A.S and lived to tell the tale?'

McCarthy nodded. 'Looks like it.'

'Blimey. So, where did Young Mundy get all the gen about Wheatcroft's connections with Finlayson? From Hoppy?'

'No. He said your mate was not particularly helpful. In fact, Stephen said he was quite unhelpful.'

'Oh.' Mowgley rubbed his chin thoughtfully, then said: 'By the way, how did your day off go yesterday?'

'Day off? I was only away for a couple of hours.'

'Oh. It just seemed longer on my own in the pub. You know how I hate drinking alone. That reminds me...'

Mowgley pulled the handle on the passenger side door and started to heave himself out of the car.

'Where are you going? There's no bar here - and I thought you said we were just going to keep a watching brief?'

He buttoned his coat up before answering. 'Nature calls and I'm too old for the empty bottle routine. Unless you've got a suitable receptacle.'

She shuddered. 'Carry on. You know where it is?'

He nodded. 'I've been here before, you know. At my age it

starts to be a regular outing.'

As he walked away, McCarthy let her window down and shouted after him: 'If there's a fag machine anywhere ...'

He stopped and looked back: 'I doubt it. Ironic as it may seem, the crematorium is a non smoking area...'

*

As she watched Mowgley walking down the steps, DS McCarthy became aware of a figure passing the car and also heading for the steps. The man had his face turned away, but from the way he walked she guessed him to be young. He was wearing what used to be called a car coat, and below it were faded jeans and scuffed trainers. His long hair was pulled back into a pony-tail. A movement on the other side of the car drew her attention, and she saw another man going in the direction Mowgley had taken. In contrast to the first man, his head was completely bald. He was shorter, but of much heavier build and wearing a leather bomber jacket and denims. Taken altogether, there was something about the two figures that suggested they were not going to attend a service in the crematorium.

Putting her unlit cigarette on the dashboard, Sgt. McCarthy took the keys out of the ignition, opened the glove box and reached into it, then pulled on the driver's door handle.

*

Detective Inspector Mowgley was about to zip up when the door swung open behind him, letting in a blast of cold air.

Instinctively, he glanced over his right shoulder, but only had time to turn slightly away from the stall before the short length of steel pipe hit him just above the right ear.

He slumped backwards until his fall was checked by the porcelain privacy screen between the two urinals. Then his right foot slid into the channel and he teetered before lurching forward. He vaguely felt the pain in his knee as it connected with the tiled floor, and could think of no better response to his situation than putting his hands over his head.

As he waited for the next blow, the door swung violently open to admit a woman. She was screaming madly, and he realised that he recognised her voice, even at that unaccustomed level and intensity.

The pony-tailed, bearded man turned towards her just as she pressed the button on the canister she was holding in her extended left hand.

CS incapacitant spray was introduced by UK Police Forces in 1999 after a six-month trial. Contained in an aerosol-type can, the version used by British police is more concentrated than the American version, and emerges as a liquid stream rather than a spray. When aimed at the face, the chemical reacts to moisture on the skin and causes a strong burning sensation. This is usually followed by uncontrollable coughing and copious nasal discharge, accompanied by extreme nausea, disorientation and dizziness. The solution is propelled by liquid nitrogen and said to be accurate and effective from a range of four metres. This stream was directed directly into the face of the man who had attacked Mowgley from a distance of no more than a few inches.

It was a text-book reaction. After his eyes had instinctively shut, the man doubled over, screeching with pain and anger as he dropped the length of pipe and tore at his face. Before he could recover, Sergeant McCarthy had brought into action the other implement she had taken from the glove box.

Victorian police in London had relied on foot-long truncheons known colloquially as billy-clubs, which was itself a slang term for a burglar's crowbar. When deployed by a member of today's Police Force, the standard issue expandable, collapsible or telescopic baton grows instantly to a length of twenty one inches. It has a solid tip to add more force to the swing, and it is not permissible for the user to strike at the head, sternum, spine or groin unless unavoidable.

Given the circumstances, Sergeant McCarthy was not overly concerned with the fine detail of standing orders in this regard. The tip of the baton caught the man squarely on top of his head, breaking the skin in spite of his thick hair. He screamed again, and fell to his knees alongside Mowgley, who was a little recovered and scrabbling for the piece of heating pipe.

DS McCarthy was raising the baton for another strike when the door was again flung open. The leading edge caught the sergeant's shoulder, sending her spinning across the room towards one of the two toilet cubicles. As she struggled to recover her balance, the shaven-headed man who had burst in took a single stride towards her, grabbed her throat with his left hand and pinned her against the tiled wall.

In the moment before she joined Mowgley and the other attacker on the floor, she saw he was smiling almost affectionately as he pulled back his fist.

nine

Named by a former Team Mowgley member who thought he had a sense of humour, The Fun Factory was housed in a depressingly neglected and cubist 1970s block overlooking the ferry port. Apart from occasional part-timers, the civilian staff consisted of Mowgley's amanuensis Jo, who was a competent and fortunately tolerant middle-aged woman.

If asked, it is doubtful that Inspector Mowgley would know Jo's second name or where she lived. He knew she was married and that the three children in the photographs on the wall of her cubby-hole were hers. There were no photographs of a husband, and Mowgley did not like to ask if that was because he had left the marital home or the land of the living. Or, he reasoned, it might be that their absence was because she did not care to look at his likeness while at work.

In the approximate centre of the otherwise open-plan floor was a flimsy-looking cubicle. The top half of three of the walls was glazed, though made impenetrable by the sheets of paper which had at some time been secured to them by adhesive putty, pieces of sticky tape and in some instances, chewing gum. So far, the oldest document to have been uncovered dated back to the start of the last quarter of the previous Millennium. This preceded Inspector Mowgley's reign by many years, but he rather liked the protective covering the layers of paper afforded.

One wall of the cubicle held a glazed door; the other sides were lined on the outside with shoulder-high filing cabinets and other bulky office ware. This arrangement made the cubicle look as if it were under a state of permanent siege, which coincided with the general view of the occupier.

Inside and in one corner stood an old-fashioned bentwood

hat and coat stand. Facing it was yet another filing cabinet, taller and in even poorer condition than those protecting the outer perimeter. On top stood an electric fan with a broken grille, an ornamental bottle-opener in the shape of a full-skirted flamenco dancer, and a small tray bearing a selection of drinking glasses.

It was common knowledge that the drawers of this cabinet contained items which the senior officer of Team Mowgley considered too essential or important to be left outside his office. These items usually included several cartons of hand-rolling tobacco, a supply of canned lager and a drawer completely filled with Cadbury's Curly-Wurly bars and Creme Eggs.

In another corner was an office chair with one castor missing. In the remaining corner was a battered armchair, the stuffing of which had long been leaking on to the pockmarked floor.

Central to the office was a desk, though this was not immediately evident as its surface was totally obscured by layers of general detritus including old newspapers, takeaway menus, empty tobacco packets and Curly-Wurly wrappers. There was also a host of paperwork, the currency of which grew ever older as the pile deepened. Some surprisingly erudite wag had once claimed that the original Charter of the City granted to Portsmouth by Richard the Lion Heart in 1194 would be found there if a thorough enough excavation were to be made.

The only other piece of furniture in the cubicle was an old captain's chair, once to be found in the snug bar of the Ship Leopard public house when there had been a snug bar. Although the leatherette on the seat and armrests was shiny with wear, it had not been Mowgley who had caused it; he tried to spend as little time at his desk as was creatively possible, and had probably put in more hours in his local than the captain's chair.

Above all this, a once-white ceiling was now a fetching shade of nicotine. Affixed to it was a dusty, cobweb-ridden and oft-flickering neon tube. Surrounding the tube like a crop of artificial stalagmites were dozens of crudely-shaped darts fashioned from the type of silver foil found in some cigarette packets. They were clinging to the ceiling by the power of

Inspector Mowgley's spit, and had been thrown there in moments of boredom or idleness: the sheer number indicated how easily and often bored he could become.

Outside and close to the door of the cubicle was the desk of DS McCarthy, Its position adding to the impression of a heavily defended redoubt. She was, as DS Quayle would have it, the dragon at the gate.

Apart from the bulky computer terminal and keyboard common to all the desks save Inspector Mowgley's, items on Catherine McCarthy's desktop usually included an out-of-date Daily Telegraph with the crossword part-completed and a collection of pens and pencils standing upright in a carved wooden cylinder. Laying at ease and looking unblinkingly at the office door would be a very large and surprisingly real-looking stuffed toy lioness, presented to her by Mowgley by way of an apology for some long-ago offence. Until recently, another object on permanent display had been a framed photograph. It had shown a handsome man in his early middle age, with a carefully disarrayed mop of thick, black, curling and gleaming hair and very white teeth. He was smiling confidently and a little roguishly at the camera, as if sharing a secret with the photographer.

The man in the frame was Capitaine Guy Varennes, a French police officer and once lover of DS McCarthy. Like the man, the photograph had ceased to have a part in her life a year ago when she had discovered the Capitaine to be married.

Several of the pencils in the cylinder were topped with brightly-coloured erasers in the shape of the heads of fantastical creatures, and there was often also a small make-up bag and compact mirror on the desktop. The bag was covered with doodles made by a felt-tipped pen.

Against a column to one end of the office was the desk of Detective Constable Mundy, and it was as orderly as that of his commanding officer's was disorderly. Looking at the way the ruler, pens, small calendar and notepad were laid out in absolute symmetry and at a precise distance from the edge of the desktop, any group of passing psychologists might immediately set up a conference to discuss the possible existence, level and sub-category of the user's Obsessive Compulsive Disorder.

Apart from Jo's work station and a computer, set of drawers and mini-filing cabinet for any temporary staff brought in during an emergency - which generally meant Jo's holiday periods or if she were ill for more than a day - the only other desk in the office was that of Detective Sergeant Dickie Quayle.

If the theme were continued in his home, it would make DS Quayle an adherent of the Minimalist style of furnishing and decor. The top of the desk was entirely clear, except for a single photograph in a very plain stainless frame of the highest quality. Unsurprisingly to the two women users of the office, the photograph was not of a relative or role model, unless it could be said that Sergeant Quayle's role model was himself. To be fair, there was an attractive young blonde woman also featured in the shot of an exotic and distant location, but she very much took second billing to the central character.

It was probably some sort of record that Inspector Mowgley and DS McCarthy were in the office in the middle of the day. They were alone because Jo was shopping; DC Mundy was attending to his continuing duties involving the past and present activities of Andy Wheatcroft. Meanwhile, Dickie Quayle was allegedly interviewing a young and attractive ferry company employee about a car which had been stolen from an overnight crossing to St Malo.

Although neither would admit it, both felt awkward about what had taken place two days previously at Portchester crematorium. Irrationally and although his sergeant would have said there was no reason for it, Mowgley felt somehow guilty about playing no part in the violent incident except that of victim.

He also did not want to visit their local in case someone made a comment on his colleague's injuries. So, in spite of it being long past their usual lunchtime, he was toying with the quick version of the Daily Telegraph crossword, while DS McCarthy was going through the office face book.

Even at a time of rapidly-increasing electronic technology, the face book was still in regular use, and its simplicity was the key to its value. Regularly updated, it now contained the mug shots of more than three hundred criminals who might attempt to pass through the port.

'Funny how they call it a "shiner" when it doesn't, isn't it?'

DS McCarthy saw that Mowgley was watching her with a

mix of concern and responsibility. She smiled reassuringly, then reached up and gently touched the almost egg-sized swelling below her left eye. The extensive bruising was dark blue, almost black, and she knew from experience that it would change hue in the coming days. It was not a fetching sight in her compact mirror, but the blood-filled eye was worse. The force of the punch had broken blood vessels in the delicate transparent tissue over the eye, and she knew it would take weeks for it to clear. 'Yes,' she said, 'I suppose it is. How's your head?'

The inspector's fingers explored the shaven area where the six stitches had been inserted, and shrugged. 'Fine. Just wish I could have returned the compliment.'

'Perhaps you'll get the chance.'

'Yeah, maybe. Any luck with the face book?'

She put it on the desk and made a wry face. 'Not yet. I shan't forget their ugly vardas, that's for sure. What about you?'

'All I can remember is a beard and a lot of dark hair. If I remember rightly, his nose was not so much broken as twisted sideways a bit.'

She nodded in accord, then said: 'What do you think it was about?'

Mowgley shrugged: 'Dunno.'

'Can you think of anyone you've upset lately...?' She paused and smiled grimly. 'Oh, sorry, what a silly question. What I mean is do you think it was connected with the Wheatcroft case - perhaps Finlayson sending us a message?'

'Maybe, but if it was, I don't see what it was supposed to say.'

'Just to show he could have us seen to at any time, perhaps. Do you think the idea was just to turn us over - or would they have taken it further?'

'That's the really interesting question. We won't know the answer until we meet the Brothers Grim again. Whatever they meant to do, it's a good job those two blokes arrived for a pee and broke the party up.'

'Yes.' The DS touched her eye again. As she had been told by a WPC at the hospital, their attackers had made an exit when two ushers had walked in. There had been a brief struggle when the younger of the two had grabbed the man who had punched McCarthy, but the thugs were obviously keen to leave, and the ushers not keen to take them on.

Statements and descriptions had been taken by the crime squad. This was because the incident had taken place outside the ferry port. It was apparently unconnected with any current investigation there, so technically not a case for Team Mowgley.

Catherine McCarthy closed the face book, stretched, then looked at her watch. 'This is not like us, is it? Fancy a pint? If you're worried about what we look like, you can wear your cowboy hat and I can put on a pair of dark glasses. People might think we're a pair of celebs.'

Inspector Mowgley looked slightly embarrassed. 'I've got to meet someone. Why don't you take the rest of the day off?'

'What, is this a secret rendezvous?'

'No.'

She gave an exasperated sigh. 'Well, then?'

'I'm meeting Sarah Wheatcroft.'

'I said you fancied her.'

Mowgley sniffed in a non-committal way. 'It's nothing to do with any of that. I just think it's a good time to have another talk with her. The doc says her mother's still too upset to speak to us, and I certainly don't want to risk meeting with Andy Wheatcroft again just yet. I thought neutral ground would be a good idea.'

'But not with me along?'

'I don't want to spook her with us both being there.'

'Ah. Of course. And where are you meeting her? Surely not the Ship? That would definitely spook her.'

'No. Southsea. You can give me a lift there is you like, and we've got time for a quick one on the way.'

'Dutch courage?'

'Of course. You know I don't like that fancy Belgian stuff.'

ten

In Mowgley's childhood years, it was a common quip amongst working-class Portmuthians that you had to wear clean underwear if you went shopping in Southsea. This was not because of risk of accident and hospitalisation, but because Southsea was posh.

Conurbations are created when neighbouring towns and villages spread and merge. Perhaps because it was an island and though the villages of Portsmouth had joined up across the centuries, each had retained and stoutly defended its identity. Each had its own social standing, and each its own collection of retail outlets reflecting that standing.

Close by the sea and hemmed in by clean-lined Thomas Owen villas and Gothic Victorian monstrosities, Southsea's shopping centre had the monopoly on classy stores and high-end purveyors of goods and services. Times had changed, but not that much, and while Tesco had chosen to set up shop in the grubby centre of the city, Waitrose had naturally settled on Southsea.

Having been dropped off by Catherine McCarthy at the crossroads from which the shopping area radiated, Inspector Mowgley wiped perspiration from his top lip and walked to the nearest cash point. It was set in the wall of a branch of the bank he currently used, and just being in the building's proximity made him nervous.

He waited his turn, then stepped forward, inserted the card and took the cash but no balance option. He gave a mental sigh of relief when the machine gave him what he had asked for, then crossed the road to wait in the appointed meeting place.

On the single occasion he had been invited to act as best

man, the bride-to-be refused to go through with the ceremony unless Mowgley dressed to suit the occasion. Almost as reluctantly as entering a bank, he had visited the shop outside which he was now standing and hired the full regalia of topper and tails. In those days, the name above the heavy plate glass door had been Moss Bros. Now it was Quality Seconds. Instead of artfully arranged striped trousers and brushed grey waistcoats in the window, there were track suits and running shoes at a price to appeal to people who were not at all prone to an athletic lifestyle.

Looking across the road, Mowgley saw himself as a small boy, breathing in the exotic aroma coming from the establishment which would have taken offence at being called a grocery shop. No broken biscuits or bottles of Corona were to be found at this emporium, and no common or garden housewife customers. The lady visitor (always a lady unless it were her chauffeur) would be escorted to a bentwood chair and invited to make her order and wait in comfort while it was prepared. It might be slices from one of the whole baked hams, glazed with brown sugar and pricked with cloves laid out in a precise and unvarying pattern. It might be a portion of mouth-watering quality cheese, cut with wire from one of the huge rounds lining the counter and wrapped in a sheet of fine greaseproof paper. Mowgley breathed deeply, and his olfactory memory bank kicked in. The bouquet was upon him, even though the premises now housed an upmarket estate agency.

All along the road, changing tastes and times were reflected by the change of shop fronts. Former salons, stores and boutiques had become fast food outlets, Indian restaurants, nail bars, tanning salons and night clubs. They in their turn would disappear, the premises emerging in another incarnation. Only the upper facades of the buildings remained unchanged.

His thoughts of times past and if they were as good as they seemed from this distance were interrupted as he saw Sarah Wheatcroft approaching from the direction of the car park behind the bank.

Although normally not something he would notice, he saw that her auburn hair appeared to have been freshly coiffed, and shone in the weak winter sun.

She was wearing a long raincoat in what he believed to be gabardine, and in a colour which Catherine McCarthy would probably have assessed as steel grey. On one arm she carried a large handbag in what even he realised was a complementary colour, and one which matched what he could see of her close-fitting boots.

'Hello.' She smiled. 'Am I late?'

'No, I'm early.'

'It's just that you had a funny expression on your face, and I wondered if you'd drifted off while waiting.'

'I have to admit I was thinking about when I was a boy, and there was a really posh grocery shop over there.' He indicated the window of the estate agency. 'In the Sixties it became a delicatessen, and they had chickens roasting on spits in the window. It was the wonder of the age to see them turning...' His voice tailed off as he resisted the temptation to take her on a visit to his past.

'Really?' she said indulgently, then: 'It is a shame how things are changing so fast. It means you feel disconnected from the past, especially if you've lived in a place for a long time.'

He thought about explaining how Portsmouth had changed a lot more than most cities thanks to the Luftwaffe, but instead gestured towards their destination.

*

Betty's Tea Rooms stood out in stark contrast to the garish frontages of the betting shop and pizza palace which flanked it. Ironically, the Dickensian-style latticework bow window and door with its bulls-eye glass panes had only been in place a decade longer than its neighbours' exteriors.

In such a changing world, Betty's was a perfectly conceived concept. Inside, the fleeting tastes and styles of modern times were steadfastly ignored. The waitresses (waiters were off the menu at Betty's) wore black uniforms with crisp white aprons and headgear. Whether it was their uniforms or clever selection by their employer, the age, attitude and even looks of the wearers suited the style and atmosphere of the location. The waitresses served the chosen variety of Chinese or Indian tea in porcelain teapots on silver-plated trays, and matching pyramids bore the plates of intransigently English fancy cakes. They were priced at an eye-wateringly high level, but that was part of the appeal.

'What a lovely idea,' she said when they had been seated and the waitress gone to fetch their order.

'Yes,' Mowgley looked around. 'It suits a lot of older people who live here-'

'I meant your idea to come here,' she smiled. 'Is your colleague not coming to join us?'

'DS, er, Detective Sergeant McCarthy? No, she's looking into something for me, and anyway, I didn't want to outnumber you.'

'Ah. No Mr Nice and Ms Nasty routine then?' She smiled almost coquettishly: 'Or was there an ulterior motive in inviting me to tea?'

He wondered for a moment if she meant what he thought she meant, then said: 'I have to admit I didn't relish the idea of upsetting your brother. But quite honestly (which was something Mowgley was prone to say when he had no intention of being honest) I just thought you might feel more comfortable to talk away from your mother's home. How is she?'

'She's not good. I think the funeral brought it home to her that dad had really gone.'

Mowgley lowered his eyes respectfully for a moment, and hoped she would not ask where he had got the wound on his head.

Instead, she looked down at her place setting and then said: 'I need of course to apologise for Andy. You will appreciate how upset he is about losing dad, and he stupidly connected it with and blamed you for bringing it about.'

'I can understand that.'

The tea and pyramid of delight arrived, and they made small talk while making light work of a Bakewell tart, a cream horn, two slices of Battenberg cake and a brace of buttered crumpets. In between mouthfuls, Mowgley heard what he had already learned from DC Mundy about his guest, and a little more.

Sarah Wheatcroft had divorced her husband after he found his secretary more interesting than her, and now lived with her cat in a small apartment in Putney. She was an analytical chemist, working for the London base of an international pharmaceutical company with its headquarters in Switzerland. Before he asked, she said, she did not cut up animals or force beagles to smoke; her main role was to examine the possible side and long-term effects of new drugs. She had no children and did not plan on having any. Not because she did not want to bring innocent life into a world of pain and suffering, but simply because she was too selfish to be anything like a good mother.

In turn, Mowgley explained that he and his small team were responsible for policing the local ferry port. With regards to his personal situation, he was single, unattached and been divorced by his wife on the grounds of mental cruelty. He agreed she had probably had a sound case for the charge, but it had been her who had left him after falling for the Frenchman who had sold them his rambling and much distressed manoir in Normandy. Ironically, he concluded, she had said she would leave him if he did not agree to buying La Cour, but had left him with the property and hefty mortgage while she took their home in north Portsmouth.

'And what are your plans for the manoir? Will you gradually restore it and then go and live there and keep chickens and grow grapes?'

He shook his head. 'They don't grow many grapes in my bit of Normandy. I've been trying to sell the place since I was lumbered with it, but I have to admit I rather like being able to call myself Mowgley of the Yard.'

'Of course. How lovely.' She looked down at the small and very traditional ash tray in the centre of the table. 'Do you mind if I smoke?'

'I thought you'd never ask.'

She took a foreign-looking packet of cigarettes from her handbag, extracted one and leaned forward towards the proffered light. A pungent-smelling cloud drifted across the table and she waved at it with her free hand: 'I'm sorry about that; I got hooked on them when I lived in Spain.'

Mowgley raised an eyebrow to show interest. 'Really? Whereabouts?'

'Oh, you wouldn't know it. Before I met my husband and went to work in London, I spent a few years living in an old farm in a mountain range about fifty miles inland from Gibraltar.'

'That sounds rather nice.'

She shrugged. 'If you like it hot in the day and cold at night and panoramic views of olive trees and cacti...and no neighbours for a mile or so. It's not everyone's idea of paradise, but I loved it. The landscape is so... dramatically barren. It's where they shot the spaghetti westerns in the 60s - so you can imagine what it looks like.'

Mowgley nodded. 'And when did you move to London?'

'Only five years ago. I'm afraid our marriage was short if not sweet.'

'And is your Spanish connection why you bought your parents the little house in Spain?'

'Yes, I suppose so. They'd come over to see me regularly at the finca, and really liked the area. Dad had a breathing problem, and the cold clear air at night helped him sleep. He loved the area and the pequena casa. I think they would have spent more and more time there, and might even have moved over if-'

Mowgley nodded again, wondered if now was an apt time and decided it might be. He took a mental breath, then watched her face as he asked: 'So the money was for restoring their holiday home?'

She did not react except for a slight and what seemed a genuine creasing of her brow. Then she said: 'Money?'

'The money your father had in his belt?'

Sarah Wheatcroft looked at him uncomprehendingly. 'I'm sorry, I don't understand. What money?'

Mowgley groaned inwardly. However he put it and however she reacted, he knew it was not going to be a pleasant exchange. 'I thought you knew. That you'd been told.'

'About what?' There was a discernible edge to her voice now, and she kept her eyes fixed on his.

'Your parents' camper was stopped at the ferry port. Customs were doing random stops, and your parents were picked out of the line. Their baggage and the camper were being looked through when your father was taken ill. When the paramedics examined him, they found a money belt.'

Her eyes remained on his as she took the cigarette from her mouth and placed it on the ashtray. 'I'm sorry, I still don't understand. A money belt? Are you serious?'

He deliberately said nothing and waited for her further

response.

There was a silence as she looked at him and down at her plate. Then she looked up: 'And how much money was in this belt?'

'Exactly fifty thousand pounds.'

She sat very still, continuing to look directly at him.

Then she looked around the table, nodded and said sharply: 'That's what this is all about, then? Not for a reassuring chat with a nice cup of tea away from the house.'

She did not wait for him to reply, but took her bag from the back of the chair and stood up. 'You thought I knew about this money, or even that I was involved some way.'

He said nothing because he could not think of anything to say, and watched thoughtfully as she walked away from the table. He waited until she left, then raised a hand to signal for the waitress.

*

'Did it go as badly as your face suggests?'

Mowgley was on his third pint, sitting at the high bar in his favourite non-pub drinking venue.

Oysters Bar had been the inspiration of Inspector Mowgley's favourite landlord and best male friend. Terry Little had spent his early years as a steward on cruise liners when only rich and famous people went on cruises. After looking after the likes of Clark Gable and Lauren Bacall and once even Bogey, he had met, fallen for and married a lady who came from a long and renowned line of city publicans. Together they had worked endless hours to make a raging success of a number of pubs.

Now, the couple were winding down. For them, winding down meant creating a very upmarket bar and restaurant in Southsea for their son and daughter-in-law to run, and a much more down-to-earth bar and pet project for Terry just a walking distance away. The original concept had been of a Spanish Tapas bar, but it had, like the best of licensed outlets, simply become El Tel's bar.

'Yes.' Mowgley emptied his glass and waved dispiritedly at the barman.

'In what way? DS McCarthy took the bar stool alongside.

'Did she turn you down for a date? Did she deny all knowledge of the dosh her dad was wearing?'

'She said she didn't know about the money.'

Catherine McCarthy sniffed. 'To paraphrase Mandy-Rice Davis, she would say that, wouldn't she?'

'Well, she didn't actually say she didn't know about the money, but she acted as if she didn't and copped the needle when she saw why I had asked to see her.'

DS McCarthy looked up at the ceiling. 'What, you mean she thought it was a date?'

Mowgley shrugged. 'Maybe, or maybe not.'

'She didn't say it was her mum and dad's life savings, or that they'd won the Lottery and ticked the anonymity box?'

'No. What was interesting is that she used to live in Spain.'

'What? When and where?'

'Before she got married. In the south, near where the Wheatcroft holiday ruin is.'

'You're right. That is interesting. So you think it was maybe her money and mum and dad were taking it out for her? But if so, why - unless it was funny money. Or do you think she genuinely didn't know about it?'

'Do you know,' DI Mowgley handed his glass to the barman. 'I don't reckon she did.'

'So how did it end?'

DS McCarthy was not to receive an answer, as her phone buzzed before Mowgley could reply. He watched his beer being poured as she acknowledged the caller, responded and then snapped the phone cover shut and told the barman to cancel the drinks.

'What do you mean, cancel the drinks? It can't be that bloody urgent?'

She shook her head as if bemused, then looked at the phone and then him. 'I fear it is. That was Jo. She says someone's just blown up the Ship Leopard.'

eleven

To a regular customer, the exterior structure of the Ship Leopard would have appeared no more distressed than usual. But the number and variety of emergency vehicles in the car park suggested something inside must be seriously amiss.

Two ambulances with their back doors open had been backed up to the main entrance. As the detectives arrived, a bemused-looking man was being helped by two paramedics towards one of the ambulances. He appeared unharmed and increasingly reluctant to get into the vehicle, and it looked more like he was being arrested than rescued.

Nearby was a gleaming fire engine with a number of flat hose pipes running from it into the pub.

A pair of firemen wearing breathing apparatus were standing by the pub entrance as if looking for something to do. One of them was dangling a lit cigarette from his hand, and Mowgley wondered how he was going to smoke it with the mask on.

Lined up next to the fire engine was a white vehicle about the same size as the ambulances. A sign on the side declared it to belong to the Royal Logistics Bomb Disposal Corps. One of the back doors was open, and a soldier in camouflage dress was fiddling with something inside.

Nearby and with its engine running stood a white pick-up truck, decorated with blue squares and red chevrons. It carried a pod with blue lights at the front and back. The signage identified it as a Royal Navy Bomb Disposal Unit. A man in a dark blue coverall was leaning against the bonnet with his arms folded, and he appeared to be looking at the soldier and his much bigger vehicle with some irritation.

Close to the entrance of the car park was an unmarked police car. Nearby were a motorway patrol car and a patrol wagon. A line of police tape had been stretched between two traffic cones which had been placed on either side of the car park entrance, and a PC was standing guard over it.

Scattered along the road directly outside the Ship Leopard were a number of obviously private vehicles, including two white panel vans, a pick-up truck, a taxi and an ice cream van with its engine running and driver at the wheel. These were obviously vehicles belonging to customers which had been shifted to give access to the emergency services. Whether the driver of the ice cream van had been in the pub or had spotted a potential business opportunity was not clear. At one end of the van a huddle of customers was gathered, some holding partly-filled glasses

As Inspector Mowgley and DS McCarthy navigated the tape, a small, elderly man was being forcibly escorted from the main entrance. Mowgley saw that WingCo the potman was doggedly hanging on to a tray bearing a dozen empty glasses. Behind him, another regular was being removed from the premises.

King Dong was a short slight man, but he was wiry and it was taking three uniformed constables to escort him from the pub. A fourth was having no luck in trying to remove the nearly full glass from the Dong's large right hand.

Inside were no signs of damage, except that the door leading to the toilets was leaning against a table in the main bar. This was not particularly unusual, especially on stag nights or the annual get-together of World War II British and German Submariners.

'Good Morning, Sir and Madam; what can I get you?'

As a fireman carrying a much-abused condom dispenser passed by, Mowgley and McCarthy saw that a man in a trilby hat and heavy raincoat was standing on the business side of the bar.

He looked to be in his late fifties, though could have been younger and of intemperate habits and sleeping patterns. He had a floribund, round and much-veined face which offset a very large nose which resembled the texture and colour of an under-ripe strawberry. The eyes set deeply into layers of lined flesh indicated an affable but observant state of being, and he looked very much at home leaning with his elbows on the bar.

Mowgley smiled. 'Hello, mate - thinking of chucking it all in and taking over here?'

The man pursed his lips then let out a small, negative puff of air. 'Do I look that stupid?'

Mowgley shook his head. He knew that many serious drinkers liked the idea of taking a pub on retirement and having the best of all possible worlds, but DI Charles Edward Williams was far too self-knowing to kid himself.

Born a year after the end of World War II, Williams had escaped National Service and started his policing career as a cadet in the Yorkshire Ridings. He had been stationed in a bleak area of moorland, dotted with farms and hamlets. As he had told Mowgley, the most serious crimes he had to deal with at that stage of his career was the odd domestic, a rash of petty thievery if gypsies were passing through, or an outbreak of sheep-stealing. Now and then on remoter farms, it might be a case of sheep shagging rather than stealing.

In 1965, he had won a transfer to the Greater Manchester force, and been attached to the squad investigating the Moors Murders. It was seeing Myra Hindley and hearing the tapes of the tortured innocents which, he said, had put him off marriage and parenthood for life.

After thirty years in various patches within the Greater Manchester area, Inspector Williams saw retirement on the horizon and thought it time to make plans for what was to come. After considering his options, he decided that the best move would be to a sinecure post on the sunny and soft south coast. There he could move in to a bungalow with a nice bit of garden and await his pension.

To his surprise, he had found Portsmouth a bit like some of the rougher areas of Manchester but without the class. He had also found that what he had got for his terraced former mill worker's cottage in Salford would not buy a caravan by the sea in Southsea.

He had settled for a small property similar to the one he had left but valued at nearly twice the price.

In general, though, it seemed to have been not a bad move for DI Williams. It was a bonus that the local Chief Superintendent was a fellow Yorkshireman. Then, three years ago, DCS Cyril 'Gloria' Mundy had taken early retirement and been replaced by a woman. Even worse, the new boss was an upper middle-class, university-educated fast-tracked woman.

Williams felt his days numbered, but was keeping his head down and his impressive nose clean in the hope that he would survive until retirement. With luck, Detective Chief Superintendent Cressida Hartley-Whitley might even be promoted to a high-profile position requiring her to say the right things during television interviews and have little real involvement with actual police work.

His was a similar situation to that of DI Mowgley, and the mutual adversity had drawn the pair together. Also, they both took more or less the same view as to the best way to be an effective police officer. Both believed in expediency to achieve justice, and neither was too fussy how those aims were achieved.

Mowgley looked around the empty pub, then said: 'A pint of drinking lager and a half of the same, please guv'nor. And one for yourself.' As the inspector and his sergeant watched Williams pull the drinks in a reasonably professional manner, Mowgley asked: 'So what's to do? We heard the pub had been blown up. Did you call it in just to get the emergency response boys going and have the place to yourself?'

DI Williams placed their drinks carefully on a bar towel, then picked up his own glass: 'No, but it's not a bad idea for the future. They do love a bit of a drama nowadays, don't they?' Williams took a drink, then nodded at the displaced door. 'It don't look much, but I'd advise you not to go for a pee, and certainly not a sit-down.' He looked towards Sgt McCarthy. 'And the same applies to you, love. The Ladies is not a pretty sight.'

'So who dunnit?' Mowgley replaced his pint on the counter and took a draw on his roll-up. 'IRA or the Campaign for Real Ale? Woman Against Men Enjoying Themselves or just a cock-up by British Gas?'

'Nope.' responded DI Williams. 'It were Dim and Dimmer, or in your local parlance, Dinn and Dinnier.'

Mowgley raised an eyebrow, drew smoke into his lungs and thought about the Brooks brothers.

Jimmy and Danny were well known to every hands-on working police officer in the City. Though barely past their teens, they had racked up more than a hundred mutual and individual convictions since becoming of prosecutable age. And those were only relating to the cases the police had bothered pursuing.

The Brooks brothers were not so much career criminals as career deadheads. The only thing to be said in their favour was that they were not violent and drew the line at conning or stealing from old people. They didn't thieve cars, but that was only because neither of them could drive. But if there was an unlocked door to hand, they would try it. If there was a neglected bag in a pub, they would take it. If there was lead on a roof and it was not too much of an effort to get up there, they would harvest it. They were avid and incorrigible opportunists, but their opportunism had so far gained them not much more than several spells in young offenders' institutions, and in more recent times, a few brief stints of real porridge.

A fair example of their uselessness as criminals came with their only foray into attempted robbery. After a session in a scrumpy cider pub, they had staggered in to a late-night convenience store on the corner of the street where they lived at the time. When they asked the owner to hand over the takings, he said he was too busy to be robbed at that moment, and requested they return in an hour. They did, and seemed hurt that the shopkeeper had arranged for the police to be waiting to meet them.

Although they pushed the petty crime rate for the City up, their sheer incompetence at their trade had led some officers to take an almost affectionate tolerance towards them, almost as a fond owner does with a naughty puppy.

'I still don't get it,' said Mowgley. 'Why did they blow the toilets up, and with what?'

'I don't think that was the idea,' Williams replied. 'As you know, they turn up here now and then with a hooky radio or mobile. This afternoon they popped in to see if anyone was interested in buying a hand grenade.'

'Sorry, but did you just say 'hand grenade?'' asked DS McCarthy.

'That I did, Sergeant. And a shiny new one by all accounts.'

She shook her head. 'Do we know where they got it from?'

'Not yet. But they did say there was plenty more where it came from.'

'Just out of interest,' asked Mowgley, 'what's the going rate for an unused hand grenade these days?'

'According to one of the locals, they wanted fifty quid for it, but said they would do three for the price of two.'

'And did he get any interest?'

'Only from Joey Sanders.'

'Ah,' said DS McCarthy. 'Mad Joey and hand grenades doesn't sound a very healthy combo to me. Especially if you factor in the Brooks boys.'

If a test were done, it was probable that Joey Sanders and the Brooks brothers would be found to be fairly matched in IQ levels. The difference was that Joey was big and violent enough to be dangerous when he felt like it.

Sanders was a creature of the streets in Portsmouth who made a sort of living from low-level extortion. Every small trader in his area of North Portsmouth knew him, and most were fearful of him. He spent his day wandering around pubs and shops, collecting tributes in the shape of a bottle of beer or a packet of biscuits or a hot pie. This he did by simply making an order or picking something off a shelf and then walking out without paying. His size, appearance and obvious instability made most victims conclude that a few pounds in occasional tribute was better than a wrecked shop or bar or the cost of dental repair work.

Joey was at his most dangerous when someone or something put an idea in his head and he followed it without thinking the likely consequences through. The best-known example had come when he arrived at his lodgings and found the door locked. Unable to kick it in and the landlord refusing to open it, Joey had walked to the nearest service station and taken a roll of plastic bin liners from the forecourt shelving. As the CCTV footage later showed, he then proceeded to fill one with a couple of gallons of petrol from the premium unleaded pump.

Arriving back at the house, he poured half the contents of the bag on to the door and lit his lighter. In the resultant fireball, Joey received second degree burns to his arms and chest and lost all the hair from his head. It was only when he was charged with criminal damage that it became clear that he had burned down the wrong door.

'So what happened next with the arms deal?' asked DS McCarthy.

'The Three Stooges went off to the Gents to discuss the transaction further. And according to the barmaid who tried to bandage him up with some tea-towels, Jimmy said that Joey started playing with the grenade and showed them how he used to pull the pin out with his teeth.'

'I didn't know he was in the army?'

'He wasn't. Didn't meet the IQ requirement level.'

'There's a surprise. Do I need to ask what happened next?'

'I suspect you're ahead of me,' replied Williams. 'Joey panicked and dropped the grenade into the cubicle they were gathered in. He must have broken all sprint records and got through the two doors and into the lounge in the five seconds before it went up. The other two made it through the Gents door before it caught up with them in the passageway.'

'Ouch', said DS McCarthy. 'And they survived?'

Williams nodded and looked at his beer reflectively. 'One of the bomb disposal lads told me that grenades can do funny things, and the amount of damage varies considerably. He had a look and reckoned the toilet bowl and the swing doors helped the boys out.'

'So how bad are they?' asked Mowgley. 'Are they sitting up and taking notice?'

Williams moved his hands in a so-so rocking motion. 'The word from the hospital is that Jimmy was probably a tad faster off the mark than his brother. He's not too bad. Danny came second and has got bad back and leg injuries. Neither of them is going to be doing any ballroom dancing for while, but they're not in any danger.'

'And what about Joey?'

'Nobody fancied trying to stop him when he legged it, but I heard just before you arrived that he's been picked up and is waiting at the nick. I thought I'd finish my pint before having a chat.'

The Yorkshireman drained his glass, then looked at it and proposed one for the road.

Mowgley accepted the offer, and Williams refilled the three glasses.

DS McCarthy lifted hers, then asked: 'Who am I supposed to say 'cheers' to?'

'I shall have it put on my weekly tab,' said her senior officer, 'unless it was tragically destroyed in the explosion.'

twelve

Jimmy Brooks was sitting up in bed having a crafty fag when Mowgley and McCarthy arrived in Ward 7b. Curiously for a geriatric ward it was on the top floor, but had a secure room with only two bed spaces. This made it a convenient place to accommodate damaged suspects.

Mowgley did his best to avoid becoming a regular visitor to the Queen Alexandra hospital. He had been reluctantly present for the removal of his gall bladder, and most of the other visits had been to interview patients who might have been able to assist in Team Mowgley enquiries. The most recent came after he had been shot by allegedly friendly fire. Mowgley adopted a policy of not visiting hospitalised friends because he found the concentration of sick people, pain and sadness not only depressing but possibly contagious.

The senior Brooks brother lay propped up in bed, the back of his head clear of the pillows and covered with a poultice of dressings which put Mowgley in mind of a larger, white version of a Jewish yarmulke. His thin face was unmarked, but both hands were bandaged, and he was having a problem holding and drawing on his cigarette. A tent-like frame holding up a blue bed sheet concealed the extent of injuries to his lower body.

The other bed in the room contained his brother, who lay on his stomach under a similar framework and was asleep or unconscious.

Danny Brooks was wearing a crash helmet of dressings, and across his spectacularly swollen and bruised nose was a wide strip of plaster. Two wads of bloody cotton wool protruded from the nostrils. A tube led from his arm to a plasma bag hanging from a stainless steel frame beside the bed.

As the officers entered the room, the least damaged patient instinctively lowered his bandaged hands to try and conceal the cigarette. Then an expression of apprehension crossed his features when he realised his visitors were not members of the hospital's medical staff.

'You're alright, son.' Mowgley spoke in his version of a soothing tone as he pointed at the warrant card his colleague was holding at shoulder height. 'It's only the Filth.'

Jimmy Brooks looked marginally relieved, slumped back on his pillow and lifted the cigarette awkwardly towards his mouth.

The detective stopped at the bedside and gave an insincere smile: 'Who did you think we were, Jehovah's Witnesses or The League of Friends?'

His remark drew no response. Although less fearful, Brooks appeared guarded and suspicious. He had the same demeanour, Mowgley thought, as a dog from a bad home. Given his upbringing and past experiences of humanity, it was probably his default expression.

'We haven't met, lad,' said Mowgley, pulling a chair alongside the bed, 'but I've heard so much about you it's almost as if we're old friends. I'm Detective Inspector Mowgley, and this is my colleague Detective Sergeant McCarthy.'

Deciding the avuncular approach was not likely to pay dividends, Mowgley sat down and waved a hand towards his companion. 'As usual, my sergeant's role will be to play nice police person to my nasty one. She will now speak to you soothingly while I think of the best way to beat a confession out of you.'

'Take no notice, Jimmy.' Catherine McCarthy smiled reassuringly as she moved to stand on the other side of the bed. 'He's just a tad upset that you and your brother blew his favourite pub up. How are you feeling? The doctor said you're not too bad at all considering, and you're in a much better state than your brother.'

Brooks looked at her as if unsure what response was expected of him, then licked his lips, shot a glance at Mowgley and said: 'The doctor said we weren't to have no visitors.'

'I understand,' said Catherine McCarthy. 'But the thing is that my boss outranks the policeman on the door, and the inspector is very anxious to find out where you got the grenade from - and if you have any more. Inspector Mowgley is in charge of the ferry port, and it's very important we know if there's any more nasty stuff stashed away there.'

'That is absolutely right, Jimbo.' Mowgley spoke breezily and patted the bed in a friendly manner. 'What you have to understand is that you have now moved into the big time. Possession of explosives at an international place of transit is a contravention of the Terrorism Act of 2000. It's not like trying to flog a bit of dodgy gear in a pub. You're right up there with Osama Bin Laden and Al Quaeda, now, son. Have you any idea of the stretch you and your bruv could be facing?'

He reached for his baccy pouch and looked at the patient thoughtfully: 'Actually, after 9/11 I wouldn't be surprised if the Yanks put in an extradition order as your offence took place on what is technically international territory. They've still got the death penalty, of course...'

*

'How do you think I did? Didn't lay it on too heavy, did I? ...and for fuck's sake mind that cement lorry!'

DS McCarthy looked fleetingly across at where Mowgley was bracing his arms against the glove box. After-work traffic was building up on this one of the three routes out of the city, and hundreds of cars would soon be gridlocked at the giant roundabout marking the point where Portsea Island joined the rest of the United Kingdom. She was enjoying the excuse to use the blue grill lights and siren, and realised that Mowgley was talking to try and keep his mind off her constant weaving in and out of traffic as they raced back to the ferry port.

'Too heavy? Of course not. Your procedural activity was spot on. Apart from a load of twaddle about extradition, there was the small matter of not cautioning him, and you really upset that doctor. Good job he was white or you could have been arrested by the uniform outside the door for racism. And I can't begin to think what's going to happen when the shite hits the fan and Head Office finds out you've been interfering with a city case as well as breaking every rule and requirement in the PACE book.'

Mowgley took his eyes off the road ahead long enough to look at her with a hurt expression. 'I phoned Charlie Williams and told him we were going for an off-the-record chat with Jimmy Brooks, didn't I? And we know where the boys found the grenades, and it's sort-of on our patch.'

'No it's not. And what's our game plan apart from getting there before anyone else? Are you going to phone it in and get all the emergency teams to leave the pub and turn up at Flathouse so you can have a pint in peace?'

'That's not fair. Let's just see what's what; we can worry about the procedural niceties when we find out if the little scrote was telling the truth about what they say they found. If he was, you can make an anonymous call to the emergency people and we can pretend we were never there. If it's a load of cack and the lad Brooks was having a flight of fantasy, we won't trouble them. And will you mind that lollipop lady for Christ's sake.'

*

H. Percy Boulnois is not a household name in Portsmouth. This is despite his innovative and extensive works as the city's municipal engineer towards the close of the nineteenth century.

It was Boulnois who constructed a paved promenade along the entire length of the seafront. It was he who turned a morass and rubbish tip into the stylish and popular Canoe Lake close by the new prom. Boulnois also devised schemes for channelling sea water to the public swimming baths, and to flush the sewers and streets of Portsmouth. Like many pioneers, his work was not always appreciated, and the wealthy residents of Southsea voiced much concern that the sea water running through their streets would rust their carriage wheels.

One project which was generally approved was the extension and improvement to the commercial docks on the north-western coastline of Portsea Island.

Before Boulnois, Slipper Quay was not much more than a ramshackle jetty. As recalled in his memoirs, the engineer increased the size and capacity of the wharfage so much so that a ship drawing up to twenty-eight feet of water could lie alongside.

From that blossoming, Flathouse Quay prospered and

grew, and had been under a more or less continual programme of change and modernisation over the intervening years. With a constant flow of goods arriving from around the world, it was bound to attract the attention of people in search of an unofficial bargain. It was alleged that people had paid just to get a job on the dockside at Flathouse Quay, and the salary was the least of their concerns. Stevedores at the Quay particularly enjoyed a status and respect normally accorded to more elevated roles.

Few of the Victorian buildings at Flathouse remained, and those that did lay mostly empty. Over the years, their more valuable components and fixtures had been fed upon by scavengers, and this tradition was what had brought the Brooks brothers to Warehouse Fourteen in the midnight hours.

The least damaged of the brothers told DS McCarthy that they had arrived at the wharf by a small boat which they had taken from its moorings some distance away along the waterfront. They had not been able to start the outboard motor so had to row, and had set off in the wrong direction and out to sea before realising their mistake.

In all, the voyage had taken them over an hour. It would have been much easier to scale an unattended gate on the land side of that area of the docks, Jimmy Brooks admitted, but the brothers had obviously liked the idea of a piratical seaborne raid.

With no further misadventures, the brothers had climbed on to the wharf, leaving the dinghy to drift away as they investigated an abandoned warehouse set well back from the water's edge. They had been there recently, and knew no lead remained on the roof. Kicking in a low window then breaking through a series of partition walls, they had found themselves in a corridor. Torchlight revealed that one side of the passageway was lined with a number of rusty up-and-over garage doors. Some were missing, some were rusted shut and others were open. Those they entered appeared to contain nothing worth stealing, and they were becoming bored and about to leave when Danny Brooks noticed that one of the doors was secured with an obviously new padlock.

With the help of their feet, a piece of steel piping and a breeze block, it had taken the brothers little time to distort the door and create a gap wide enough for them to squeeze through.

Inside, Danny had stumbled into what seemed to be a stack of crates. The torch had illuminated a chest high collection of rectangular metal containers. All were of a drab olive colour with stencilled white letters and numbers on the tops and sides. The one they chose to open contained rows of what they recognised as hand grenades.

Frightened but elated by their find, they sat on the floor, had a smoke and considered their options. They had no vehicle with which to shift the boxes, and nowhere to take them if they had. The best idea, they concluded, would be to remove and sell the items little by little, feeding off the cache until they perhaps found a bulk buyer.

Consequently, the brothers filled their pockets with grenades, put the lid back on the box and, after squeezing through the gap, restored the battered door to its original shape as best they could.

They then walked home to the bedsitter they shared in a road not far from the docks. Finally becoming thoughtful of the possible volatility of what they carried, they refrained from smoking until they had stored all but one of the grenades safely in the refrigerator, next to an elderly pizza and a small piece of compressed cannabis resin.

Then, with a spring in their steps, they had set out to get started on their new and hopefully almost explosively successful business venture.

*

DS McCarthy's warrant card having gained them entry to Flathouse, she parked the car outside a row of near-derelict Victorian buildings partly obscured by twin mountains of shingle and sand. Far above, a crane driver looked incuriously down on them before returning his attention to shifting a container from banana boat to quayside.

It was not an unfamiliar task, as seventy percent of the bananas eaten in the United Kingdom came through this entry point. The man in the control box had begun to foster an illogical dislike for that variety of fruit, and, as he told his drinking mate down the pub, had eaten enough bananas to last him a lifetime.

The inspector and sergeant found the warehouse and the row of storage units without trouble. But of the alleged cache of weapons there was no sign. None of the doors carried a padlock, and the garages held no more than brick rubble, graffiti, the evidence of small fires, any number of used condoms, three badly stained and partly disembowelled mattresses and the inevitable shopping trolley.

'Bugger.'

Inspector Mowgley ignored the handkerchief his colleague offered him and wiped his hands on the front of his overcoat.

'Are we sure this is the place?' asked DS McCarthy.

'Unless there's another derelict Victorian warehouse in the vicinity. If the stuff was ever here, it's been moved.'

'You don't believe Jimmy Brooks, then?'

'Mowgley shrugged. 'It's possible he was telling the truth, or his version of it. Everything he said about the building and the lock-ups was pucka. But even if there was something here, they could have found only a box of the grenades - or even just the one they showed to Mad Joey.'

DS McCarthy took out her cigarettes and offered Mowgley the packet: 'So what do we do now?'

He took a cigarette and leaned forward for a light. 'Pass. And by that I mean we'll pass it over to my mate Charlie. If we all keep shtum about our interview with Jimmy, Chas can have all the fun of checking out the fridge at their flat; if it's true about what's in there, he can take the credit for saving the neighbourhood.'

Catherine McCarthy directed a plume of smoke towards a hole in the false ceiling lining the passageway: 'I still don't know why you didn't just tip him off and leave it the City boys to sort out.'

Inspector Mowgley looked down his nose at her and frowned sadly: 'How little you know me, even after all these years, sergeant. To begin with, the Leo is on our patch, which makes it our business. Though he didn't invite us to speak to the Brothers Dim, Charlie knew I'd not be able to stay away. And as it was a fairly pressing matter, he knew I wouldn't go by the book if I talked to them. If you remember, he made a point of telling us what ward they were in before we left. Not that he's devious, but by putting us on the scent he kept his own nose clean if there were any repercussions...or, come to that, percussions.'

'Okay, I can see you wanting to put your name to it, but the City would have taken it over anyway. What was the point of rushing down here?'

'As I said, firstly to see if Jimmy Brooks was telling you porkies. It could have been that he fancied you and wanted to impress you by coming on like a prospective big-time arms dealer.'

DS McCarthy wrinkled her nose in distaste. 'And what about secondly?'

'What about secondly?'

'I mean what was the other reason you wanted to have a look before calling it in?'

'Elementary, my dear McCarthy. If it had been stacked floor to ceiling with weaponry, the emergency services would have come blundering in and maybe destroyed valuable evidence. And if there had been an arsenal here, it's a bit of a coincidence it was so near the water - and our ferry port.'

'I get that, but I also suspect you wanted to be the first one to pass the information on to the Special Unit friend you were telling me about the other day.'

'Hmm.' Mowgley removed the imaginary pipe he had been smoking and looked at it. 'Perhaps your powers of deduction are better than usually demonstrated, sergeant.'

thirteen

When the appointment was announced, Catherine McCarthy had wondered why Cressida Hartley-Whitley had chosen a man to be her key support officer.

The DS had initially supposed the Chief Superintendent had wanted to show gender even-handedness to reassure senior male officers they were not under threat of a cull. Of course, in a perfect PC world, the choice may have been made because, regardless of gender, the new incumbent was considered the best person for the job.

When DS McCarthy had met and seen Detective Superintendent Raymond Brand in action, she had realised that neither of these possibilities were at all likely. She concluded that CS Hartley-Whitley had simply taken on the most incompetent, unimpressive and thus least threatening applicant.

Superintendent Brand, or SuperBland as he inevitably became known, was a tall, slim and generally artificial-looking man in his early fifties. He carried himself deliberately erect and had a full set of too-white teeth and a full head of equally suspicious black and glossy hair. His features were small and regular and, like their owner, generally unremarkable. In another time he would perhaps be considered handsome by the more mature women in the typing pool. Those old enough to remember would have said he closely resembled the manager of a motel in a popular 1960s television soap opera.

Overall, his attempted air and style of command aimed at patrician but came out as condescendingly distant and consequently out-of-touch. He had come to his new posting from Essex, and the word was that his people were not sad to see him go. As his new team said when they thought it safe to do so, he was not an inspirational leader; it seemed that his main talent was for making sure at all times that his narrow-buttock arse was impregnably covered. In senior policing circles this was, of course, nothing new.

Waiting outside his office, DS McCarthy bet herself that it would be as generally bland and unappealing as the man. Feeling vaguely guilty that she had let him down by not being at his side during the interview, she had given Mowgley a tentative tap of assurance on the small of his back as he left her. Now she sat in the corridor, longing for a cigarette and toying with the pages of a very old copy of the TV Times.

Inside, Mowgley saw a young female inspector sitting against one of the walls. She looked out-of-place and awkward, and as if he would much rather be elsewhere. The new Super had clearly set the scene as if Mowgley were a suspect to be questioned in an interview room.

In fact, the meeting fell short of an official carpeting so there were no set rules of engagement. Brand had summoned Mowgley to his office with no given reason or warning. But he obviously wanted a witness, and even some sort of back-up in case things got out of hand. Mowgley's reputation as a loose cannon had obviously reached the new senior officer. Perhaps, the inspector thought, he should have been accompanied by a representative from the Endangered CID Officers Protection Federation. But that would have been difficult, as no such organisation existed.

He made a childish gesture by leaving the office door ajar, then caught the eye of the young inspector and nodded and smiled over-effusively. He had met DI Geraldine Prosser on a couple of occasions and knew she was a rising star as the first female officer to reach the rank of inspector at such an early age. She did not return the greeting, then looked quickly away as if shamed by her small act of moral cowardice. She would, Mowgley reflected, have to learn to ditch any such small examples of conscience if she wanted to reach the heights of the man waiting to speak to Mowgley.

Detective Superintendent Brand was standing behind his desk. Mowgley assumed this was not a gesture of common politeness, but to enable the taller man to look down on him.

Brand nodded curtly at the chair in front of his desk, and waited for Mowgley to take it. He knew this would be so Brand could look down on him from an even loftier height. Just to wrong-foot the senior officer and establish his general lack of compliance, Mowgley silently counted till ten, then slowly unbuttoned his overcoat, took it off and looked round the office. Seeing a row of hooks on the back wall and alongside Inspector Prosser, he walked around the desk and hung his shabby garment on top of the Superintendent's stylish trench coat. As he did so, he winked extravagantly at the inspector, who again looked quickly away.

Mowgley walked ponderously back to the seat, lifting his feet as if the carpet was as sticky as the one in the Ship Leopard. Finally, he sat down, crossed one leg over the other, smoothed the front of his jacket and looked guilelessly at his superior officer. It was all rather juvenile, he accepted, but best to start off on the right, or rather, the wrong foot.

Obviously angry at what he would see as a display of dumb insolence but unable to voice his irritation without losing face, Brand sat down and regained his composure and the upper hand by picking up a Report folder. Opening it, he studied the single sheet it held as if seeing it for the first time. Mowgley knew that he would have looked at it at least once already as he planned the order and content of his questions. He had probably also written down key phrases and points he did not want to forget to make.

While this was happening, DI Mowgley directed another vacuous smile at DI Prosser, then turned his attention to the surface of Brand's desk. It was predictably neat, organised and characterless. Then he thought about his own desk back at the Fun Factory and hoped it was not true what they said about telling a man's personality from the state of his desktop.

After some moments, Brand put the open folder down. Mowgley had earlier had a bet with DS McCarthy as to how Brand would open the proceedings, and was pleased to find he had predicted correctly.

'Thank you for coming in, Inspector.'

Mowgley knew that the proper response to this preliminary was none, but adopted a mock-obsequious expression before saying 'Not at all, sir, and thank you for asking me.'

He was pleased to see irritation again register on the face of his opponent, and settled down to, if not win, than at least try to draw the encounter.

*

'Come on then.'

'What, is it my turn already?'

'You know what I mean. Who won?'

'To be honest, I think it was a no-score draw.' Mowgley took a long pull from his glass and picked up a menu and price list from the high table at which they sat. 'Good in here, isn't it? The beer's much cheaper than the Leo. Pity they don't do pasties, though. And it's all a bit clean.'

When they had left the Station House, Sgt McCarthy had suggested they find the nearest pub so she could get a blow-by-blow report on the encounter.

On the main road through the north of the city, The Careful Tailor occupied the site of a former furniture store. It was one of a phenomenally successful pub chain which had hit all the right buttons to ensure a full house and huge turnover. The format and structure was as unvarying as it was inspired. Each of the outlets was in a key urban location and on a site which had never traded as a pub. They were all open-plan, with high ceilings and a strange hybrid decor combining the traditional look of a country pub and a Victorian gin palace. There would be a long bar dotted with pumps selling cut price beer, and the food was equally thoughtfully chosen and inexpensive.

Already, this outlet was busy with a mix of students and office workers, and the sort of perennial drinkers with high blood pressure and a low tooth-count. The outlets did not have the idiosyncratic appeal of somewhere like the Ship Leopard, but they provided exactly what people wanted from a pub in changing times.

'If you don't give me a full verbatim report immediately, I won't let you have another beer before the next meeting.'

Mowgley looked shocked. 'Crikey, you know how to get your way, don't you? But I can't until you tell me something.'

'What?'

'What does verbatim mean?'

'Ha ha.' DS McCarthy reached out as if to confiscate his glass, and Mowgley held up a defensive palm. 'Okay, okay. For a start, your old mate Hot Lips Prosser was in the office, pretending to be a witness but really there in case it went pear-shaped and I decked him. I smiled at her, but for some reason she appeared not to know me.'

'What a tart. But I guess she would not have had a lot of choice and you can't blame a girl for wanting to get on. So anyway, what did the bland one want to know?'

'He kicked off by asking how we knew the Brooks brothers were in hospital and why we went there.'

'We'?

'Actually he left you out.'

'So what did you tell him?'

'I didn't want to drop Charlie Williams in it, so I said one of the regulars said they had seen the brothers being loaded into the ambulance and we had used our deductive reasoning to conclude that they would have been taken to the nearest hospital.'

'I bet you didn't say it like that.'

'Well, not the deductive reasoning bit.'

DS McCarthy frowned into her glass. 'Anyway, why wouldn't an investigating officer tell a colleague about what he knew of a case happening on his doorstep?'

'Quite, but I didn't want to give Bland the slightest reason for blaming Charlie for any of our actions.'

'I can see that. And how did you get over us turning up and barging past the uniform on the door - and in spite of the doctor's instructions?'

'I said that, given that the offence took place on my patch and that it involved potentially lethal explosives, it was a matter of the utmost urgency for me to interview the suspects and ascertain they were not part of any organised terrorist group.'

'Getaway.'

'No. True.'

'And it worked?'

'Not much he could say, was there?'

'I suppose not. And what about the set-to with the doctor afterwards...and us going to the lock-up without phoning it in?'

'I reminded him of the urgent nature of the enquiry and said how vital it was that we covertly check out that there was no activity at or around the lock-up; and anyway the place was on my patch and so it was down to me to selflessly risk my life to investigate any serious threat to the ferry port and its users.'

'But Flathouse Quay isn't on our patch.'

'No, but he doesn't know that.'

'Mmmm.' DS McCarthy drained her glass and looked at her watch. 'So how was it left?'

'He apologised for thinking ill of me and dragging me in for no reason, kissed me on both cheeks and congratulated me for thinking on my feet, using my initiative and risking my life by exposing myself to the lethal dangers of a cache of high-explosives, a possible gang of ruthless terrorists - and your lethal driving at speed.'

'You're kidding.'

'Yep.'

'But he was okay about it all?'

'Absolutely.'

This was not strictly true; Mowgley had not mentioned that Brand had concluded their meeting by saying he had intended disciplining and perhaps suspending the inspector when he had heard of the sequence of events. The only reason he was not taking the matter further was because of information from Detective Superintendent Stanton of the Special Unit that DI Mowgley had been working under her direct instructions.

Inspector Mowgley pushed his glass across the tabletop. 'Now what was that about a pint before the meeting? And I just saw a bloke come in eating what looked suspiciously like a pasty. By its shape and size and aroma, I reckon there could be a Gregg's nearby. Time for some more investigative activity I think, Sergeant.'

*

According to office legend, there was a book containing weekly procedures and routines to be followed by those whose job it was to police the country's continental ferry ports. The book varied slightly depending on circumstances and location of each port, but was supposed to be followed to the letter.

If there was such book, nobody in Team Mowgley had seen it. If it had ever existed, the common opinion was that their leader had either burned or defenestrated it long ago.

One standing order which had survived in intent if not always in practice was the weekly briefing. It was an occasion when the full-time members of Team Mowgley could assemble in the office to exchange information on current cases and discuss mutual concerns. Tradition required that the sessions ended not with a morale-building group hug, but a visit to the Ship Leopard.

Mowgley and DS McCarthy arrived from lunch with the inspector still working on his follow-up Gregg's pasty.

They found DC Mundy in the body of the office transferring notes from his pad to a whiteboard. DS Quayle had one buttock resting on his desk as he exchanged texts with a female crew member on board a French ferry boat in mid-Channel.

Their part-time cleaner Fran was making hot drinks in the corner which served as a tea station, while Jo the office administrator was at her work station, preparing to take notes of the meeting. She signalled for Mowgley's attention as he passed, handing him a sheet of paper detailing the nature and content of all calls that had come in while he was out of the office. Mowgley filed the information in his overcoat pocket, finished off the pasty and said: 'Thanks, Jo. Any luck with Hoppy?'

His assistant looked slightly discomfited. 'I tried again an hour ago, and was told DI Hopkirk was not available. The woman at the other end said she would let him know you had called.'

Mowgley paused in mid-stride. "Not available'? Did she know it was me or was it a snotty temp?'

'Yes and no. It was actually DS Ross.'

The inspector frowned. Karen Ross had been a member of the city drug squad for almost as long as Dave. They had had a passionate fling in the early days, but both had decided it was their nature to be free of commitments. Or at least that was the cover story.

'Hmmm.' Mowgley rubbed his chin thoughtfully. 'Okay, Jo, thanks.'

The office administrator took the phone from its cradle. 'Do you want me to try again?'

'No, it's okay. I'll try his mobile after the meeting.'

'It was his mobile number that I called - and DS Ross who answered it.'

*

The meeting having been declared open by Inspector Mowgley before he retired to his office, DC Mundy stood at the Nobo board and gave a summary of noteworthy activities at the port over the past week.

At the lower end, several dozen ferry passengers had been temporarily detained and the excess tobacco and alcohol items they were carrying confiscated. A more ambitious attempt had been made by a former police officer from Cheshire. Customs officers had found 85 kilograms of hand-rolling tobacco in suitcases, boxes and a laundry basket in the back of his Land Rover. It was calculated he had been trying to evade more than £17,000 excise duty.

As DS Quayle would be reporting, a man was being held on board a ferry which had turned back in mid-Channel in the early hours. He was part of a stag party, and had allegedly set off a major alert when he set fire to his cabin. When asked why, he said, it had seemed like a good idea at the time.

The major event of the week had been the detention of a man attempting to smuggle sixteen Vietnamese nationals through the port after arriving on a ferry from Cherbourg. The thirteen men and three women had been discovered packed into a purpose-built coffin-like box under some crates of dried noodles. The driver of the van had at first said he had thought the box contained a bulk order of compressed duck for local restaurants, but later claimed he was merely giving the passengers a lift so they could have a day out in Portsmouth.

DC Mundy concluded by confirming that all these matters were being dealt with by the appropriate bodies, and that there were no major all-ports alerts concerning fugitives travelling in either direction.

After a break for tea and cigarettes, it was time for DS McCarthy to bring her colleagues up to date with regard to ongoing matters in which Team Mowgley were directly involved.

To deal with the most recent first, she said, there were no developments on the explosion at The Ship Leopard. The two suspects were being held in custody but had not yet given statements about the alleged cache of weaponry from which they had taken the grenades.

Neither had there been any significant developments in the matter of the money belt containing £50,000. The money was still being held by Customs, and no charges had been laid. This was clearly because there were no indications to whom the money belonged. Mrs Wheatcroft had been questioned and denied all knowledge of the belt or the money, as had her son and daughter.

It was possible that Andrew Wheatcroft was involved, but he had proved particularly uncooperative when questioned by DS Quayle with an escort of two uniformed officers. She would say no more as she believed he had information on the matter, and ended by asking for any questions.

DS Quayle adopted a clearly mock-sympathetic expression and asked: 'Only how your eye is, and why you think you were attacked at the Crem?'

Mowgley had been adding a Curly-Wurly bar to the desk redoubt, and leaned through the doorway, still chewing. 'The truth is we don't have a clue, Sergeant, but thank you for asking.'

'I only wondered if you thought it might have some connection with the money belt, sir.'

'Do you think it has?'

Quayle raised his hands in a don't-know gesture. 'Just a thought.'

'Well, we haven't found either of the attackers in the Book or on the wire,' said DS McCarthy, 'which means they're either not known or we've missed 'em.'

'Moving on,' Inspector Mowgley looked pointedly at his watch, and then at Quayle, 'can we have any further information on Andrew Wheatcroft, Sergeant?'

Without bothering to stand, Quayle delivered his report. 'As usual, the Army is being totally unhelpful. Nobody at the Signals Corps wants to know, and when I asked about any Special Services connection the curtain came right down.

'So is that it, or is there more?' asked Mowgley. 'You're looking a bit smug.'

Quayle gave his trademark oily smile. 'Like you always say, sir, I've been using my initiative. I've been talking with a member of the Military Police and she may be able to help.'

'She?' said DS McCarthy, 'Why am I not surprised? So what's the connection? Does she know Wheatcroft?'

'No, but she does have access to all records relating to offences by service personnel. If he's crossed the line in any respect, there'll be details on file - and they'll include where he's been and with who.'

'I think that should be 'whom', Sergeant.' Mowgley looked at his watch again. 'So when will you know more?'

'Probably by tomorrow, sir. I'm meeting my contact in a pub near the Redcap barracks in Chichester this evening.'

'I look forward to seeing your expenses claim,' said Mowgley dryly. 'Now boys and girls, if there's no more business, I suggest we adjourn to the pub. I have reason to believe the doors are now unofficially open, and arrangements have been made for the Ladies to become unisex while the Gents is being recreated.'

'Shouldn't that be 'whilst', sir?'

'What?'

'Shouldn't it be 'whilst the Gents' and not 'while the Gents'?'

Mowgley was thinking of a suitable response when Jo appeared from her work station to tell him there was a call.

'Ah, is it Hoppy?'

'No. It's Charlie Williams.'

'Did he say what he wanted?'

'A pint I think. He said he was calling from Portsdown Hill, next to the Churchillian.'

Mowgley followed her back to her cubbyhole and picked up the phone.

'Hello Chas. What's to do? I hear you fancy one at the Churchillian?'

'I do, mate, but it's business. We've got a body here.'

'Blimey, a lot of it about at the moment, ain't there? Anyone I know?'

'Dunno, Jack, but he seems to know you. There's a photo of you on his mobile phone...'

fourteen

Apart from having a road and a public house named after him, Henry John Temple is best remembered in Portsmouth for what became known as his Follies.

When Prime Minister in 1860, the Third Viscount Palmerston had given active support to the creating of a number of fortresses and batteries to counter the threat of a French invasion. Four were built in the waters of the Solent, while others lined the crest of Portsdown Hill. Two of these became unjustly known as Palmerston's Follies because the giant guns pointed inland rather than in the direction from which the French fleet would come.

Never firing a shot in anger, the forts remained as monuments to the scope and scale of Victorian engineering.

One of the most impressive was Fort Widley, which was disarmed in 1907. During the early years of WWII it housed a bomb disposal unit, and was later a holding place for prisoners of war. In more recent times, it became home to an equestrian centre and Southsea's Sub-Aqua diving club. Its vast subterranean quarters have even been the venue for midnight ghost hunts.

The fort became the focus of the city police force and local media on that bright February day as the result of what began as an unremarkable event. A dry moat ran alongside the rear of the giant building, and into it that morning had trespassed a three-year-old black-and-tan Doberman Pinscher called Bubbles.

As the owner later explained to a local television presenter, Bubbles was an incorrigible bird chaser. To the horror of his master, he had leapt effortlessly over the railing in pursuit of a noisy herring gull. Somehow, the dog had survived the fall and had got up, shaken itself and gone off in pursuit of a passing rabbit.

The caretaker was summoned and let the owner in through a hefty wrought iron gate at a level with the underground arsenal. Shortly afterwards, they emerged into the moat and found Bubbles lapping enthusiastically at a dark stain close to one of the sheer stone walls. Ten feet above the stain was the body of a hanging man. The hands were trussed behind his back, and he was hanging head downwards, a rope leading from one ankle to a beam projecting from the moat wall at the level of the railings.

By coincidence, Bubbles' owner was a butcher. As he had said to the investigating officer and later to the on-the-spot television presenter, it looked to him as if the man had been bled like a pig.

By the time Inspector Mowgley and DS McCarthy arrived, the Scenes of Crime Officers had done their initial work in the area below the body. The corpse had been lowered to the ground and afforded the relative dignity of a standard issue cadaver pouch.

Normally portrayed in television dramas as black plastic, the body bags favoured by Hampshire police were generally white, and made of a non- porous material. The colour was chosen so that any small debris or items coming away from the body or its clothing in transit from scene of discovery to mortuary would show up readily.

The non-porosity was to prevent the leakage of body fluids or blood. This would probably not be a problem with the hanging man. At a guess from the senior SOCO, most of the seven pints which had once circulated through his body was now soaking into the earth below where he had been found dangling.

Mowgley and McCarthy found DI Williams standing alongside the body bag, regarding it with a lugubrious expression. The bag was laying on the ground behind the SOCO van, and the detective was talking to a slim figure enclosed in a hooded white coverall. Her mask had been pulled up to the top of her head, revealing young, fresh and comely features. The Scenes of Crime Officer was showing Williams something in a clear plastic evidence bag, and as the two detectives approached, she turned, smiled brightly and gave a little wave.

'Hello you two. We must stop meeting like this, Mog. People are beginning to talk.'

Mowgley held his arms up in mock surrender: 'What can I say, Truly Scrumptious?'

Trudy Sixsmith pointed at the evidence bag. 'Looks like I've got competition and you've got a fan, maybe even a stalker. Unless the real subject of the photo was Cath.'

Mowgley looked at the plastic package and then the body bag. 'So what's it all about, Charlie?'

DI Williams spread his hands. 'A bit of a funny one, mate. Male in his mid-thirties. Found a couple of hours ago by a dog walker. Bonzo-'

'Bubbles, actually, Chas,' interrupted Trudy Sixsmith.

Williams frowned. 'Whatever. Anyway, dog jumps in to moat after a rabbit or something. Somehow it doesn't break its neck, and the owner calls the caretaker. They find Rover-' DI Williams cast a warning glance at the SOCO '-having a lovely time slopping up the blood from the ground beneath the body.'

'Could he have fallen in or jumped?' asked DS McCarthy.

Williams shook his head. 'I think we can rule out suicide. He had his hands tied behind his back, and was hanging upside down on a rope by one ankle.'

'The Hanged Man.' DS McCarthy said thoughtfully, looking up at the beam. There was an extension ladder leaning against the wall and, by now, photographs would have been taken from all angles and the rope secured in an evidence bag.

'Yes,' said DI Williams as if the sergeant had stated the obvious. 'His throat had been cut and he'd bled like, well, as the dog's owner put it, like a stuck pig.'

DI Mowgley grimaced: 'So with all that blood, he must have been alive when the deed was done.'

'You're getting better at this, Mog,' smiled the SOCO. 'I am well impressed.'

Mowgley gave the faintest hint of an acknowledging bow, then turned back to DI Williams. 'And what's this about a photo of me on his phone?'

'A photo of the pair of you, in fact.' Trudy Sixsmith held the clear plastic evidence bag up. Sealed Inside was a mobile phone. She looked at DI Williams for clearance, then asked:

'Do you want to see it now? I'll send you a copy anyway.'

Mowgley nodded. 'So how did you find it?'

DI Williams looked at the package. 'The phone was in his jacket pocket. Don't ask me about the photo, mate. I'm still getting used to having electric windows on my car.'

While swiftly pressing buttons through the plastic covering, Sixsmith raised her eyebrows in Catherine's direction: 'Bloody Hell, what a pair of old codgers, eh?' She held the bag out towards Mowgley. 'It's only a phone with a camera in it, but it is a good one. It's actually state-of-the art, or it was last year. He must have liked new boys' toys. This is a Sanyo SCP 3500. If I remember rightly it's got a tad under half a megapixel capacity on the camera and would have set him back about £300. It's a fairly new procedure that we have a look to see what's in any phones at the scene. Just in case there's anything the investigating officer needs to act on right away.'

Mowgley looked dubious. 'You mean like a text saying *Meet you at the fort. Please bring some rope. Love Deidre*?'

Trudy Sixsmith widened her eyes. 'Gosh, inspector, I am even more impressed. You actually know what a text is.'

Mowgley wagged a reproving finger and reached for the evidence bag.

DS McCarthy moved closer to him, and together they looked through the plastic covering at a fuzzy image on the phone's small screen. It showed Mowgley getting into the passenger side of DS McCarthy's car. She was standing by the driver's door, looking at something off-camera.

'Is that all you get for £300?' Mowgley frowned. 'My old Box Brownie would have done better. For that sort of money I would have expected it to make the tea.'

'Another few years and they will,' said the SOCO officer, 'but it'll be espresso coffee and not tea.'

'Is there anything else on there?'

Sixsmith took the bag from him and shook her head. 'Not really. At least not at first sight. The text messaging and call boxes and records had been wiped, and yours was the only photo.'

Mowgley frowned 'Is that it, then?'

'By no means,' said Trudy Sixsmith. 'It might be that the victim has a nice convenient account with a company which will send him the details of all the action with the monthly bill.

It could be pay-as-you-go, but the SIM card should tell us a good bit. Of course, that's assuming the phone belongs to the person in whose pocket it was found.'

'What puzzles me,' said DS McCarthy, 'is why the killer would leave it on the victim - and with only the photo on it.'

'Exactly,' said DI Williams heavily. 'We'll run our man here through the works and see if he's known. Do you want a look before we send him off?'

'Might as well.'

Williams nodded to Trudy Sixsmith, who bent down and pulled at the tab of the heavy duty zip fastener. The two sides parted easily, revealing a mass of dark hair. In parts it looked sticky and clumped, and Mowgley realised it had been caused by the blood running from the man's cut throat.

A bone-white forehead streaked on each side with vertical lines of dried blood appeared, and then closed eyes. Further down and as a narrow-bridged, slightly twisted nose came into view, the tab stuck.

'What's the problem?' asked Williams.

'The fastener's caught in his beard, I think. Hang on a minute.' Sixsmith fiddled with the tab and then gave it a wrench, automatically apologising to the corpse as the head lolled to one side as if in protest. 'There,' she said.

They looked down at the dead face, the whiteness of the cheeks and brow contrasting sharply with the crusty lines of blood and the darkness of the hair and blood-matted beard. Then DS McCarthy looked at Mowgley.

'What?' He returned her look.

'Don't you recognise him? It's the bloke who attacked you at Portchester Crematorium.'

*

'A bit strange, isn't it?'

'Bubbles surviving a fall of thirty feet? I read somewhere that they always land on their feet.'

'That's cats, Jack, not dogs. I meant the way the victim was found. Idiot!'

'Steady on, sergeant, it was an easy mistake to make.'

'I meant the driver, not you.'

'So did I.'

They had left the Hill and were driving back towards the Fun Factory.

'And what was that about The Hanged Man?' asked Mowgley. 'You said it in capital letters.'

'It's a tarot card. You know, the set of pictures that people use to see into the future. I don't know much about it but I think you pick some and they predict what's going to happen to you.' DS McCarthy took evasive action as an oncoming truck bearing an overloaded builder's skip lurched towards her side of the road.

Mowgley instinctively ducked, then said: 'What, if you pick the one with the bloke on the rope you're going to be hung?'

'Hanged. No, not at all. They all mean something, but not necessarily what they show.'

'Oh, I get it,' said Mowgley in way that suggested he did not. 'What I don't get is why whoever did it would have left the phone in the victim's pocket. And why the photo of us on it, and why he took it.'

'You don't know that he took it. It could be someone else who took it and sent it to him for some reason.'

'What do you mean?'

'I'll explain the technology later, or get Trudy Sixsmith to. But what if the killer wanted the photo to be found? What if it was some sort of warning?'

'Yes,' said Mowgley thoughtfully, 'I had thought about that.'

fifteen

As they neared the roundabout which led to the ferry port, Mowgley looked at his watch and pointed at the flyover leading into the city. 'Can you drop me off at Southsea?'

'Yeh, if you tell me what for? Going shopping or meeting Ms Wheatcroft again?'

'No, just got to see a man about a dog.'

'What man? Bubbles's owner?'

'Of course not. It's just an expression.'

She changed lanes and took the flyover, then looked at Mowgley and said: 'Question Time, then? Usual rules and stakes applying?'

'Okay, that's one.'

'What?'

'You just asked me a question.'

DS McCarthy shook her head. 'What are you like? Right, here we go. Are you going to get measured for a new suit?'

'Don't be silly, Sergeant. And that's two.'

'Are you going for another tea and buns session with Sarah Wheatcroft?'

'You already asked. That's three.'

'Alright then. Are you going for another tea and buns session with Jane lairy Stanton?'

'Nope. Four.'

A pause and then: 'Are you really going to meet a man about a dog?'

'Nope. Five.'

'Hmmm. But you are going to meet someone?'

'Yes. Six.'

'Male or female?'

'Female. Seven.'

'Is it about what we've been working on?'

'Tangentially. Eight'

'What do you mean, 'tangentially'?'

'I mean tangentially. And that's nine.'

'Whoa. You can't count that as a question, can you?'

'Yes. And that's ten. You owe me copious drinks of my choosing at the place to be decided, which probably means the Ship Leopard.'

'Hang about. I have another question.'

'I told you, the game is over.'

'No, I mean I want to know something. If the game is called Twenty Questions, how come I only get ten when it's my turn?'

Mowgley regarded her as a teacher regards a pupil who cannot grasp the most elementary of concepts: 'Because, you silly goose, them's the rules. And what is life without rules? I didn't make them up, I just follow them.'

'But you did make them up.'

'That's not the point. Carry on, Sergeant, and do try to pay attention to your driving. You just missed that lollipop lady; do you want to go back for another try?'

*

The bus pulled up and Mowgley alighted. It was a journey of no more than two miles from the shopping precinct to where the ferry boat shuttled passengers between Portsmouth and its smaller neighbour, Hayling Island. But Mowgley was early and it had been some time since he had caught a bus. Had he known the cost for the short journey, he would have taken a taxi. He was also upset that the driver had asked him with a perfectly straight face if he had a senior citizen's bus pass.

He walked across the road, past the lifeboat station and to where a burger van was pulled up alongside the beach looking over the narrow entrance to Langstone harbour. It was only a few hundred yards to the south-western tip of Hayling Island, but the current got up to double figures when the water was emptying from or draining into the harbour. It was said that nobody had ever swam across the narrow channel and lived to tell the tale, but that was probably as much of an urban myth as the accusations about Palmerston's Follies.

As a teenager, Mowgley had tried it when full of beer and

false optimism. It had been slack tide but still too much for him, and he had had to be rescued by the ferry boat. To make the humiliation complete, the captain had charged him for the short distance to the Hayling pontoon, and then again for the trip back to where his clothes and wallet waited on the Portsmouth side.

Mowgley smiled indulgently at the past, and ordered a tea and a double cheeseburger with double onions. As he waited, he looked along the beach to where a car had drawn up on the shingle, its bonnet pointing toward the channel. The woman at the wheel made a negative gesture when Mowgley held up his polystyrene cup and pointed at it.

He walked across the shingle and opened the passenger door.

'Oh mate, have you got to eat that in here?'

Mowgley shrugged. 'It's either that or keep me hunger at bay with a fag, ducks.'

Karen Ross made a face and lowered the driver's window. 'Just promise me you will not fart before you get out.'

'I'll do my best, K, but you know how it is with fried onions.'

'No, I don't actually.'

'Okay, calm down. You sound a bit tense. You want to go for a drink at the marina?'

'No, I'm alright.' She looked through the windscreen at the water then said: 'You live down here don't you?'

'Mmm,' said Mowgley through a mouthful of meat, onions, melted cheese and bread.

'What, next to the marina? I thought the flats cost a fortune?'

'They do. No, I live just over there.' Still engaged with his burger, he pointed with a thumb over his shoulder.

'In one of those wrecks?'

'They're not wrecks, actually. They're houseboats.'

'Didn't you used to doss above The Midnight Tindaloo in Southsea?'

Mowgley did his best to look hurt with a full mouth. 'I still do, but it's undergoing significant redecoration and refurbishment. DS Gargery owns that big black one with the windmill on the roof. He's kindly letting me stay in it for a while.'

'But isn't that his shagging station?'

'It is, but we have an arrangement that I am not there when he wants to be.'

'Oh.'

There was silence for a moment as Mowgley finished his burger, wiped his face with the serviette it had come in, then put the crumpled piece of paper carefully on the dashboard. Then he looked across at DS Ross thoughtfully, and said: 'Okay mate, do you want to tell me all about it? Where's Hoppy?'

She continued to look straight ahead through the windscreen. 'I don't know.'

'Oh come on...'

'Really Jack, I don't.'

'Have you tried his phone?'

'He left it behind.'

Mowgley looked at where a figure in a wetsuit sat astride a jet-ski, churning up the water as he performed aquabatics for the benefit of the customers sitting outside the pub on the opposite shoreline.

'So where is he supposed to be?'

'On leave. He put in for a fortnight.'

'So what makes you think he's not coming back?'

'I didn't say that.'

'But it's what you think, isn't it?'

Ross was silent for a moment and then looked across at him: 'Can you roll me a fag?'

'You don't smoke...and you hate people smoking in your car.'

'I know.'

Mowgley reached for his tobacco pouch, and said: 'Go on, then. Tell me the lot. Are the rumours right about him getting little envelopes from Mickey Finn?'

Again the silence, then: 'Yeah.'

Mowgley groaned. 'But what the fuck for?'

DS Ross took the cigarette and leaned across so he could light it. She sucked on the roll-up, then let the smoke dribble through her lips. 'How the fuck should I know? You'll have to ask him.'

'But you must have asked him. I take it you were unofficially back together again after the public split?'

Another deep inhalation, then: 'Yeah. He said it seemed

better to keep it quiet. And of course I asked him why he got into it.'

'And what did he say?'

'He said it just got out of hand. He came away from seeing one of his narks and found an envelope under the wiper blade. There was a grand inside.'

'And?'

'He said he was going to report it, but then he looked at the money and thought how nice it would be to have a bit of cash.'

'And when was this?'

'A couple of years ago. Maybe more.'

'And you didn't know?'

'Not at first.'

'What happened after the first envelope?'

'He said he got a call from Finlayson and they had a meet out of the City. Finlayson said he didn't want much.'

'And what was the deal?'

'Hoppy would be on a 'retainer', and in return Finlayson just wanted to be left alone and hear any info that would affect him. He even said he'd give Hoppy a regular stream of sacrificial goats - dealers from outside or those he worked with who had upset him. Nobody would know if Hoppy was sensible.'

Mowgley grunted 'Buying a new flat on the seafront and a big beast of a motor wasn't that sensible was it?'

Karen Ross lowered her window and tossed the cigarette stub out, then watched it as it lay smouldering on the shingle. 'He was quite sensible, as it happens. He took out a huge mortgage on the flat and the car was on the book. He kept bugger all in his account, so he'd look clean and just a bit silly with all his debts if anyone had a look.'

She looked down and sighed heavily as Mowgley started to roll another cigarette. 'What happened to the retainer, then? It must have been quite a lump to get him to take the risk. He couldn't have spent it all on clothes and taking you away for dirty weekends?'

She grunted bitterly. 'Not much of that.'

'So how much was it and what did he do with it?'

'There's a place in Spain he goes to. A villa on the coast.'

'And does he own it?'

'He said so. He had a lot of money over there as well - I saw a Spanish bank book when I was at the flat in Southsea.'

'How much was in it?'

'A couple of hundred grand in Euros.'

'That's a big retainer ain't it?'

She nodded, then said: 'I think he was also doing a bit of business on the side with confiscated coke.'

'What?!'

She nodded again. 'He'd pick stuff up when he got a tip-off and only turn some of it in. The rest would go with him to Spain for selling. He said it was never any trouble getting through Customs when he flashed his card, and he always went through Dover.'

'And have you been there - to his place in Spain?'

'To the villa? No.' She took the cigarette and waited for a light. 'But I know where it is, sort of. Before it all got nasty he was going to take early retirement and move out there and said I could go and stay with him.'

Mowgley drew on his own cigarette. 'So when did he go, and what did he tell you?'

'Last week. Officially, he'll be away for another week.'

'But you reckon he won't be coming back.'

'I know he won't be coming back.'

'Is that what he told you?'

'No. But I know he's gone for good. I went round to his flat yesterday and all his best gear was gone.'

'Well you know how Hoppy likes to be smart wherever he's going.'

'Even he wouldn't take that much gear for a fortnight.'

Mowgley let silence settle for a moment, then said. 'Are you going to tell me the lot, or what?'

DS Ross looked across at him, then down at her hands on the steering wheel, then she said: 'I was with him the night before he went.'

'Go on.'

'He got me to drive him to a tower block in Somerstown, then wait outside. He was gone for about twenty minutes, and came back with a box.'

'Do I need to ask what was in it?'

She lowered her window, repeated the performance with the stub of her roll-up, then said: 'He said it was coke.'

'How much?'

'About 300 grand's worth.'

'Shit. Is that street value?'

'No, wholesale. He had a job to carry it. It was about 10 kilos-nearly a couple of stone.'

'Jesus wept. Who'd he get it from?'

'He said it was Finlayson's, fresh in from London. Hoppy knew the delivery date and where it was going to be before distribution around the city. He said he'd never touched Finlayson's stuff before. He said he told the guy there was a team waiting in the car, and if he didn't hand it over he was going to take him in. He said he even let the guy keep a couple of packs.'

'But what was it all about? He knew he'd have to stay out of the country for the rest of his life, and lose his pension. And you.'

DS Ross laughed humourlessly: 'He said he knew that Internal Affairs were moving in on him, and he reckoned Finlayson suspected he was doing a bit of business on the side as well as taking the retainer. He said he'd done a bit of business with the guy they found under the pier, and it was Finlayson letting him know he knew what was happening, and he might be next.'

'And what was he going to do with the coke?'

'He said he had a buyer. I don't know if it was here or over there.'

'But did he really think he could just swan off to Spain and be safe? For fuck's sake, I hear Finlayson is bigger there than he is here.'

'I know, I know. But Dave said Spain was only a staging point. He said he was going to lay a false trail. As soon as he unloaded the coke he was going to fly to South America or somewhere. I could go out and see him regularly, then we'd both be together when I jacked it in.' Her head slumped forward. 'You have to understand what a state he was in. He just wasn't thinking clearly. It was Internal Affairs and Finlayson on to him, and he was taking the stuff himself to keep going.'

Mowgley sat and took it all in, then said. 'I still can't believe he let it get to this stage.'

'I know. He said it just sort of built up on him. And he was taking more and more of the product. One minute he was rolled up on the sofa crying. The next he was buzzing and full of big plans for the future. He really started living in his own little world.'

Mowgley watched as the jet-skier took a spectacular tumble, then said: 'So what's your plan?'

'Mine?' She shook her head. 'I haven't got one. I just needed to talk to someone about it, and he always said you were his best mate. He said he always knew where to come if he was in trouble.'

'Yeah,' said Inspector Mowgley, 'but I think he may have put himself beyond help this time, love.'

Miguel Altamarino Fracuelo coasted to a stop in a cloud of dust and reached for his water bottle.

Tilting his head to drink, he narrowed his eyes against the sun and reflected that it was going to be a hot day for the time of year, even for this part of Andalucía.

He took a long pull at the bottle, then leaned forward and patted the handlebars of his new Orbea Sherpa as if acknowledging and rewarding its performance. It was the most expensive bike he was likely to buy, but more than worth it. The old track could be demanding at times, and the lightweight aluminium frame and suspension made the going easy and carried a lifetime warranty. And everyone knew the name and how much it cost.

Clipping the bottle back in place, he lifted his Spiuk sunglasses so he could check out the handlebar odometer. Then he looked at his watch and was pleased with the progress he had made along the former railway line.

Now reincarnated as a sometimes spectacular walking and cycling track, the Via Verde stretched for 36 kilometres and linked two Andalucian white villages. Roughly following the route of the Guadelete and Gaudalporcun rivers, the level track passed over deep valleys and through mountains, with 30 tunnels and four viaducts along the way.

Miguel looked at his watch again, lowered his sunglasses and stood on the pedals. If he kept to his schedule, he would be in time to watch the vultures feasting.

Although the lines had been ripped up to forge weapons during the Civil war, the original five stations were still there. Two were in a sad state of repair, while three had been restored to provide food and drink and accommodation for cyclists and walkers. The station at Penon Zaframagon had become a nature centre, dedicated to the observation and study of a large colony of Griffon vultures nesting on the rocky lime outcrop for which the station was named.

The Griffon is an 'Old World' vulture with a wingspan of up to nine feet. The average male weighs in at around seven kilograms, but some have been known to reach more than

30lbs. Like all scavengers, vultures are opportunists and live off the misfortune of other species. Dead rabbits, sheep, goats and the odd dead dog form a typical part of their providential diet, but sometimes they strike lucky with more substantial finds. In a well-documented case, a 52-year-old woman was hiking with friends in the French Pyrenees when she slipped and fell nearly a thousand feet. The leader of a rescue team said her body was almost completely consumed by a small group of Griffon vultures in less than 45 minutes. The only remains were scattered bones, some torn clothing and the victim's hiking boots.

Miguel blinked, then frowned and consulted his watch as he emerged from the first tunnel beyond the station at Zaframagon. From the frantic activity on a slope by the start of the biggest viaduct, it looked as if feeding time had started early. Or it could be that the vultures had found a pre-lunch appetiser. During previous rides, he had seen a number of scrawny sheep looking for grazing on the sparsely grassed hillside above the viaduct. He'd also noted a small group of wild horses in that area, and once a young bull which had obviously broken out of one of the fenced-off fields lining the track.

Braking gently, he slowed, stopped, dismounted and propped his bicycle against the rusting steel girder at the start of the viaduct. The usual feeding point was further along the track and in deliberately inaccessible spot so that visitors could not get too close and disturb the birds. But here they were jostling for pride of place no more than twenty metres from the track.

Moving slowly, he eased his digital camera from its pouch and moved up the slope. The camera had a zoom feature, but it tended towards fuzzy shots if taken without a tripod or something solid to steady it on.

As he had hoped, the vultures were too occupied with their meal to pay attention to him, and were anyway used to human spectators. From ten metres away, he could make out a bloody shape at the centre of the melee, and the gobbets of flesh being torn off the carcass and swallowed whole. One particularly large bird was bracing itself and using its wings as stabilisers as it yanked at and tried to dislodge what looked like a giant blue-red worm. Finally, the length of intestine came *away and the bird fell away from the bubbling mass of guts.*

Holding the Samsung NX300 steady, Miguel focussed quickly on the temporary gap and reeled off a dozen shots. Looking down at the screen to review the photographs, he was puzzled to see a familiar shape amongst the entrails, flesh and blood and bones. Pressing a button to enlarge that part of the frame, he peered down at the screen. Then he realised exactly what he was looking at and recoiled in shock, dropped the camera and was violently sick down the front of his Castelli Prologo cycling top.

sixteen

The day loomed depressingly full of meetings for Inspector Mowgley.

The first took place at 11am at the Fun Factory, when the team gathered for the second time in two days to discuss case developments.

In fact, the only officer to make a report was DS Quayle, freshly returned from his liaison with the female military police officer based in Chichester. As he said to DS McCarthy on arrival, the lady had come up trumps and delivered the goods. Inspector Mowgley forbore asking if events after the meeting had been as satisfactory.

Corporal Andrew Wheatcroft had once been a Sergeant with the Signals Corps, said Quayle. He had lost a stripe as the result of a fracas in an Aldershot pub, when three local youths had made the mistake of demanding he surrender the pool table. It was the redcap's informed opinion that Wheatcroft would have got away with it had he not broken the arm of one of the MPs who arrived to break up the brawl and rescue the aggressors.

Wheatcroft had then moved on to the injured man's colleague, and it had taken another three redcaps to make the arrest. This act of turning on his own had cost Wheatcroft a stripe and a spell in the last remaining military correction centre or glasshouse at Colchester Barracks. Since then, he had earned his stripe back.

There were a number of incidents of rumoured violent behaviour listed on his sheet, but nothing that stuck. As DC Mundy had reported, Wheatcroft had been and still was regularly assigned to specialist communications work for the

Special Services.

'So, Dickie,' said Mowgley in a non-serious tone, 'it looks like you spent a few bob in finding out what we knew already. But then as long as you got something out if it...'

'In fact, sir, there is a bit more.'

Looking at Quayle's face, Mowgley knew that he had as usual left the best till last, giving him the opportunity to parry and override the inspector's inevitable dig.

'There's a surprise.' Mowgley said. 'Do your rabbit from a hat bit, then. Are you going to tell us that our man's been mixed up with drug peddling in the mob?'

'Not for drugs, sir, but he was pulled in for questioning about a raid on an arsenal a couple of weeks ago.'

Quayle relished the suddenly increased level of attention, then said: 'Shall I carry on, sir?'

Mowgley put his chair on to four legs, swung his legs off Quayle's desk and reached for his tobacco pouch, then said: 'Don't take the piss, sergeant.'

Quayle smiled in a deliberately smug and oily manner and continued: 'The stuff was taken from a depot in Herefordshire. The raiders got away with more than a dozen cases of light arms, ammunition and hand grenades.'

DS McCarthy held up her cigarette in a polite gesture of interruption, then said: 'I don't remember reading about it or seeing any all-ports alerts?'

'Nor would you have. They only released the news this morning.'

There was a short silence, then DS McCarthy asked the obvious question: 'Why?'

Quayle again enjoyed the closeness of the attention of his audience. He paused before saying: 'They didn't know about it till yesterday.'

DS McCarthy looked puzzled. 'Again, why?'

'It was a switch. The boxes were replaced with replicas with bricks inside. Although the daily tally was done, they didn't need to open any of the crates until someone spotted that the serial number was out by a couple of points. Then the shit hit the fan and they went through everything.'

'Do they have any idea of who did it?' asked DS McCarthy. 'Dissident IRA or any organised group?'

Quayle shook his head. 'I got the idea they think it's an

inside job.'

'What makes you think they think that?' Mowgley asked.

'Just the things she said and the way she said them.'

'You mean she told you that nobody actually noticed anything suspicious at the time of the raid? Don't they have those things called sentries? And if so, may one ask if this sort of thing happens often?'

'I think the sentry's gone missing, sir. And yes, I think it happens more than you'd think. My contact said, off the record, that guns and ammunition and even vehicles go missing all the time. There was even a tank nicked from a depot up north some time ago, and nobody noticed for days.'

'Makes you feel really secure, doesn't it? I wonder if the navy has lost any ships or atomic submarines we don't know about.' Mowgley got up, walked to his office and returned with a Curly Wurly bar. Unwrapping it, he looked thoughtfully at DS Quayle, took a bite from the bar and said: 'Okay, I think we get the picture. But how does it connect to our man?'

Quayle shrugged. 'It doesn't...directly. I only found out about it because my contact said a team of military investigators is coming to Portsmouth later today. They're meeting with Superintendent Brand and want to have a look at the lock-up where you didn't find the cache. She didn't say they've got anything on Wheatcroft, but she wanted to know why I wanted to know about him. I think they've got something to make a connection with him, but she wasn't saying. I think their version of Internal Affairs is on Wheatcroft's case, but they want to keep it to themselves.'

DS McCarthy exchanged glances with Mowgley, and said: 'Well, at least that explains your return summons to Bland's lair this afternoon.'

'As I said, sir,' continued Quayle, 'there is no connection with the raid and Wheatcroft, but as the grenades turned up on our patch, I thought you'd like to know what the MPs are thinking.'

'Spot on, sergeant,' said Mowgley. 'Just one last question. How did you manage to get all this out of an employee of the MOD, and a redcap on top of that? I know you've got a way with the ladies, but...'

Quayle gave his faux-unctuous smile again, then said: 'Apart from anything else, I think she thought she was getting stuff out of me sir. She also mentioned that she was fed up with the Army and fancied a job in CID.'

'Ah. And you told her your dad was Chief Commissioner and said you would use your influence?'

'I said I would give her any information which might be of help.'

'I bet you did, sergeant. And did you give her any?'

'Not really sir, though she did ask about you.'

Mowgley paused with the remnants of the Curly Wurly bar half-way to his mouth. 'Me?'

'Yes sir. She seemed to know quite a bit about you.'

'Ah, does she now?' Mowgley digested the information with the remains of his chocolate bar, then called the meeting to a close.

*

The detective's second meeting of the day took place in the now officially re-opened Ship Leopard.

The restoration of the men's lavatory was still under way, but the landlord had come up with a solution to any unease that female customers might have felt about sharing their facilities. Two-Shits had simply hung a hand-made sign on the outer door leading to the Ladies. One side of the card read GENTS and the other LADIES; all the user had to do was turn it to the appropriate position when entering. As the landlord of the Ship Leopard reported, the scheme had worked fairly well so far except for a minor incident when Peter the Pouffe had complained about sexual orientation discrimination and threatened a protest in the form of a sit-down occupation.

Also present at Mowgley's permanently reserved table were DS McCarthy and DC Mundy. Apart from not enjoying his company, the reason the inspector had not invited DS Quayle was that he did not want the sergeant to hear DS McCarthy's findings regarding the identity of the Hanging Man. He also knew that DC Mundy had news of Dave Hopkirk's movements after he had said goodbye to Karen Ross. Neither case officially affected Team Mowgley, and in any case, the inspector would be happier if Quayle was ignorant of the details.

When Stephen Mundy had returned with the drinks, DS

McCarthy took a folder from her voluminous handbag and handed it across the table to Mowgley. He opened it and immediately said: 'Aha. I take it this is our Hanging Man?'

DS McCarthy nodded and Inspector Mowgley continued: 'I can see why you didn't spot him in the face book. I assume he wasn't sporting the beard in there?'

'He was clean shaven and had short hair in our shot.' said DS McCarthy. 'But then he likes, or rather liked to change his appearance regularly.'

Mowgley put the information sheet on the table top and took the top off his beer. 'Why's that, apart from the obvious?'

'He's more than a regular visitor to our shores. In fact, he's been deported three times. I hear they've started calling him the Yo-Yo Man at the Home Office.'

Mowgley raised his eyebrows and his glass. 'He must like it here, then?'

DS McCarthy nodded, sipped at her lager then reached for a packet of pork scratchings. 'I reckon they'd give him a Frequent Traveller discount on the ferries if he used the same name.'

'So who is he and why did he take such a dislike to my face?'

Sgt McCarthy picked up the sheet of paper and held it so Mowgley and Mundy could see the head-and-shoulders photograph in the top left hand corner. 'Meet Baksim Bushani. He's 32, or rather he was 32 on his last and final birthday, and could truly be described as a career criminal. His career brought him here from his native Albania as not much more than a teenager. In 1992 he was jailed for three-and-a-half years for doing some serious damage to a Class 'A' dealer in South London. On his release he was deported to Albania, then popped up before the courts in 1997 for possessing fake ID. Nobody knows how long he'd been back, but he only got a measly fifty-four weeks. He was put on a plane to Tirana in 1998, then almost immediately puts in an appearance at Staines Crown Court, charged with battery. He got just sixteen weeks for that, and was deported for the third time.

'But he couldn't stay away?'

'Nope. He was arrested in Birmingham in early 2000 and charged with possessing a K of cocaine. They also found £14,000 in cash in his flat.'

'Don't tell me he only got a year's worth of porridge?'

'No. This is the 'would-you-believe-it?' bit. He was doing five years in Winson Green and was released in error.'

'In what?'

'In error. There was a mix-up with another eastern European who was due for parole, and they let Bushani out. And the other guy was not even Albanian...just had a similar name and appearance.'

'I can hardly believe it. Next you'll be telling me the NHS regularly cuts the wrong limbs off people and the Army mislays tanks.' Mowgley reached out for the sheet. 'So what brought him down here to end up doing, if you'll forgive the grisly pun, a suspended sentence? And more importantly, why did he have a photo of us about his person?'

'According to local intelligence and the Drug Squad records, he worked for our chum Mr Finlayson as an enforcer and general gofer. I haven't a clue and neither has anyone else why he and his mate had a go at us.'

'Hmmm.' Mowgley stroked an imaginary beard. 'Curiouser and curiouser. And do we know anything about his folliclychallenged accomplice?'

'I fear not. As Jill Computer at Head Office said, baldheaded, stocky and thuggish-looking could describe half the adult men in Portsmouth, let alone those with a record.'

'Quite.' Inspector Mowgley finished his pint and pushed the glass across the table towards DC Mundy. 'Good work, Sergeant. Now, Stephen, before we hear what you've been up to, do you think you could do the honours again? Just tell Twiggy it's on Sergeant McCarthy's tab as she's still paying off her debt from our last Twenty Questions session.'

*

An hour later, DS McCarthy's debt was cleared and DC Mundy had concluded his report.

'And how was Dover?' Mowgley asked conversationally.

'It was...busy sir.'

Mowgley nodded thoughtfully. 'I was thinking about asking for a transfer there, but there's no place like home. And it's so big and busy. All we get is a bit of smuggling people and things and the odd bizarre murder.'

'Just to recap, Stephen,' said DS McCarthy. 'DI Hopkirk was making trips through Dover to Calais every month or so.'

'Yes, sergeant.'

'And always to Calais?'

Mundy nodded.

'And he always took a one-way ticket?'

Again Mundy nodded.

Mowgley grunted. 'Seems a bit of a slog to drive from Calais to Spain - if that was where he was going. It must be a thousand miles. Why not just hop on a plane?'

DS McCarthy looked quizzically at him: 'If he was carrying quite big boxes full of white powder?'

'Ah, silly me. But then he would still have needed a friendly customs officer to wave him through.'

'Not really. If he flashed his card and said he was on business...'

'Silly me again,' said Mowgley. 'And even I can work out why he didn't go through Portsmouth.'

'Absolutely. There's no boat to Spain from Dover, but anyway he wouldn't want anyone knowing where he was going to end up.'

Mowgley nodded to show he agreed with the logic, then turned to DC Mundy. 'And his latest - or probably last - trip from Dover was at the back end of last week?'

'Yes sir. A mid-morning crossing.'

'That figures. Not so much chance of a bored or tired and irritable Customs officer ignoring the card and insisting of having a look in the boot. That's a point.' Mowgley looked thoughtfully into his glass then at DC Mundy: 'Have you got a record of all his crossings for the past year?'

Mundy looked as if he might have been guilty of dereliction of duty, then said: 'No sir- I-'

Mowgley held up a reassuring hand. 'Not a problem, Stephen. Is there any way of finding out if any one Customs bloke was on gate duty every time Hoppy went through?

Mundy, thought for a moment, then said: 'Yes sir. I would need to collate all the times that DI Hopkirk used the port and then ask for a shift rota for all officers, but it could be done.'

'May one ask why?' DS McCarthy looked at Mowgley with arched eyebrows. 'You don't think...?'

Mowgley shrugged. 'Who can say?' He reached over and

patted DC Mundy on the shoulder. 'Don't look so worried lad. Just a thought, and put it on hold till we've had a good think about it.'

seventeen

'It must be really boring.'

Mowgley looked out of the window and made his John Mills village idiot face at the driver of a Jaguar who was undertaking their car as he joined the M27. The man glowered at Mowgley and sped by even faster, as if he thought their proximity would infect him and his shiny car.

Mowgley was being chauffeured to his third meeting of the day, which he speculated would be a little more demanding than the previous two.

'What?'

'Just rushing about and going to meetings all day - you know, like all these executive blokes in suits.'

'And women.' Said DS McCarthy.

'Alright, sergeant. And women.'

'But isn't that what we do?'

'What?'

'Dash round going to meetings all day?'

'Not really.' Mowgley stuck a thumb in each ear and waggled his hands at another undertaker. The driver of the battered pick-up builder's truck merely shook his head as if at the mental shortcomings of humanity, then took one hand off the steering wheel and gave Mowgley an obviously practiced one-fingered salute. 'Have you ever noticed,' the inspector said as the truck pulled sharply in front of them, 'how they all have brooms sticking up from one of them bits of upright pipes behind the cab? Yet I bet they never use them. Perhaps it's like a badge of office.'

Receiving no answer, he addressed DS McCarthy's question: 'Ah, we might go around meeting people, but it's usually because there's been a robbery or a murder or some form of crime against society and the ferry port. You can't say that's not interesting. All those executives have to make out all sorts of reports and give an account of what they've been up to on behalf of their company.'

'So do we,' said DS McCarthy dryly. 'Or at least the rest of us do.'

They drove on in silence for a moment and then Mowgley said: 'Why did you join the Force, Cath?'

'You know I don't like it when you call me that. Is that why you're doing it? And you know it's the Police Service, now, not the Force.'

'Of course. Perish the bloody thought we should ever force any bum holes to behave themselves.' He sighed heavily, looked around for any other motorists to annoy, then continued: 'Go on then, why did you become a member of the ...Service?'

'Do you know,' she replied, 'I often ask myself that.'

'And what's the answer?'

'It must have been in a weak and unthinking moment. But somewhere and at some time I think I thought I could make a useful contribution...'

'In a minute you're going to say it was so you could make a difference and protect the weak and innocent, aren't you?'

'Bollocks.'

'That's sir, if you don't mind.'

'Okay, bollocks, sir.'

More silence and then: 'So what about you?'

'What about me?'

'Why did you join up? To help keep law and order and stability in the community and all that?'

'No, not really.' Mowgley waved to a child standing at the window of a people carrier.' If I remember rightly it was so I could tell lots of people what to do and beat them up if they didn't do it.'

*

Inspector Mowgley was on the way to his fourth and hopefully final meeting of the day.

DS McCarthy had picked him up from the Station House after his interview with Superintendent Brand and the members of the Military Intelligence squad who were looking in to the theft of the arms from the armoury at the Hereford barracks.

'How did it go, then?' she asked. 'Do I still call you sir, or do I now outrank you? Or will you be looking for a new job soon? I know they need a shelf stacker at my branch of Waitrose.'

'Do you think I'd really work as a shelf stacker for Waitrose? All them snotty women dressing up just to go shopping and thinking they're better than you 'cos they buy wholemeal bloody bread? Now, Tesco or Asda I wouldn't mind. Or B&Q. I like them orange aprons. It would be a bit like being a Mason in Northern Ireland.'

'Yes, but what I was asking is did you get out of there alive?'

'More or less, I think. I did refer to Useless Eustace as Superintendent Bland once, but I don't think he picked it up.'

'And what about the MI people?'

'No, I don't think they picked it up either.'

DS McCarthy sighed. 'Ha ha. And..?'

'And they didn't seem that much interested in me. Bland told them about Dumb and Dumber and Mad Joey Sanders and that there were no other interesting prints or forensic stuff at the lock-up. They didn't like the idea of the boys being on bail, but as I said, they're too stupid to run away anyway.'

'And you don't think they reckon we had anything to do with it?'

'In what way?'

'Well, we could have been in on it and the reason we went to the lock-up without calling it in was to get rid of the evidence.'

Mowgley shook his head. 'No, I don't think they thought that. The way they treated me, I reckon Bland told them I was an irresponsible loose cannon always going off and doing my own thing without telling anyone. They wouldn't have thought I was up to any major league arms raids.'

'So how was it left?'

'We all stood up and I invited them for a pint, but they turned me down. Funny thing, though, they did ask about old Mr Wheatcroft dropping dead at the ferry port with a small fortune round his waist.'

DS McCarthy swerved to avoid a young woman pushing a pram off the kerb as if defying drivers to run in to it. 'Getaway.

Now that is interesting. So the MI people are making links between the missing weapons and Wheatcroft. They can't be as stupid as they look, then.'

Mowgley shook his head in reproach at the young woman as they passed. 'It's a good job I can't lip read. No, I don't think they could be as stupid as they looked. I suppose that's why they're called Military Intelligence.'

*

Inspector Mowgley toyed with his pint and watched the customers coming into the city centre pub. It was not a place that he would choose to use if there were any viable alternatives, and he would probably never visit it again. But it suited his purpose. It had been his say-so where the meeting would take place, and for that it was just right.

Location was probably the reason the pub was able to keep its doors open, he reflected. It was on a corner overlooking a shopping precinct which thousands of people must visit each day. That was the ultimate in passing trade. Plenty of customers would come in for a drink or a sandwich or one of the more exotic items on the blackboard menu outside. It was funny, he thought, how the more appetising the dishes were made to sound, the crapper they would be.

Come to think about it, the pub was a bit like the precinct. Well worn and without any hint of character. It looked as if it used to be part of an office block, but was obviously custom built. The Crown followed the 1970s fashion of lots of glass, aluminium and red bricks as a frontage, as if trying to disguise the fact that it was a public house.

Inside, the decor would have been regularly updated, but was as soulless as the exterior. This year's theme seemed to be Benefit Office Chic, with utilitarian chairs and tables and drab hessian on the walls. Even the woman behind the bar looked like she was going to ask you when you had last worked rather than what you wanted to drink.

As he watched an old couple not enjoying each other's company, he became aware of a figure standing over him. Round one to IA.

'Inspector Mowgley?' The man spoke with an almost mellifluous Scottish accent, and Mowgley noted the red hair.

He kept his tone and manner neutral. 'How did you know? Was it the carnation in my buttonhole, or have you been looking in my file?'

The man gave half a smile. 'You just looked more like a policeman than anyone else in here. And of course, I've been looking at your ID photo for a while.'

'Lucky you.'

Again the half-smile, but this time it looked genuine. The detective nodded at Mowgley's glass. 'Re-fill?'

'Only if you're going to have something alcoholic...sir'

The man reached down for his glass. 'It's a pub isn't it?'

Mowgley watched as he walked to the counter. Gentley was tall, probably in his late thirties and strongly built. He would weigh in at around 15 stone, and looked sporty. The broken nose could have come during a rugby match, or an arrest. The arrest, of course, could have been of a fellow officer.

He suspected women would find him handsome, and maybe even personable. Whatever else, he was not most people's idea of a member of Internal Affairs, or what in his homeland they called The Complaints.

The officer returned and Mowgley held a hand out for his pint. So far he had not stood up, and had no intention of doing so. 'Is your first name George?' asked Mowgley, though he knew the answer.

'No, it's Iain. Why?

'No matter.'

DCI Gentley held his pint of IPA up to the window and looked at it quizzically.

'That'll teach you to order real ale in a pub you don't know,' said Mowgley.

'Is that why you're drinking lager?'

'No, I drink it all the time. It's cheap and doesn't upset my stomach, and it annoys people like you.'

Gentley stood up. 'So it's true what they said about you.'

'Who and what?'

'Anyone I asked. They said you could be an awkward bastard when it suited you. And you were awkward most of the time.'

The DCI started towards the bar to change his drink, then paused and looked back: 'Do you fancy a short with that? Or are you driving?'

'No I'm not driving, and as I said before, only if you're having one.'

'I don't see why not. It's not often I meet celebrities.'

*

Mowgley raised his whisky glass, then said: 'Someone asked me today why I joined the Force. Sorry, I mean Service.'

'Force will do me,' said Gentley. 'And what did you say? That you wanted to do your bit for society?'

'No,' said Mowgley for the second time that day, 'so I could beat people up and get away with it. What about you?'

'What, do I like beating people up? Sometimes.'

'No. Why did you go into Internal Affairs?'

Gentley shrugged. 'It just sort of happened.'

'Didn't you know it would make you more unpopular than Millwall?'

The Scot considered the question, then said. 'I never really thought about it, to be honest. I liked the idea of weeding bent coppers out, though.'

'Is that why you're here? To weed me out?'

'Not really. I specialise in officers involved in drug-related corruption. Anyway I think you'd be a tough old weed.'

'Less of the 'old'. And you don't think I am?'

'A tough old weed?'

'No. Bent.'

'Well, if you are, you're bloody good at disguising it.' Gentley looked at Mowgley's overcoat, then said: 'I think you like to do things your way. My dad was like that.'

Mowgley held a defensive hand up. 'Steady on, are you trying to say I'm a fuckin' dinosaur?'

'They ruled the Earth in their time, didn't they?'

'Yeah, but you don't see a lot of them about nowadays, especially in the Force.'

'True.'

*

Another two pints and chasers later, and Inspector Mowgley was feeling somehow guilty to be enjoying DCI Gentley's company. It was not that he was prejudiced like some policemen; he accepted that working in IA was a job that needed to be done and that someone had to do it. But that was true of traffic wardens, and he couldn't imagine meeting too many of them he would fancy having a pint with.

'What are you thinking?'

Mowgley smiled. 'To be honest with you, I was thinking how strange it is that I'm enjoying sitting with an IA man who's also a Jock.'

'You're not Scotophobic, are you? With your name and physog, I should think there's a good bit of Celt in you.'

'Funny enough a lot of people have said that I'm a bit of a Celt...or something like that.' Mowgley put his empty glass on the table: 'Come on, then.'

'What, are we off, or is it my turn again?'

'I love it when people add the 'again' on. It's like they're saying you're trying to get out of your round.'

'Sorry, Paddy. So what do you want me to come on about?'

'It's Hoppy, isn't it? Your lot reckon I was in it with him?'

Gentley put his glass down as his expression changed momentarily and Mowgley saw that he was unaffected by the drink. 'I think we thought you might be when we started having a look at him. You saw him regularly and were old mates from school.'

'That doesn't make someone bent, does it?'

'Of course not. What I meant is that when we heard about him, it was natural we had a look at everyone he had any dealings with.'

'Including the rest of the drug squad?'

'Of course.'

Mowgley wondered if IA had been watching when he had the last drink with Hoppy at the Bridge Tavern, or when he met with Karen Ross. But he was certainly not going to bring her name up.

'Before we go any further, can you tell me if your lot took any candids of me and my sergeant?'

Gentley looked genuinely puzzled. 'Photos? Not that I know of. Why?'

'It's not important. So if you don't reckon I was at it with

Hoppy or anyone else, the next question is obvious, ain't it?'

The DCI raised one hand invitingly. 'Why not ask it, then?'

'Why are you here?'

Gentley lifted his glass and drained it, then looked at Mowgley levelly. 'I know you've been, shall we say, pursuing your own enquiries about DI Hopkirk...'

'No crime in that, is there?'

'Not at all. No, I asked to meet you just to say I didn't want you thinking we were interested in you and yours.'

'And that's it?'

'No. I wanted to see you face-to-face so I could tell you we've found your friend.'

Mowgley sighed as if he knew what was coming but did not want to hear. 'Blimey, you don't hang around, do you? Was he in Spain?'

'Yeah.' DCI Gentley held his hand out for Mowgley's glass.

'So, to coin a phrase, did he come quietly?'

'I'm afraid he did, Jack.' Gentley squared his shoulders, leaned forward as if he hoped increasing their proximity would lessen the impact of the message: 'I really am genuinely sorry to be the one to have to tell you that DI Hopkirk is dead.'

eighteen

'Sometimes,' said the short man in the long shorts, 'they fill the planes with the engines running.'

He did not make it clear if he meant the planes were filled with people or baggage, cargo or fuel with the engines running. Or whether it was the engine of the fuel bowser or the airplane which were kept running during the filling process. Or perhaps both.

Mowgley was the most nervous of air travellers - or any sort of travel where he was not at the controls. So it was unfortunate that he and Catherine McCarthy found themselves in close proximity to a voice of doom in the departure lounge at Gatwick airport as they waited to be called for the 11.45 flight to Malaga.

Apart from the confrontation with the man in the ticket office and the woman in the platform coffee shop and the youth with the leaking earphones and the commuter who needed to tell his wife he was on the train, it had been an eventless and even relaxing rail journey.

Passing through the Sussex countryside close by the Arundel canal had reminded Mowgley and his colleague of how much of England was still so green and fairly pleasant.

The journey from the station to the North Terminal had been less relaxing for DS McCarthy, as Mowgley had insisted on standing in the middle of any escalators, hindering the passage of those vying to win the race to the check-in counters. As Mowgley had said over-loudly, suitcases on wheels were banned from the escalators. Also the people so rudely pushing past couldn't all be late arrivals, so the plane was not going to go without them. And the seats having already been allocated, there was no purpose in trampling old people and pregnant women underfoot.

They had, however, reached the terminal without any serious encounters, and passed through Check-In and Security surprisingly smoothly. As DS McCarthy had observed reflectively, the terminal dealt with nearly eighteen million passengers a year so even Mowgley could not throw any metaphorical spanners in the works.

She came back from the bar with coffee to find the voice of doom still declaiming all the reasons why people should not travel by air.

The owner of the voice was a middle-aged man with the same colour of skin as an over-ripe blood orange. His thinning hair was dyed and cropped short, and he was wearing a pair of aviator-style sunglasses pushed up on to the crown of his head. In the lobe of one ear was a small stone of diamond-like appearance. He seemed to be dressed to allow for any weather conditions, as below the heavily padded ski-jacket he sported long, narrow-legged khaki shorts. On his feet were sandals made of clear plastic.

As he told the elderly lady opposite him about the most lethal areas to find yourself in an airplane as it fell from the sky, Mowgley sighed and nudged his travelling companion: 'Can't you arrest him?'

DS McCarthy shrugged. 'What for? Spreading alarm and despondency?'

'Either that or wearing sunglasses in an offensive manner.'

'What's wrong with wearing sunglasses on top of your head?'

'Unless you're Alain Delon with a sweater tied round your neck by the sleeves in a 1960s French film, it strikes me as more than a little pretentious. Anyway, you must be able to do him for having legs likely to cause a breach of the peace.'

DS McCarthy studied them. 'Blimey, I see what you mean. I've seen thicker pipe cleaners. And what crap tattoos. I suppose I could do him for offensive artwork, or just complain to a passing security guard or crew member that he was frightening the passengers.'

Mowgley shook his head. 'Remember how cheap the flight was. He could be a crew member - or even the captain.'

Catherine McCarthy gave him a reassuring pat on the knee and rewarded his weak joke with a smile. She knew he was clowning to take his mind off the impending flight, but also the loss of an old friend.

'So remind me why we're going to Spain,' she asked, 'or at least what our excuse is for flitting off to Spain?'

'No excuse needed, sergeant. We are going to be pursuing our enquiries into why Mr Wheatcroft was on our patch on his way to Spain with a very large wad of dosh about his person.'

'But how will a visit there help?'

'Well, we've drawn a total blank so far, but we know where the money was going, or at least where the Wheatcrofts were going. Who can say what we may uncover at their holiday home?'

'Holiday ruin, according to your chum Sarah Wheatcroft. But unless you've been grilling her, we don't even know where the place is.'

Mowgley looked smug. 'We do, actually. Or we know a man who does. I put young Mundy on to phoning all the estate agents in the town where Sarah said it was. As there are only a handful, it wasn't hard to find the one who flogged her the wreck. I got Stephen to say they had been recommended by Ms W. The one who recognised her name was obviously our man.'

'Clever boy. But why didn't you just ask her for the address before we left?'

'Use your loaf, sergeant. If she has been up to no good with Mum and Dad or even her brother we don't want to spook her. Besides, I've arranged for the estate agent to pick us up at the airport. That'll save the taxpayer a hefty cab fare, and being English the agent must be a safer ride than a Spanish taxi driver.'

'So why's he putting himself out like that? Did you tell him you were a cop?'

'No, I got Young Mundy to tell him we were thinking of buying a place in the town.'

'That was a bit rotten.' DS McCarthy looked thoughtfully at the man with the sunglasses on his head. 'Actually, I can see you in Spain rather than France when you retire.'

'I won't ask why.' He proffered his cup: 'Your turn for a refill I think - and can you see if they've got any Curly Wurlys in the duty-free shop?'

*

An hour passed, and the man with the sunglasses had gone off in search of other travellers to fill with unease. DS McCarthy had finished the Telegraph crossword, and Inspector Mowgley was reading a discarded copy of The National Enquirer.

Putting her newspaper aside, DS McCarthy stretched, yawned fairly discreetly, looked at her watch and said: 'You never told me how it was left with the bloke from Internal Affairs.'

Mowgley looked up in mock resentment. 'Do you mind? I'm just enjoying feeling desolated for this woman who had a boob job which didn't turn out well. Though I would have thought ending up with three would have made her more attractive to most blokes.' Mowgley held the open magazine at arm's length, grimaced, then tossed the magazine onto the seat opposite. 'Anyway, I did tell you about McTavish.'

'You told me he said they weren't interested in you, and that you got on alright with him. And that he was going over to Spain to look into Hoppy's...death.'

'Yeah.' Mowgley's face darkened, then he said: 'I certainly never thought I would find myself enjoying a wet with a Jock - and a Jock from IA.'

'So what is he like?'

Mowgley shrugged and reached for his tobacco pouch. '"Like"? What do you mean, "like"?'

'Well, how old is he and what does he look like? Is he tall or short or fat or thin or bald or with a big bushy red moustache or what? Did he wear a kilt...and is he nice?'

'"Nice"? What does that mean? I suppose he's quite good looking for a Jock if you're a bit short-sighted and forget the hump and the cross-eyes.'

'I wonder what he tells people you're like. And what's his first name?'

'It's one of those with an unnecessary letter to show he's a posh Jock.'

'Like F-fyfe, you mean?'

'Not that posh. It's Iain with two i's. But I think his dad is a wealthy lard.'

'A lard? I think you mean laird.'

'Catch up, sergeant. I said I think his dad is a wealthy lard - dripping with money, geddit? For sure he owns a fair bit of land up there. I know because I had Young Mundy check him out. But why all the questions - are you on the lookout now that you and Guy are no longer at it? If so, I think you'll find he's far too young for you; unless you reckon you could handle a toy boy.'

DS McCarthy's intended response was forestalled as her phone rang. She exchanged greetings, listened, said 'okay, here he is,' then handed the phone to Mowgley. 'It's your SOCO toy girl.'

'Hi Mog. Where are you?'

'Waiting to fly to Spain.'

'Ah. I won't ask why, but don't forget to bring me back a straw donkey.'

'Only if you've got some good news for me about the phone in Yo-Yo's pocket?'

'Yo-Yo? The poor chap was at the end of a rope, not a bungee.'

'Long story. But did you find out who the phone belonged to?'

Trudy Sixsmith paused then said: 'In brief, no. But do you want to hear the full monty?'

Mowgley looked up at the departure board and nodded at his phone: 'Yes please.'

'Okay. So pay attention. As you know, there was nothing on the SIM card except the photo-'

'Simca? Isn't that a make of foreign car?'

There was a deep sigh in response. 'Never mind. Suffice to say that there was nothing on the phone to give us a clue if it belonged to the dead Albanian or anyone else.'

'So, that's it then?'

'Not quite. To put it very simply, every mobile phone has a unique tag on it. It's called the IMEI code. The owner can register it in case it gets nicked.'

'What, like a chassis number in a car...?'

'Sort of. The point is that if the owner actually did register the code, it'll be on file with his contact details.'

Mowgley groaned theatrically. 'Oh yes, it's obvious that a drug-dealing, people-bashing professional scumbag is going to register his phone, isn't it?'

A brief silence, then: 'Did you know that 'sarcasm' means 'flesh-tearing' in Old Viking?'

'No.'

'Well, you do now, grandfather. If you applied a smidgeon of the deductive powers that you like to credit yourself with, you would have worked out that any phone found on such a person as Mr Yo-Yo might possibly have been nicked from its original owner. And that that owner might be able to give you a lead to where it went missing and perhaps even who took it.'

'Er, of course. Just testing, Trude.'

'Sure you were. So do you want me to pass the IMEI code on to the cute DC Mundy with your compliments and say you want him to follow it up?'

'Cute? Surely, kittens are cute, not hairy-arsed coppers.'

'I bet his bum isn't as hairy as yours.'

'If you play your cards right you may yet find out.'

'Can't wait. I'll take it as a 'yes' with passing the code on to the dishy DC- and don't forget the straw donkey.'

Having said goodbye, Mowgley returned the phone to DS McCarthy, who looked at it and then him. 'You do realise she's young enough to be your daughter - and possibly your granddaughter? And you accuse me of wanting a toy boy?'

'Just a bit of harmless flirting, sergeant. And you should be aware that 50 is the new 30.'

'Who says so?'

'Me.'

The conversation was put on hold by the announcement that passengers for the 11.45 flight to Malaga should make their way to Gate 28.

They stood and had begun walking across the departure lounge when Mowgley let out a groan.

DS McCarthy looked up at him, then asked 'What's the matter? Stomach pains? Don't worry, all the data proves that flying is the safest form of transport –'

'It's not that,' said Mowgley. 'matey with the offensive legs is right behind. You can bet he's going to be sitting near us for the whole journey going on about death and disaster on airplane flights.'

'Never mind,' said Catherine McCarthy brightly, 'it could be worse.'

'How?'

'Like you said earlier, he could be the captain.'

nineteen

Many aficionados claim that Olvera is the most beautiful of all Andalusia's White Villages.

A pleasing jumble of angular whitewashed properties with red tiled roofs, the classic pueblo blanco occupies the slopes of a steep hill amongst the mountains and plains of the Sierra de Cadiz, about sixty miles inland from the Costa del Sol.

This arid part of southern Spain abounds with olive trees, cacti, dust and aloe vera plants the size of small houses. Between the groves of countless olive trees, parts of the more barren landscape could be taken for Mexican desert. This is why it was chosen as an ideal location for the series of 1960s 'spaghetti western' movies. They were made by Italian directors with an international cast of actors, and the post-dubbing and synching of the dialogue into gruff English was so bad it has become legend.

Long before appearing on postcards, Olvera was a popular place for tourists, and is referred to warmly by Pliny in his 1st-century History. The region was overrun by Visigoths in the 5th Century, and then along came the Moors.

Nowadays, Olvera has a peaceful and easy-going air. Visitors are drawn to a spectacular castle and church overlooking a skein of narrow winding lanes and alleyways. The two symbols of war and religion also look down on the one hundred bars and restaurants that the residential population of 10,000 manages to keep afloat throughout the winter months.

This number and variety of drinking outlets ensured its immediate qualification as Inspector Mowgley's kind of town.

Two hours after arriving at Malaga airport, he and DS McCarthy were sitting in a cool and almost cavernous bar set at the bottom of a flight of steps leading up to the gilt and gingerbread church.

With a cold beer and smoking cigarette to hand, the detective was more than content, excepting for the cost of his refusal to follow DS McCarthy's advice on dress code for their brief stay. After the near-freezing temperatures at Gatwick they had encountered a wall of sweaty humidity when walking out of Malaga airport. As Mowgley had conceded, his overcoat and scarf were not suitable wear for southern Spain, even in February.

They had been met at the pick-up point by the estate agent and his wife, and she had driven more slowly and sedately than Mowgley could have wished for. The problem was that her husband was even more of a nervous passenger than the inspector, and kept up a remorseless running commentary of directions and possible hazards en route. He also had an alarming habit of grabbing the steering wheel when he thought his wife would miss a turning, causing the car to lurch in accord with Mowgley's stomach.

The journey had at last ended, and the two detectives deposited outside a modest hotel. After arranging a rendezvous for the next morning, they had watched as the car hiccupped away, then booked in before starting the long walk up to the top of the town. This was not for the purpose of sight-seeing, but because that was where Mowgley had been told the majority of Olvera's bars were to be found.

Apart from the steepness of the gradient, the most remarkable aspect was how well-kept the buildings were, and how haphazardly arranged and badly secured were the power and telephone lines connecting them. The cables were, he thought, like giant liquorice strands, sagging dangerously in the heat of the afternoon sun. The houses they were draped over were mostly terraced and flat-fronted, with blazingly white plasterwork and deep ochre clay tiled roofs.

The doors were invariably ornate, and as if there were a competition to have the most elaborate entry point in the street. Some were monumental constructions of planked wood with giant studs and wrought iron ring handles more suited to a castle than a small casa. Others were more demure with carvings and coloured glass panels. All the properties they passed on the long trek had their windows protected with elaborate grills of wrought iron. This would almost certainly be an echo of the town's Moorish past, and for decorative rather than security purposes.

All the way up the hill the street was lined with cars, parked as badly and apparently thoughtlessly as the power cables above them. All no-parking signs were casually ignored, and drivers were dumping their cars where they could before walking to their homes.

After a while, Mowgley realised that this was not a refusal to accept and observe the rules, but a pragmatic recognition of the circumstances. Had residents insisted on maintaining parking rights outside their homes, one transgression would have set off a domino-effect and probably led to bloodshed. The unspoken arrangement was a satisfying example of organised anarchy that obviously suited all.

There was, it occurred to him, something of a pilgrimage about their slog up the sloping streets towards the neoclassic 19th-century church. The fussy embellishments were made to look even more garish by the clean, solid lines of the neighbouring medieval Arab castle.

As they laboured on and upwards, they found themselves under the incurious scrutiny of residents, looking out from dark and cool-looking interiors or down from the balconied roof gardens. It was, the detective observed to DS McCarthy in between shuddering gasps, all very different from the average street in inner city Portsmouth.

*

Mowgley looked around him with deep approval. 'I reckon this is almost too good to be true.'

He had found the bar by ignoring DS McCarthy's reservations and entering what looked like an old apartment building at the start of Olvera's main shopping street. Down a gloomy passageway and past the numbered front doors of residents they had come across hidden treasure.

The ceiling was two storeys above their heads. The bar area was huge and to a specialist dealer the hand-painted floor tiles would be treasure trove. More tiles dressed the lower half of three walls, and the front of the long, straight counter which occupied the fourth. It was topped with a thick and apparently seamless layer of marble, which would have thrown any trendy kitchen designer into a paroxysm of envy.

The wall facing the bar was divided into cubicles, from two of which came regular bursts of staccato rapping. Investigation revealed games of dominoes in animated progress, the players probably having a combined age much greater than the nearby church. Though his companions were intent on the game, the oldest looked up at Mowgley and grunted a greeting. He had one eye tightly closed, and it made him look as if he were aiming an invisible gun.

Scattered about the room were other mostly aged customers, all male and sitting at sets of mismatched chairs and tables.

Mowgley liked the way their arrival had been mostly ignored by the customers and barman, either because they were used to tourists or simply disinterested in who they were and where they came from.

He had ordered two ice-cold beers by pointing at the pumps, and they were now seated at a marble-topped table in the porch-way of the building.

'In what way do you find it too good to be true?' asked DS McCarthy.

Mowgley sipped at his beer and savoured its intense coldness as he watched two boys playing on the steeply sloping road. Looking more closely, he realised that the round objects they were pursuing downhill were olives and not marbles.

'Well, for starters,' he finally responded, 'beer at under a pound a pint, and baccy at half the price of England. Lovely weather and nobody seems hostile, just not interested. In France the punters would have been staring at us like they were looking for a fight. The only drawback I can see is the food.'

'But you haven't tried any yet.'

'True, but I bet you can't get pasties or Indian here, and take a decko at the pathetic size of the portions.'

Catherine McCarthy looked to where a young man at a nearby table was eating from a side plate. On it was a very small hamburger in a bun and a handful of chips.

'If Two-Shits served that there'd be a riot,' Mowgley observed. 'No wonder we haven't seen any fat people yet.'

'Are you having me on? You must know that he's having a

tapas and not a main meal.'

'I'd heard of tapas, but I thought they'd all be sardines and olives and stuff, not a hobbit-sized burger and chips.'

'Just keeping up with changing tastes, I suppose. As you may not know, Andalucía is the home of the tapas tradition. It is said that the custom came about when King Alphonse the Tenth was ill and couldn't manage a full meal. He would have little tempting titbits, and when he got better he decreed that all wine served in the region should come with a snack.'

'A bit like getting a packet of pork scratchings or Salt 'n' Vinegar with your pint?'

'I suppose so. 'Tapas' means 'cover' and each glass of wine used to arrive with a slice of ham covering it.'

'Blimey, you sound like a guide book.'

'That's because I'm quoting from one.' She reached into her handbag and produced a small blue book: 'I like to find out about a place I'm going to visit before I get there.'

'Very commendable, Sergeant. And what do you make of the people so far?'

'Too soon to say, but different from us and the French for sure. I notice that all the older people move really slowly downhill as well as up, but that's probably because of the heat in summer. Loads of scruffy but inoffensive-looking men hanging around the Lottery stall or on benches under orange trees. The whole atmosphere and attitude seems to be very laid-back. As you said, nobody seems much interested in us, which I like.'

'Me too.' Mowgley drained his glass and stood up. 'I am in such a good mood that I intend buying the second round, and while I'm at it I'll check out the tapas.'

'I did while you were at the bar. There are at least fifteen selections, and all at about fifty pence a go. I'll come with you and pick something.'

'Don't bother. What's the Spanish for 'At these prices I'll take the lot, matey'?'

twenty

As Sarah Wheatcroft had said, the house she had bought her parents was little more than a ruin.

The pequena casa stood in a narrow alley off the street leading down from the church and castle. Two doors away from the house, the alley simply came to an end. There was a waist-high balustrade preventing cars and people plunging into oblivion, and from it some spectacular views towards the morning-misted mountains.

The nervous estate agent had met them outside the church and seemed more hurt than angry that he had been deceived. He knew about the deception as DC Mundy had phoned him earlier to reveal the inspector's true identity and his wish to see the Wheatcroft property.

He was a short, twitchy man in late middle-age with tufts of thinning hair, prominent ears and eyes and a strong Birmingham accent. In curious contrast, his shorts revealed thin, almost stick-like legs while his paunch strained against the buttons of his shirt. Perched on a snub and redly-veined nose, he wore the sort of half-glasses that barristers, academics and other poseurs like to peer over. Apart from the accent, Mowgley thought he would make a good Mr Pickwick.

As they walked, the agent explained that he and his wife had come to live permanently in their holiday home five years earlier with plans to set up a business. The idea had been to import camels from North Africa and through Gibraltar on to Spanish territory. They would then offer adventure holidays featuring camel treks through the vast and dusty plains of the area.

The enterprise had fallen at the first hurdle due to problems with obtaining a licence to bring the beasts in to Spain and use them for the proposed business. The venture had to be abandoned because, as he admitted, camel-trekking without camels was not really a goer.

Not wishing to take a bar or run a bed and breakfast operation, the couple had followed the route of so many expatriates in their position and started trying to sell Spanish houses to other Britons. The big mistake people made when they moved to another country, he concluded, was to think that living where they had been on holiday would be just as much fun.

Before they reached their destination, Mowgley gave the man a fifty euro note to, as he said, cover the cost of the petrol to and from the airport. The agent almost smiled as he took the money and tucked it away. If he were a betting man, Inspector Mowgley would have laid out the same amount again that Mrs estate agent would not know about the transaction.

*

The interior of the Wheatcroft's holiday ruin was as unappetising as the face it showed the world. Some people can look at a sadly neglected set of rooms and see what could be done with them given enough time, money and enthusiasm. Being a veteran owner of a wreck in a foreign land, Mowgley could only see a money pit.

Looking round for possible hiding places, it soon became clear there would be few. The upstairs of the house had no floorboards, and the ground floor was of undisturbed and ancient concrete. There was no yard, and the tiny roof garden obviously held no secrets. There was an absence of pots and pans in what had been the kitchen, and no sleeping bags or mattress. Overall, it was clear that Mr Wheatcroft had not made a start on any restoration work on the pequena casa, or slept on the premises.

Outside, Mowgley thanked the agent, shook his hand and

was turning to leave when the man said: 'But don't you want to see the other place?'

'Beg pardon? What other place?'

The agent pointed at the house next to the ruin. It was far bigger and immaculately presented. The flat roof was higher than any other in the row, and would afford magnificent views across the valley to the next village.

'Did you not know?' said the estate agent, 'this one also belongs to Mr and Mrs Wheatcroft.'

twenty one

'You don't look happy. Are the churros not to your liking?'

The two detectives were taking a late breakfast outside a bar overlooking the valley plain.

Mowgley toyed with the length of sugar-coated, deep-fried dough. 'It's not a proper breakfast is it? And all that sugar can't be good for you.'

'Unlike your healthy, life-lengthening fry-up at Ginger's caff, you mean? Anyway, what did you think of the Wheatcroft's second, second home? I suppose it proves Sarah Wheatcroft was in on the money-smuggling routine?'

Mowgley abandoned the confection in favour of a roll-up. 'Not at all. Why do you assume that?'

'Because she didn't tell us about the posh house next to the ruin.'

'That could be because she didn't know about it. She could have bought mum and dad the wreck and not known that they had used their commission from the money smuggling to buy the place next door. That could actually suggest she was innocent of any complicity.'

'Yeah, right. Do you really believe that?'

'No, I just said it's possible, that's all. At least the posh place next door tells us that it wasn't a maiden voyage for the Wheatcrofts when they got caught. The estate agent said the asking price for the flash house had been the equivalent of seventy-five grand. As they bought it cash and had no other income, it would have taken the kick-back from a fair few trips with the money belt to pay for it. Perhaps Mrs W was even in on the act and bringing readies over in her bra. Whatever, they must have had a proper little business going there.'

'Okay. But you know what really gets me in all this?'

'No. What?'

Catherine McCarthy finished her hot chocolate and reached for Mowgley's tobacco pouch. 'That a very ordinary old-fashioned apparently honest couple would get up to all this malarkey. I bet she never pinched a packet of sugar from the Co-op all the time she was there. What changed that?'

'As you are constantly pointing out, times are a-changing. They would have been fed up with having worked all their lives and then seeing people get thousands of quid compensation for having their feelings hurt, or getting more on benefits than they ever earned for a hard week's work. And I reckon it's also all the Guardian readers refusing to be 'judgemental' about the naughty stuff people get up to. I reckon the Wheatcrofts just got pissed off at being poor and seeing everyone getting up to all sorts and getting away with it. Along came the chance - probably courtesy of their darling son - and off they went.'

'You don't sound as if you blame them.'

'I don't think I do. I blame their boy for setting them up - if he did - and Mickey Finn for taking advantage of them. Simplistic thinking, you may think, but whichever way you look at it, it's Michael Finlayson whose the bad boy.'

'Hmmm.' She looked thoughtfully at the smouldering end of her cigarette. 'Okay. So where are we now? We know that the Wheatcrofts were doing the money run regularly, which does not bode well for Mrs W when she comes to trial - even allowing for the sympathy vote. But we don't know who they were doing the trips for, although we have a pretty good idea. And we don't know what happened to Hoppy.'

'Well, we do know what happened to Hoppy, but not who did it and why.'

DS McCarthy frowned at the chocolate sludge at the bottom of her breakfast bowl then stuck a finger in to it. 'We're pretty sure it was Finlayson, aren't we?'

Mowgley looked thoughtfully out across the valley to the distant peaks. 'The money or the murder or both? The odds are not long. But we should know a bit more after lunch.'

'Why?'

'We're going to see the investigating officer.'

'And where might he be found? Oh, my word...'

DS McCarthy paused with a chocolate-smeared finger en route to her mouth. Her attention had been taken by the gleaming blue convertible which had pulled up on the other side of the street with a squeal of tyres and a cloud of dust.

Mowgley looked at the car and then his sergeant. 'It's only a motor, Sergeant.'

'I know, but look who's driving it.'

The man behind the wheel was young, with a shock of curly red hair much deranged by the wind. Apart from the broken nose he had neat, even features, and was wearing what looked like very expensive sunglasses. Before getting out of the car he smiled at them, revealing a set of almost suspiciously white teeth. Then he stretched lazily, got out of the car and walked towards them.

'My word again,' purred Catherine McCarthy, 'he's tall as well.'

'As well as what?'

'As well as being drop-dead gorgeous.'

Mowgley sniffed disparagingly. 'He's not my type, really.'

Arriving at the table, the man lifted the sunglasses and smiled even more broadly. Then he indicated the car with a flourish. Talking to both of them but looking only at DS McCarthy, he made a half-bow and said: 'Your carriage awaits.'

*

DCI Gentley gunned the hire car along the almost empty CA-447 and earned a yelp of reproach from the back seat.

By none-too subtle manoeuvring when they approached the hire car, DS McCarthy had ensured she would be sitting alongside the Internal Affairs officer. From his demeanour and the way he was driving like a madman, it looked to Mowgley as if his sergeant's interest in the young inspector was reciprocated.

'So where are we going?' asked DS McCarthy, turning to look at the driver as she tried to hold her hair in place and wished she had brought a head scarf. She was wearing sunglasses, as he had handed her his in a gallant gesture as they set off.

'Ronda,' replied DCI Gentley. 'It's about 40k from here if we take the scenic route through the mountains and past a rather nice big lake.'

Looking more at DS McCarthy than the road, he explained that Ronda was the headquarters for the Guardia Civil. The GC, as he was sure she knew, was the national police force of Spain. It was a military organisation and the equivalent of France's Gendarmerie. While the national civilian police force attended to matters in urban areas, the Guardia Civil took an interest in the countryside, and specialised in investigating drug and arms smuggling. Because DI Hopkirk had been found on the Via Verde and also because of the circumstances surrounding his death and his role in the British Police Force, the case was being handled by a very senior officer in the GC.

Mowgley looked at the watch he did not have on his wrist, then reached forward and tapped DCI Gentley on the shoulder. 'There's no panic, you know. I thought you said our meeting was not till one o'clock?'

Gentley looked back over his shoulder and spoke loudly above the engine noise: 'Actually, we're being given lunch, and I believe our host takes his food very seriously.'

A huge blare and a flash of light returned his attention to the road, and he adeptly steered the car out of the path of a giant juggernaut. As it flashed by, the klaxon sounded again and a hand appeared from the driver's window. It was making the standard Continental sign to show exasperation, when the owner makes a gesture as if throwing an invisible ball into the air.

Mowgley waited until his breathing returned almost to normal, then opened his eyes so he could locate his baccy pouch. Having rolled a cigarette, he put the ill-manufactured result in his mouth and tried to light it. Finally succeeding, he held the packet over the passenger seat head rest. 'Do you want a fag to steady your nerves, Sergeant?'

DS McCarthy set her lips in an almost prim line, looked over her shoulder and said disapprovingly: 'No thank you, sir.'

The DI shook his head in recognition of the change in his sergeant's attitude to smoking a common roll-up. Also, he mused, she had obviously already deduced that DCI Gentley was a non-smoker.

*

They drove on across the vast plain, the barren landscape appearing to change in form, texture and even colour as they passed by. Now and then they would see a farmhouse or bar, but it was the loneliest place Mowgley had ever driven through. It was almost a moonscape, he thought, and there was little relief of tree or dwelling as it stretched to the distant, mist-shrouded mountains.

Forty minutes later, and they had reached civilisation in the shape of the town of Ronda.

'We're crossing the canyon through which flows the Guadalevin river, lying approximately one hundred metres below us in the Tajo canyon upon which the town stands.' DS McCarthy was reading from her guide book, using the sort of extravagant gestures used by airline stewardesses when demonstrating where the emergency exits are to be found.

'Constructed in the Neoclassical style in 1784,' she continued, 'the Plaza de Toros de Ronda is the oldest bull-fighting ring in all Spain. The great Hollywood film director Orson Welles was a summer visitor to Ronda for many years, and his ashes were buried in a well on the property of a famous bullfighter friend who lived in the town. Another famous visitor was Ernest Hemmingway. His novel For Whom the Bell Tolls describes the execution of Nationalist sympathisers by throwing them into the Tajo gorge.' DS McCarthy shuddered, shut the guide book and put it in her handbag, replaced her sunglasses and said: 'I wonder if that's true.'

'About the executions?' Iain Gentley asked. 'It's true that people seem to do the most terrible things to each other in civil wars.'

'Yes. I suppose we could ask our host.'

'I would find out which side his dad or grandfather were on before you ask,' said Gentley. 'I think feelings still run deep in some people and places.'

*

The Guardia Civil barracks at Ronda put Mowgley in mind of the way western movie makers like to portray a typical Mexican hacienda.

It was a long two-storey flat-fronted building, whitewashed to within an inch of its life, with a red tiled roof and flanked at either end by two accommodation blocks.

Unlike a typical French Gendarmerie barracks, there was no gate or even swing-arm barrier to navigate. The only guard was a short, prematurely balding young man in shirtsleeves, with a sidearm holster dangling from his belt. He was lurking inside the compound by the entrance to the car park, and directed them to the reception area without asking to see any identity.

'Just as well we're not Basque Separatists with a bomb or two about our persons,' observed DS McCarthy as they walked across the yard.

'Why would he think that?' said Mowgley, 'Basques are known for their big noses and ears and feet, and for being hairy.'

'Exactly,' said DS McCarthy, looking pointedly at her superior officer.

*

Though not particularly hairy, Teniente Coronel Juan Antonio Romero did sport over-large facial features. Obviously not far from qualifying for retirement, he had a small head with strands of black, well-oiled hair plastered back across his damp pate. His long, large-lobed ears were worn close to the sides of his head. He had an overcast brow and deep-set dark eyes and very full lips, the top one kept company by a long, narrow moustache. His nose was extremely pronounced and his chin small. The overall effect, Mowgley thought, looked as if the midwife had pulled him from the womb by his nose and his face had set that way. On further reflection, he decided the senior officer was almost a dead ringer for Jose Ferrer playing the consumptive Turkish officer in Lawrence of Arabia.

Fortunately for the visitors, the Lieutenant-Colonel spoke excellent English, which he demonstrated when DCI Gentley made the introductions.

'I am most happy to welcome you to my country,' he said in a formal but amiable manner. 'I am sorry that you have lost your fellow officer, and will be pleased to tell you all I know of the circumstances of his...death.'

As the senior British officer in years of service if not rank, Mowgley gave their thanks for his assistance and co-operation and asked if they might continue their discussions over lunch.

'I cannot imagine a better solution,' said the Coronel, raising an eyebrow as if surprised there might be any other option, 'and I have taken seats at a restaurant where we may find typical Spanish food on the menu. Sadly, that is not always the case in urban Spain nowadays. Unless, of course,' he smiled to show he was not to be taken seriously, 'you would prefer a Big Mac?'

*

Literally yet liberally translated, De Locos Tapas becomes Mad Caps, which was where the Lieutenant-Colonel took his guests for a real taste of Spain.

With just five tables, the restaurant was as small inside as its reputation was large throughout the town of Ronda and beyond. This was made evident by the compliments in the visitor's book.

Waving away a menu and giving the owner full rein as to the food and drink chosen, Senor Romero explained that what they were about to receive was a selection of pintxos, the Basque equivalent of tapas. 'In fact, as the Basques say,' he said, 'pintxos are like tapas, only far better.'

Playing a hunch, Mowgley asked if the policeman was a Basque. 'Oh, no, certainly not,' smiled the officer, clearly unoffended, 'I am a Madrileño. I am from Madrid. But I believe there is Basque in my family some generations ago.' He made a casual gesture at his face, then said: 'You are obviously a detective of merit, inspector.'

'May I ask what brought you to Ronda, Coronel?' asked DS McCarthy. 'Were you posted here?'

'I asked for a posting here two years ago, Detective Sergeant.' Romero inclined his head graciously as if in apology for appearing to correct her. 'The pace and quality of life in the big town was becoming less and less to my taste. My wife is from this area, and we wanted a home away from people and traffic and noise. Now we live in the mountains, and my life is an easy one. Our crime rate is not high here and murder is relatively rare. That is why we were so shocked at the death of your colleague - and the nature of his discovery. But perhaps we can speak of that when we have eaten.'

*

Less than an hour later and the table was occupied by two empty bottles of rich Andalusian red, a bottle of sweet dessert wine and twenty side plates bearing the remains of a repertoire of tapas that even Mowgley had found as rewarding to the taste as well as the eye.

Now the party had moved on to intensely rich black coffee, with a plate of sweetmeats for DS McCarthy. The proprietor had been to graciously accept their plaudits, and in return had invited their opinion of his Gran Duque d'Alba 18-year-old XO brandy.

Given the quality of the food and drink, It seemed inappropriate even to Mowgley to introduce his baccy pouch to the gathering, so he joined the Guardia Civil officer in trying a Partagas Spanish Rosado cigar. As the Coronel explained, 'Rosado' referred to the hue of the wrapper, and the 'Spanish' was a nod to the influence of that country in the history of Honduras.

'Now, my friends,' said the Spanish policeman, blowing a discreet cloud of fine blue smoke toward the slowly turning ceiling fan, 'I think you will wish to hear what we know of your colleague's death.'

twenty two

Teniente-Coronel Juan Antonio Romero lifted a limp hand to his mouth and gave a soft, almost deferential cough. In so doing, he reminded Mowgley even more of the Turkish officer in Lawrence of Arabia.

'As you know,' said Romero, 'Your colleague's body was found on the Via Verde by a cyclist. It was some way from the track and the cyclist was alerted by the vultures... squabbling over something.'

The officer paused, took a sip of his brandy and looked quickly at Mowgley under hooded eyes. He obviously realised that what he was saying would be painful. He took a draw at his cigar, then continued: 'The cyclist saw what the birds were fighting over, and drove them off when he had recovered from the shock. He called the police and stayed with the body. He is available if you wish to question him further, of course. Forensic officers attended and your friend was identified by his police officer registration on the international DNA bank.'

Mowgley knew what the Spanish officer was saying without saying it. 'So there was not much of him left by the time the cyclist had intervened?'

Again the softly apologetic cough. 'No.'

'So no point in asking to see him?'

'No.'

Mowgley emptied his brandy glass and reached for the bottle.

'Do you have any leads?'

The Spanish officer frowned. 'Leads?'

'Do you have any information or evidence of who might have done this to our colleague?'

Romero shook his head. 'No. Not yet.'

'When you say 'not yet' do you mean that you have an idea of who did it?'

'No. I meant that we have no information or evidence at this time.'

Mowgley nodded. 'I understand that. So how was the body found?'

'"Found?" It was, as I said, found by the cyclist...'

'Sorry, I mean were there any other pieces of material evidence on or near the body? Was there anything in his pockets?'

Again the cough, then: 'Detective Hopkirk was completely without clothing. At this time of year the temperature drops severely in the mountains overnight, so it is possible he would have died of hypothermia before the morning.'

'He was naked?' Mowgley digested the implications. 'So it is most likely that he was killed and then dumped by the track. Why would they leave him alive to get away and find shelter?'

Romero looked at the end of his cigar as if considering whether he should say more. Then he put the cigar down in the ashtray, looked Mowgley directly in the eyes and said: 'Senor Hopkirk had been... secured. He was staked out by his hands and feet. It appears a piece of tape had been put over his mouth.

There was silence, and then Mowgley said: 'So he could have been alive.'

Preceded by a gentle, somehow sympathetic cough, the Spanish officer said. 'I think not. I hope not. There is some evidence that his stomach had been opened to expose his entrails before they left him to the birds...'

*

The sky above the mountain range was blood red. Like the scenery, Mowgley thought, sunset came on a grand scale in this part of Spain.

They had returned to Olvera, and were sitting outside a bar run by a large, hairy man who had told them in spectacularly mangled English that his name was Pedro. Whether this was his real name or he used it to amuse or patronise British tourists was hard to tell. A couple of young men at the bar had smiled when the proprietor had introduced himself. Perhaps,

Mowgley thought, the name had some ribald connotation in everyday Spanish. Or perhaps it would be like the landlord of a tough dockside pub telling a visitor that his name was Cecil or Justin.

'You know what gets me?' he said.

'Loads of things and more so as you get older,' said DS McCarthy.

'No, what I mean is how complex and subtle any language is. It's not just about understanding the words; there's all the ways a word or a sentence can change its meaning depending on how it's said.'

'Quite true,' said Iain Gentley. 'Imagine how hard it was for me when I came across the border. It was bad enough in London, but Portsmouth has a language of its own.'

'Several, actually,' said DS McCarthy, 'it's mostly the Navy, you know.'

It had been a sombre journey back from Ronda. Mowgley had been dwelling on inescapable thoughts of his friend staked out and left to die in agony, alone and far from home. Death was death and it should not matter where it caught up with you. But nobody wanted to die in a foreign land.

'So now you have spoken to the Lieutenant-Colonel, what's next for you?' asked DCI Gentley.

Mowgley looked at his glass and shrugged. 'I was just thinking about that. I suppose there's not much we can do here. But I'd like to look at Hoppy's villa before we go back. What about you?'

'I've just about done.' Mowgley noticed that the young Scot shot a glance at Catherine McCarthy before continuing. 'I had to...close the file on DI Hopkirk, and there's some related stuff I need to do while I'm over here.'

'That all sounds a bit mysterious,' said Mowgley. Are you up to something big to do with all this? Is it more than Hoppy being on the take?'

'If I told you I'd have to kill you, Inspector. But if you want a lift down to see the villa tomorrow...?'

'That would be good,' said DS McCarthy rather too quickly. Then, speaking to both men: 'Did you get the idea that Senor Romano was holding something back?'

'I did,' said Gentley. 'Though perhaps it was the language or the culture giving that impression. He's obviously a very reserved man.'

'Even so,' said DS McCarthy, 'though he tried hard not to show it, he certainly reacted when you asked him if he knew of Finlayson or Wheatcroft. Is that why you asked him?'

Mowgley answered for the DCI. 'It wasn't such a long shot that a very senior officer in the Guardia Civil should have heard of an international drug smuggler - and a possible gun runner. That's what the GC do, remember. Investigate illegal drug and arms trading.'

'That's right.' DCI Gentley got up and reached out for Mowgley's empty glass. 'Same again?'

'No thanks. I don't fancy any more. Must have been that big lunch. It filled me up.' Mowgley stood up and buttoned his overcoat. 'Gets chilly at night here, doesn't it?'

DS McCarthy looked up at him and raised her eyebrows. 'Did I hear right? You just turned down a drink? So where are you going? You can't be going to bed - it's barely eight o'clock and the hotel doesn't have SKY television.'

'I just thought I'd make an effort and climb the steps to that castle. It must be quite a view from there, even after dark.'

'Okay.' DS McCarthy put a hand out towards her handbag. 'Do you want me to come with?'

'Don't bother, Cat. I just fancy a stroll on my own. Lots to think about.' He turned towards DCI Gentley and nodded. 'Thanks for the lift and the help,' he said. 'We'll speak in the morning?'

'No problem.' The Internal Affairs detective looked at his watch and then his glass. 'I think I've had too many to drive back to my hotel in Putanges; perhaps I'll be able to get a room at your place. Then I can take you to the villa whenever you like in the morning.'

'That's a good idea,' said Inspector Mowgley, then, in an almost avuncular voice, he added: 'Have a nice time, the pair of you.'

twenty three

'Act your age, you silly old bugger!'
Mowgley's shout was lost in the slipstream as the soft-top Porsche Boxster slid effortlessly past, the sound of its engine hardly rising above a throaty purr.
The elderly driver had close-cropped grey hair and his leathery, tanned face put Mowgley in mind of a pickled walnut. He was wearing a large pair of aviator-style sunglasses on the top of his head. They looked a permanent fixture, as much for display as the large stud in his right ear. Perhaps, the detective thought, he had another pair to put on when the sun shone.
They were cruising down the A-428 from Olvera to Marbella, and being regularly overtaken by a selection of top-of-the-range cars. All were heading south to the playground of the rich and sometimes infamous, and it had been noticeable how the quality and type of vehicle had changed as they neared the coast.
At the start of their journey from the hinterland, the few vehicles encountered were mostly unremarkable. Some of the cars and vans were spectacularly distressed and reminded Mowgley of rural France of a decade or so before.
But as they neared the sea, their sleek powder-blue hire saloon looked a poor relation amongst the growing number of growling high-performance cars.
Without exception they had their hoods down, and Mowgley wondered what the ratio of convertibles to hard-top cars was in Spain compared to wet and cold Britain. He also wondered if not having a proper roof contributed significantly to the traffic-related death toll. Apparently not, when considering the comparative lack of carnage on Spanish roads.
Before leaving, he had asked DC Mundy to look up the

relative figures, intending to use them as a cautionary tale for Catherine McCarthy if they had needed to hire a car. When Mundy came up with a cross-referenced, precise and very detailed raft of data, Mowgley had been surprised to learn that the death toll on the roads in Spain was lower than in the UK. He had at first put that down to Spain being twice the size of the United Kingdom with about the same population. But though as roomy as Spain, France killed twice as many of its citizens on the roads. Italy came a close second in the death hit parade. Obviously it was nothing to do with traffic density, and the French and Italians were intent on establishing who were the baddest and maddest drivers in Europe.

Today, Mowgley was pleased to note that DCI Gentley was driving almost sedately. It was true they were in no hurry and had no appointments to meet; but he preferred to think the young man's calmness at the wheel was a result of developments after he had left Gentley and Catherine McCarthy together on the previous evening.

Already he had noted that their relationship had altered, albeit subtly. The day before had been spent playing the eternal game and establishing if, how soon, where and what would happen between them. Clearly something significant had occurred in the hotel, and the two detectives were displaying the signs that they were now, for however long, a couple.

At breakfast they had sat closer together than would be natural or seemly for work colleagues. At one point, DS McCarthy had even brushed some crumbs from DCI Gentley's chin. She had, Mowgley admitted to himself, often attended to him during a meal, but more in the manner of a mother with a messy child than a lover.

'So how far is it now?' Mowgley leaned back and dangled his arm over the side of the car. For once, he was almost enjoying being driven.

Gentley looked at the satnav. 'It's about an hour to the coast, and about forty minutes to the villa.'

'So the place is a bit inland then?'

'Yes. I suppose he didn't want to be too upfront. According to Senor Romero, it's an old granja - a farm - converted into a villa.'

'You mean all tiles and white walls and a swimming pool?'

'Exactly. The Coronel said it's a lovely place and in a good location.'

Mowgley started his second attempt to roll a cigarette since they had left Olvera. 'So what links it with Hoppy?'

'Don't know yet. Romero must have been keeping watch on the place. They certainly seem to know a lot about it and who's been using it.'

'Isn't it a bit close to Finalyson's bar and nightclub in Marbella for Hoppy's good health?'

DCI Gentley lifted a hand off the wheel in a don't-know gesture. 'Now, yes, but not when he and Finlayson were on good terms. Maybe DI Hopkirk had left things here he needed to pick up, so it was worth the risk. Or he thought it was.'

DS McCarthy nodded agreement, then raised her voice over the sound of the engine and wind. 'Perhaps it was having the villa and getting a taste of the good life which started him doing his own dealing.'

'Yeah, you're probably right,' said Mowgley. If he owned it.'

'What do you mean...if he owned it?'

'We don't know he does-or did. Anyway, it's funny how a bit of money can make people do such silly things.'

DS McCarthy looked back at him, pulled her hair from her face and smiled affectionately: 'Don't worry Mog, I can't see it happening to you...'

*

If its surroundings would still be familiar, the former farm would have been unrecognisable to the original owner.

Surrounded by a high whitewashed wall broken only by a massive wrought iron set of gates, the villa sat atop one of a line of hills leading to the mountain range through which they had just passed. It was clear that the view from the roof terrace would be stunning. That view would have been unspoiled by any activity or noise, as the nearest property was half a mile away, and the nearest road further still.

They had bucketed their way up a winding track through dozens of almost geometrically-straight lines of olive trees, and pulled up alongside a dusty Guardia Civil patrol car. It was unoccupied, and parked to one side of the gleaming black and ornate gates, one of which was open.

As they got out of the car, Mowgley saw that the name of the villa had been fired into a highly glazed set of tiles on the wall next to an intercom system.

He pointed at the sign. 'Anyone know what granja dinero means?'

'Money Farm,' said DCI Gentley.

'That's a bit cheeky isn't it?' DS McCarthy neatened her hair and lifted Iain Gentley's sunglasses to the top of her head, earning a disapproving scowl from DI Mowgley. 'I suppose Hopkirk thought he was remote enough here to get away with the gag.'

'Perhaps,' said DI Mowgley. 'Or perhaps it wasn't his.'

Catherine McCarthy frowned 'I can't see an impoverished Spanish farmer calling it that. Or perhaps he was being ironic.'

'No,' said Mowgley, 'what I meant was that perhaps it was renamed by the owner before Hoppy got it. It could have been Finlayson.'

'You mean the keys were in recognition of service rendered and to come?'

'Maybe.'

Catherine McCarthy's frown deepened. 'Still seems an extravagant gesture. This place must be worth at least two hundred thousand pounds.'

Mowgley looked at the house, rubbed his hands together briskly and nodded. 'At least. Now then, shall we visit the money farm and see if anyone's left any produce lying around?'

*

They walked along the gravelled driveway, past a tennis-court and a fountain and towards the wide steps leading up to the entrance. The deep green of the lawns on either side of the drive were a demonstration of conspicuous consumption, in this case of the valuable resource of water.

There were no plants on show except two lofty palm trees, one at each end of the raised terrace which ran the length of the villa frontage.

'I wonder why people do that?'

'Do what?' Iain Gentley followed Mowgley's nod towards the very ornamental stone balustrade.

'Put something which would look over-the-top outside a 17th-century chateau on a building which is supposed to look like a Mexican hacienda.'

Gentley looked sideways at Mowgley, then said 'Perhaps the owner liked it. I wouldn't have thought of you as a snob.'

'Everyone's a snob in some ways, son. It just takes different forms with different people.'

At the top of the steps, a bored-looking Guardia Civil officer did not bother to ask for any identity. His blue, short-sleeved shirt strained across a massive paunch, and Mowgley thought he was probably thinking about what he would be having for lunch. To be fair, so was he. The man had obviously been warned of their visit, and just made a slight adjustment of his shoulders in recognition of their rank before nodding at the tall, black wrought ironwork protecting the panelled wooden doors.

Tiled from floor to ceiling and the walls bearing huge and ornate gilt-framed mirrors, the lobby reminded Mowgley of the decor in what was then called a house of ill-repute he had helped raid as a young policeman. The next set of doors rose to the lofty ceiling, and opened to reveal a vast open-planned area.

An acreage of marbled floor lay before them, dotted with heavy and heavily carved furniture. An enormous glass-topped low table bore an empty fruit bowl set exactly in its middle. Doors led off from this living area, and beyond it was a grand, winding staircase.

A balcony ran in a semi circle from the top of the stairway, giving access to what would presumably be bedrooms. There were no discarded newspapers or DVD stacks near the monstrous television, and even the cushions on the seats of the chairs and sofa were plump and undented. The overall impression was of the show house on a very upmarket development, or a glossy photograph in the sort of magazine which tried to persuade Britons it would be a good idea to sell up, leave friends and family and start a new life in a foreign land.

'Well,' said DS McCarthy. 'I don't know what the rest of the place looks like, but either Hoppy was as fussy about his living space as he was with his clothes, or Spanish SOCO has a thing about leaving things really neat and tidy.'

'Yes,' agreed Iain Gentley, 'I don't think there'll be much

left to pick over.'

Behind the first of the doors leading from the living area was a kitchen which reminded Mowgley of the flight deck of a starship in a very modern science fiction movie. Opening the next door revealed a room almost the size of the living area, with a full-sized snooker table in its centre, and a marble-topped bar complete with chromium stools taking up one wall. If they had ever been occupied, the rows of shelving and glass-fronted cooling cabinets were bare. When Mowgley pointed out the lack of bottles, DCI Gentley said they would have been taken away for forensic examination and perhaps would be returned after being scanned for prints and DNA.

'Quite,' said Mowgley ironically. 'I always admire the way you IA people are so trusting and think the best of people.'

Next to the bar and recreation room was a home cinema, complete with a screen occupying one wall and red-plush retro-style folding seating for twenty. As with the bar, the shelves and units which would have contained DVDs were empty.

Alongside the cinema was a cavernous shower wet room, its walls and even ceiling lined with stainless steel. Alongside was a toilet almost as big and certainly as comprehensively equipped as a stop-off at a motorway service station. There was a commercial condom dispenser on the wall above the two urinals, and Mowgley noticed the coin slot had been blanked off. Setting the selector for a French Tickler, he pressed the button and found no response. After watching him try all the selections, Catherine McCarthy said: 'El SOCO are being overly optimistic if they've taken them all away for DNA testing.'

'Maybe.' Mowgley ran a finger through a sprinkling of white dust around the dispensing outlet. 'Or perhaps it was dispensing another commodity.'

At the top of the grand marble stairway, six very large bedrooms awaited. Each had its own bathroom with duplicate washbasins and toilets. All were as lavishly furnished and pristine as the downstairs rooms and areas. Back on the landing, a spiral staircase led up to the roof terrace, and the three detectives ended their inspection of the property there.

'Mmmm.' DS McCarthy breathed deeply, turned her face to the sun, leaned on the wrought iron balustrade and looked to where a distant and faint line suggested the meeting of sky and sea. 'Well, I don't know about you, but the inside of the place was even grander than I expected. And it seemed set up to accommodate a dozen people at a time. No matter how useful your mate was, I just can't see Finlayson handing over the keys to a palace like this.'

Mowgley joined her at the balustrade: 'Perhaps it wasn't Hoppy's.'

'Eh?'

'Well, he told Karen Ross it was, but perhaps he was only using it. Or sharing it.'

'With who, or do I mean whom?'

'No good asking me, sergeant. What I mean is that it could have been a little treat for other people to who - or do I mean whom - Finlayson owed a favour.'

'You mean whom, I think. So the Money Farm could be a sort of grace and favour holiday home for faithful retainers and high-rolling customers?'

Mowgley shrugged. 'Something like that. Or it may have been a home-from-home for other useful coppers like Hoppy.'

McCarthy's eyes widened and she looked to DCI Gentley. 'Is he saying there may have been other drug squad officers at the trough?'

'Or non-drug squad officers. It's something we've been looking at,' said Iain Gentley. 'Other handy contacts in the Force even beyond the city and the county coming over here for the ultimate luxury breaks. Drinks, food, girls - or boys - and some snorting stuff all thrown in.'

Catherine McCarthy whistled. 'And you thought my boss here might have been involved in all this?'

'Not really. Unless he did it very craftily, Jack has never been to Spain before. And if he was getting a payoff, he hid it very well.'

The detective sergeant frowned. 'And what about me? I've been to Spain a few times. Have you been looking into me?'

Gentley held up his hands, palm out at shoulder height in a pacifying gesture. 'No, of course not.'

Mowgley smiled, enjoying DCI Gentley's discomfort. 'Well, if he wasn't showing an interest in you officially, he surely is now, sergeant.'

DS McCarthy did not take the bait. She stretched, looked

around her and said: 'I suppose you can almost see why people do it.'

'Do what?' asked Mowgley.

'You know, go bent, or get involved in dealing in a big way.'

Iain Gentley walked across and stood beside them. 'Do you mean you would if you had the chance?'

'Are you asking in a conversational or professional context...sir?'

'I was just thinking what mortal dangers the suppliers take on, and what a price people will pay for a packet of powder to put up their nose.'

Mowgley raised an eyebrow. 'That's a bit of a Calvinistic stance, is it not, young Iain?'

'Oh, I don't know,' the detective replied. 'I just think how bizarre it all is. Billions of pounds spent and tens of thousands of deaths worldwide because drugs are banned.'

DS McCarthy gave him a sharp look. 'Are you as a senior police officer saying you think all Class 'A' stuff should be legalised?'

'No, not necessarily, but I certainly think something radical has to be done. As they say, if it hadn't been around and in general use for so long, alcohol would surely be a prohibited substance. And look what happened when they tried to ban it in America.'

'Someone else on the job made that point to me not so long ago. And she was a senior officer.' Mowgley looked reflectively across the foothills towards the shimmering mountain tops. 'But what an awful thought.'

'What,' asked DS McCarthy, 'banning booze?'

'Of course. Can you imagine what pubs would be like if you couldn't get a proper drink in them?'

twenty four

Marbella sits somewhat smugly in the foothills of the Sierra Blanca, looking out across a usually pellucid Mediterranean.
   Its location endows the town with a benign microclimate, helping make it one of the most popular tourist destinations in Spain. Another attraction to some visitors is looking at what lots and lots of money can buy. The town has a population of around 140,000, which more than quadruples in the peak summer months. Marbella's so-called Golden Mile actually stretches for more than six kilometres and is where some of the most luxurious residences in the world are to be found. Some say this strip of the Spanish coastline actually smells of money, and often bent money.
   More than any other Spanish town, Marbella has been rocked by a series of scandals involving drug trafficking and money laundering and corruption at the very highest of administrative levels. It is estimated that more than 30,000 properties in the city boundaries were built without proper planning permission. It is not known how many former and current British gangsters own or live in properties in the Marbella catchment area.
   Mowgley began to button his shirt and ran a finger through his disobedient hair as they passed the Grand Casino. 'Do you think they'd let us in?'
   Catherine McCarthy looked up at the soaring, curlicue-d and rococo-ed frontage they were passing. 'Do you really want to go in there?'
   'Sod the casino. I meant they'll probably bar us from the town for not being flashily-dressed or orange enough.'
   DS McCarthy looked at where a gaggle of exotic creatures with very white teeth, identical retroussé noses and expensively

tousled hair were rattling their jewellery at each other outside a bar. Alongside the conspicuously parked Gucci, Armani and Birkin handbags was a row of parked cars which included two Maseratis, a Rolls-Royce and a customised Ferrari. She regarded her superior officer for a moment, then nodded and said: 'Perhaps it would be best if you could duck down out of sight till we get to the poor quarter - if there is one.'

They had reached Puerto Banus, or to give it its proper name, Puerto Jose Banus. To the southwest of Marbella, the marina and adjoining temple of shopping and eating and drinking extravagantly was created in 1970, and now attracts an alleged five million visitors a year. Many are fabulously rich and celebrated; most come to see and be seen while pretending to be rich and celebrated.

Using his specialist knowledge as an IA drugs-related corruption officer, DCI Gentley had been taking them on a tour of the high and lowlifes centres of the town. As they slowly drove alongside the marina, Mowgley scented the air, then said, 'Is it my imagination, or can I smell funny money and white powder?'

'I would not be surprised,' replied Iain Gentley. Once upon a time you might spot Ava Gardner, Laurence Olivier or Audrey Hepburn dining here. Now it's likely to be trustafarians, fading pop and movie stars and some really premier league Class 'A' dealers.'

He pointed to a distant hillside, dotted with villas. 'There's a place belonging to a Brit trafficker who you could say is the northern counterpart of your Mr Finlayson. He came out here when the climate got a bit hot for him in Liverpool, and kept a luxury yacht called Dancing with Waves in the marina. He did a lot of big-time trading between Morocco and here, and was busted in the late 90s for importing 500 kilos of hash. He was sentenced to ten years, but escaped from an armed escort a couple of years ago by jumping on a jet-ski and disappearing across the straits of Gibraltar.'

DS McCarthy raised an eyebrow. 'And they haven't made a TV series out of his adventurers yet? So where is he now?'

'That's what a lot of people would like to know.'

'And do you think he's a rival or a trading partner of Mike Finlayson?'

'Pass. For sure he was known to be an international fixer

for traffickers on a worldwide basis. It may be that Finlayson wants to take over his contacts and connections now that he's on the run. It's clear that Mr Finlayson seems to be intent on growing his businesses over here very quickly.'

DS McCarthy looked at a huge white yacht moored in the azure waters beyond the marina. It was like a giant queen bee being tended by a dozen droning speedboats ferrying guests to and from its gleaming decks. The boat was, she thought, only slightly smaller than a cross-Channel ferry. 'Do tell me,' she said,' we're staying here for the night?'

'There is a place along the road where they say the gold taps alone are worth a quarter of a million,' said DCI Gentley. 'You can rent it, but the high season rate is 15,000 quid a day, I fear it's a bit beyond our expenses limit. I just thought you'd like to see the place before we retreated to somewhere more our style - or rather our price range.'

*

The El Cordobes bar was in a much more modest area of Marbella, and owned by a former bullfighter. Or at least that was the story. Related items on the walls included posters advertising corridas, a cape with a very obvious tear in it, a crossed pair of barbed darts and a so-called suit of lights complete with the strangely-shaped hat.

As far as Mowgley could see, none of the matadors on the posters resembled the proprietor, and the massive-bellied man behind the bar could certainly not have got even a foot into the knee breeches of the traje de luces. He walked with a quite dramatic limp when moving to serve customers, but Mowgley suspected the incapacity was more likely due to arthritis than an old goring injury. Fortunately, the inspector's almost total lack of Spanish restrained him from telling the owner that if he ever attended a corrida he would cheer for the bull.

'So, when do you plan on going back?' Mowgley shut his eyes and put a baby squid into his mouth. It tasted every bit as bad as he thought it would.

As the inspector chewed with grim determination, DCI Gentley glanced at Catherine McCarthy. 'I'm just about done, but I've got a final meeting with Colonel Romera tomorrow.'

'So, you're going back to Ronda?

'No, it's here.'

'Oh, right. And what's it about?'

Gentley looked embarrassed. 'I know this is going to sound really arsey, but I can't tell you.'

'Of course you can; you mean you won't.'

'I've been asked not to tell anyone about the meeting, that's all.'

Mowgley gave up the battle with the squid, spat it into a cupped hand and put the mangled remains on the side of his plate.

'Okay, I'm not really that hurt. But why the sideways leer at my sergeant?'

Gentley hesitated and DS McCarthy filled the silence. 'We - I - was wondering if you'd be alright to get back on your own.'

'What, to the hotel?'

'No, to the UK. I've got loads of time due, and it seemed a shame to dash back if you can do without me.'

'Do you mean getting on the plane? Don't they have people to do that for old and infirm passengers?'

DS McCarthy's lips thinned. 'You know what I mean.'

It was DCI Gentley's turn to pick up the thread. 'I-we- just thought it would be nice to take a look along the coast for a couple of days. I could run you to Malaga in the morning-'

'There's a flight at noon,' interjected DS McCarthy, 'and there's plenty of room. Of course, you don't have to go...'

Mowgley smiled almost benignly, then looked at the remains of the baby squid. 'Do I look like a raspberry? It's been a nice couple of days, but I'm beginning to miss the Ship Leopard and proper food. So yes, of course you can hang on here, but only on one condition.'

DS McCarthy shook her head despairingly, then said to DCI Gentley. 'He means gooseberry and he does that sort of thing deliberately. Irritating isn't it?'

Turning to her superior officer, she continued: 'anything within reason, and I bet I know what's uppermost in your mind. I spotted a Brit bar down near the beach as we passed, but I don't know if they do Cornish pasties.'

*

As a regular visitor to France, Mowgley had become something of an expert in the sort of bars which aim for the custom of British expatriates or holidaymakers already missing familiar surroundings.

In general he found they fell within two broad categories. One was an attempt at evoking the sort of rural village pub the like of which had never existed. The other was an equally cack-handed attempt at appealing to both British and native taste.

Entering Union Jacks, Mowgley had realised he could add another category to his portfolio. This was night club posing as pub. Or the other way round.

After the brightly lit street, the gloominess of the interior was amplified, like the bass thump which they had followed from the car. Above, the darkness was relieved by a number of spotlights trained on a giant and hopefully ironic mirror-ball. Strategic locations like the top of the bar, the emergency exit and the door to the toilets were marked with neon tubing, and a pathway from the entrance to the bar was laid out like an airport runway with twin rows of small lights set in the wooden floor. A row of cubicles occupied the wall opposite the bar, and in between were two chrome poles ascending from raised platforms to the artificially-starred black ceiling. Mercifully, it was too early for the DJ or the pole dancers to have begun their routine. It had been immediately clear to DI Mowgley on entry that, whatever else was on offer, Cornish pasties would not be on the menu at Union Jacks.

DS McCarthy and DCI Gentley had kept him dutiful company for half an hour, and had been clearly relieved when he had ushered them on their way. Making sure his phone was charged and he had the address of their hotel, Catherine McCarthy had ignored Mowgley's invitation to tie a label to his lapel in the manner of a wartime evacuee.

An hour on and the level of the piped music was steadily increasing to match the inflow of customers. Outnumbering the men, the groups of young women seemed to have come from the same mould. All seemed to be competing to wear the least clothing, and all had skin of the same orange hue. The men's faces were either leathery brown or any shade of sunburn from rare roast beef to fire-engine red. Virtually all the women had blonde hair, cut and shaped in identical cascades of curls and crinkles. With their eyes made big, they reminded Mowgley of Cocker Spaniel puppies fresh from the water. Everywhere, teeth were whiter than bone, and the ultra-violet lighting gave the dancers smiles like Halloween masks.

Having spotted the DJ setting out his stall, DI Mowgley was about to drain his glass and make good his escape when he felt a presence behind him. Looking into the mirror at the back of the bar he saw a familiar face.

'Hola Jack,' the owner said, 'what's a nice boy like you doing in a place like this?'

twenty five

'How did you know where to find me, or was it another massively unlikely coincidence?'

She shrugged. 'As I said last time we had a drink together, I'm a detective.'

Detective Superintendent Stanton lit a cigarette and regarded Mowgley through the smoke. 'To be honest, I've been watching you all day. Or at least, I know a man who has.'

'You mean the short swarthy bloke with the receding hair and the pony-tail and earring, with the Hawaiian shirt and the bomber jacket, camouflage cargo trousers and ropey trainers? I spotted him trying to look like a tourist at Puerto Banus, then outside the matador's bar up the road.'

She looked puzzled. 'Nope. That doesn't match anyone I know. Perhaps it was a pimp. Or someone else has got a reason for traipsing round after you.'

They had escaped from the British bar before the disc jockey and dancing girls had launched into action, and were sitting outside a restaurant on the grand promenade. The atmosphere was not relaxed, but getting easier.

When Jane Stanton had suggested eating at the Restaurant Garum, Mowgley had hoped for a tikka masala and proper chips; it was with disappointment that he learned that the name came from an ancient Roman fish sauce, and that the establishment specialised in salmon and sea bass rather than Bombay Duck. But there had been hope in the shape of a classy-looking bacon and cheese pure beefburger with coleslaw and anorexic but acceptable chips.

When they had eaten and he had rolled a cigarette and lit her Malboro king size, they looked across the table at each other, each waiting for the other to get down to business.

'Oh go on then,' Jane Stanton finally conceded, 'start grilling me.'

Mowgley took a deep draw on his roll-up, then said: 'No point in me taking notes, putting you under caution or oath or checking that posh handbag for a tape recorder, I suppose?'

'I bet you've never taken a note in your life, and we don't use tape recorders now. It's all cutting edge digital stuff. Anyway, you suppose right. But feel free to ask what you like, though I may take the Fifth if it suits for awkward questions. Like my age, for instance.'

'I already know that. And where you live, or used to live. And who your mates at work are. And who can't stand you.'

She looked at him coolly. 'I thought you'd probably do your homework on me.'

He returned the look. 'I like to know a bit about people I've shared a meal, a drink and a bed with. Especially if they've shot me.'

She put on a mock-exasperated face and voice: 'Oh you're not going to keep bringing that up, are you? It was only the once, and it meant nothing to me.'

'That's what they all say.'

He leaned over and refilled her glass. In truth he was enjoying her company and the badinage. She took a sip and watched as he poured wine for himself. 'Lummy, that's the first time I've seen you drink wine. Are you getting to like it?'

Mowgley nodded at his beer. 'Only as a chaser. And at these prices and as you're in the chair, I wanted to make the most of it.'

'Actually, the good old taxpayer is paying, one way or another. But that should make it taste even better.' She looked beyond the palm trees and across the moonlit sandy beach to the wine-dark waves. 'It's nice, isn't it?'

'What, here? I suppose that's why so many villains live here. On that note, what are you doing here?'

The Special Projects Units officer let out a long plume of smoke. 'I reckon you know the answer to that one. Probably the same reason that you're here.'

'I doubt it. I came to find out who killed my mate, and I reckon you already know. It was Finlayson, I guess?'

'You guess right.'

'And because he was nicking his gear and setting up shop

on his own?'

'That's right as well.'

'And the bloke with no tongue under the pier? He was acting as Hoppy's nark and passing on advance information about incoming shipments?'

'Right again.'

Mowgley emptied his glass and reached for the bottle.

She winced. 'You're supposed to sip and savour that, you know, not neck it.'

'I don't do sipping.'

She smiled. 'That's true.' She looked across the terrace at the doors to the restaurant. 'As you've already put his back up, I'll wave to the waiter for an encore. You carry on.'

'Thanks, Ma'am. So what made Hoppy come over here and why was he stupid enough to go to the villa?'

She shrugged. 'We don't know that he did. There's lots of DNA and marks of his in the Money Farm, but that could have been from previous visits. My best bet is that he came on what was meant to be a flying visit to pick up his cash stash or some more product or perhaps both. Obviously, Finlayson was tipped off by one of his minions or contacts here, and that was it for your chum.'

'And do you know if he was alive when they left him staked out on the old railway line?'

She frowned. 'No. I hope for his sake he wasn't.'

The conversation stopped as the waiter arrived with a fresh bottle of wine. He looked down his nose at Mowgley as if debating whether it was worth the effort of pouring him a sample for approval. He obviously decided not, put the bottle down audibly and huffed off.

Jane Stanton waited while Mowgley topped her glass up and re-filled his own, then said: 'Okay, next question.'

'Did the villa really belong to Hoppy?'

'No. It belongs to Finlayson - or rather, to a company in the Seychelles which is another front for him and his operations.'

'And was it - is it - a rest and recreation centre for fellow British-based gangsters and bent police and even the odd Customs officer of note?'

'Yep. As I said, there's a good bit of surveillance film on the place, and a load of forensic which is still being analysed by Spanish SOCO.'

'Are they any good?'

'What, you mean are they a load of bumbling garlic-eating incompetents? Not really. Not up to our standards perhaps, but then I would say that, wouldn't I? They're foreign and from a hot country. Next?'

'The Wheatcrofts.'

'What about them?'

'Was it Finlayson's money in the belt, and if so how does he launder it? And how involved is the Wheatcroft's son?'

She lit another cigarette and appeared to be considering her response. 'Yes, it was one small consignment of the flow of drug money exported by Finlayson and destined to come back after laundering.'

'And do you know how he's been laundering it?'

'Yes, pretty well, and he's been pretty inventive. As well as a handful of bars and clubs along the coast, he's got an import and export business and a security set-up here.'

'What, you mean like supplying bouncers at other bars and clubs as well as his own?'

'No. Like supplying and installing sophisticated surveillance and Intruder alert systems for some of the biggest and flashest properties all along this Costa.'

Mowgley frowned. 'Really? Set a thief to catch a thief sort of thing?'

She nodded. 'Something like that. Sheiks, deposed kings and princes, Russian Oligarchs and the cream of the old brigade of London gangsters.'

'Does it do well?'

'Not half. Money's no object to the mega-rich customers, and the has-been hoods love lashing out the dosh to show they've got it, and they're still important enough to need the latest in electronic protection. Then there's the regular updates to the electronics.'

Mowgley started to roll another cigarette. 'A good business to be in if he wanted to do a bit of burgling.'

'I'm sure he's considered that as a pension scheme if it all goes to shit with this drugs empire.'

Mowgley lit his roll-up. 'So how exactly does his ill-gotten gains from the UK get laundered?'

'It couldn't be simpler. He adds the cash to the genuine turnover of his businesses here, and then it's squirted back electronically to Portsmouth clean as a whistle and to support his and justify his clearly lavish lifestyle.'

'What about the taxman in the UK? Doesn't he ever want to take a look at the books to see that they add up?'

'That's the beauty of it. The money comes into the country tax-paid in Spain where the businesses are based and operating. Finlayson pays peanuts in the UK.'

'And I suppose he don't pay as much tax as he should to the Spanish government?'

'Spot on. This is Spain - and particularly Marbella.' She stretched and leaned back in her chair, looking across at the lights dancing on the crest of the small rippled waves responding to the offshore breeze. 'So is that it for Question Time - at least for the time being?'

'Just a couple more.'

She groaned theatrically. 'Okay then. Shoot, if you'll pardon the expression.'

He did not smile. 'You didn't say about Wheatcroft junior.'

'If he's in with Finlayson? Very much so, but more of that tomorrow.'

'What's happening tomorrow?'

'I'll tell you in a minute. Before you ask, your lady friend Sarah Wheatcroft appears clean as paint.'

'So you had a good look at her?'

Jane Stanton gave a slight shrug. 'Of course. A high-level chemist who spent some time in Spain? It was a no-brainer.'

'So if she's straight, the parents bought the posh place next to their ruin without her knowing.'

'Yes, silly as it sounds, it appears they bought it for cash and just didn't tell her. She's never been over to see the ruin since she bought it, so how would she know or find out?'

'And it was Wheatcroft junior who fixed his dad up with Finlayson?'

'It would follow. Personally, I think acting as a mule and buying the place next door here was the poor old sod's way of cocking a snoot at the Establishment and Fate for his rotten boring life and all those grinding years of crap wages. You'd be surprised at how many oldies are up to no good nowadays. They've had to build special wings for pensioners in some nicks.'

Mowgley rubbed his chin thoughtfully. 'So I hear. Okay

then, nearing the end. What about the Hanging Man in the dry moat - and why did he have a photo of me in his phone? Was it another of Finlayson's creative killings?'

'Probably. Like the guy under the pier, the bungee - jumping Albanian was two-timing him.'

'With who. Or should that be whom?'

'Whichever takes your fancy. The Albanian was working for Finlayson, but at the same time doing stuff with the Eastern Europeans we bumped into the year before last. He could have been done by either side.'

'And my photo?'

'I honestly don't know. But we'll find out. Is that it now?'

'Except for what you're really doing here, what's happening tomorrow that includes DCI Gentley but not me, and where did the grenades and the other stuff come from and go to?'

Stanton stubbed her cigarette out and reached for her handbag. 'In case you hadn't noticed, I work for the Special Projects Unit, and we specialise in drugs and guns. Why wouldn't I be here? You'll find out about the grenades and the arms cache tomorrow.'

'And what is happening tomorrow?'

'A meeting of minds.'

'So why wasn't I invited?'

She put a Gold American Express card on the table and nodded to the hovering waiter.

'To be honest again -'

'Why do I always feel you're about to tell a big fat porky when you say that?'

She smiled. 'Okay, I give in. The fact is we didn't want you blundering in and fucking things up when Mr Wheatcroft popped his clogs in the ferry port. Also, and think about it, with you being so close to DI Hopkirk we weren't going to take you into our confidence. Then it all got worse when the deadheads took the grenades as souvenirs and your mate turned up dead. Then when you came over it really caused a shitstorm. Now my bosses and opposite number in the Guardia Civil have decided the best thing to do with you is bring you in instead of trying to keep you out. You have to realise this is really, really serious stuff. It was either let you join the game or knock you off, and I persuaded them you were worth keeping.'

Inspector Mowgley looked at her to see if she was joking,

but her face gave no indication.

'Okay,' he said, getting up from the table as the waiter returned, 'can you drop me off at my hotel, wherever it is?'

She laid two twenty Euro notes on the table, then slid the credit card back in its holder and put it in her handbag. 'I was going to suggest a nightcap at my hotel. It's on the prom and rather nice, unlike where you're staying. Fancy it?'

Mowgley looked at her thoughtfully for a moment, then shrugged and picked up one of the banknotes. 'Well, okay Ma'am. But only if you promise to be gentle with me - and that includes no accidental shootings...'

twenty six

The projection room in the Guardia Civil base at Marbella was not as up-to-date and well-equipped as the one at the Money Farm. Perhaps, Mowgley thought, this was because this branch of the national police force did not have as big a budget as Michael Finlayson.

The meeting was about to begin and those attending were sitting round a long, oval table. The top was blemished with a number of cigarette burns, and it was scratched in places. There were no writing materials in evidence, just a heavy glass tumbler and a folded paper napkin in front of each seat. Ashtrays sat on either side of two large glass jugs filled with water and ice. Mowgley noticed that someone had taken the trouble to add slices of orange and lemon.

A large screen occupied one end wall of the rectangular room, and what looked like a projector was set into the suspended ceiling. There was an air conditioning vent high up on one of the longer walls, but the temperature and fug of smoke suggested it was not working. The top half of the other end wall was covered by a mirror. Mowgley assumed it was not there for either decorative or reflective purposes.

At one end of the table, Teniente Coronel Juan Romero was sitting with legs crossed, rubbing his chin and looking thoughtfully at the blank screen. He was flanked by two men. One was about Mowgley's age, with a slight build, long thin face and heavily oiled hair sleeked flat to his head. He had prominent eyes beneath rimless glasses, thin lips and slightly prominent teeth. He wore a smartly-cut uniform unmarked by badges of rank or any fol-de-rols which meant he was probably a very senior officer. With the double-breasted grey uniform, hair style and severe glasses, Mowgley thought he looked a little like Josef Goebbels.

Sitting directly behind the officer like the rider on the back of a tandem bicycle was a man in a shabby suit. He was older than the Goebbels lookalike and had a nervous air. He was holding a clipboard in his lap and referring to it as he darted glances at the foreign visitors. As Mowgley watched, the man looked directly at him, then leaned forward to whisper in the officer's ear. Inspector Mowgley wondered for a moment if the man was some sort of political advisor, then realised he was probably a translator.

Across from the duo was a heavily-set man. He was perhaps a decade younger than Mowgley, and wearing a well-cut and obviously expensive lightweight suit. Though otherwise well-groomed and with neatly arranged medium-length hair, there was a slightly coarse and thuggish air about the way he sat sprawled back open-legged in his chair, which he had pushed away from the table.

Mowgley had no idea who Goebbels or the other man were, or what they did for a living. When the three British detectives had been ushered into the room by Juan Romero, the officer had made no introductions. The two strangers would have been briefed as to who Stanton, Gentley and Mowgley were, but just as obviously did not care to share their identities or positions within the Spanish law enforcement services.

First to enter the room, Mowgley had taken the seat at the furthest point from the three Spaniards. As if in a show of solidarity, Jane Stanton and DCI Gentley had sat on either side of him.

Speaking in English after making his trademark deprecatory cough, Romero opened the proceedings by welcoming their British colleagues. As he paused, the translator leaned forward and spoke quietly to his client. The officer appeared bored and looked at Romero as if urging him to get on with it.

This the Lieutenant-Colonel did by raising one hand above his head and snapping his fingers. Almost immediately, the lights dimmed and the screen grew bright.

For no logical reason, Mowgley had been expecting a grainy, wobbly picture; the opening shot was in fact in crisp and steady focus. He recognised the front gates of the Money

Farm framed in the shot, and wondered if they had rigged up the surveillance camera in one of the olive trees on either side of the track to the villa.

Apart from the occasional buffet of wind, there was no sound until an engine in low gear preceded the appearance of an expensive-looking car. The limousine drew up at the gates, and a man in a chauffeur's hat got out. Walking as if on familiar territory, he crossed to the gates, pressed a button on the intercom box and spoke into it. The gates slowly opened as he walked back to the car, got in and drove into the grounds.

Then the shot cut abruptly to the same scene at another time, with the sequence of arrival repeated except that the cars and callers were different. In one, DI Hopkirk got from the car and walked to the gates to punch a sequence of buttons on the intercom box. As with the other clips, there was a read-out at the bottom of the sequence giving the date and time it had happened. Again there was a sudden cut as Hopkirk walked back towards his car, and then the scene changed.

The shot showed the front doors of the villa, and from the low level and movement Mowgley assumed the camera was concealed in a bag or case. As the bearer neared the doors, one swung open and a man stepped out, smilingly extending his hand towards the camera in a gesture of welcome. This sequence was repeated twice, with the same man opening the door on two occasions. Then the scene changed to a very rocky shot of a large motor yacht. Another cut and the next scene showed a brightly illuminated saloon, assumedly on board the boat. From the height of the shot it appeared the camera bag was resting on a table. It revealed Andy Wheatcroft, glass in hand, lounging on a white settee alongside a pair of glazed doors leading on to a deck area.

After a moment, two men came into shot, framed by the glazed doors. Mowgley recognised one of them as Michael Finlayson. The drug trafficker smiled through the glass as if to the camera, then opened one of the doors and ushered his companion in. Andy Wheatcroft got to his feet and all three men took a seat at the table. Finlayson and Wheatcroft were partly out of shot, and the man sitting between them took up most of the screen. He was in his middle years, shorter than Wheatcroft and Finlayson, dark in colouring and large-featured.

There was no soundtrack, but as the men began to speak in English, subtitles in Spanish appeared at the bottom of the screen. The content of the conversation meant nothing to Mowgley, but he did his best to appear interested. It was warm in the room, and after the heavy meal and late night in the hotel, he felt himself slipping away.

A sharp dig in his calf brought him back to life, and he covered his groan with a cough. The video of the meeting ran for another ten minutes, and ended with the three men in vision standing and reaching forward to shake hands with the owner of the camera bag.

The film stopped at that point, the screen darkened and the lights came up. There was a brief silence, and then Teniente Coronel Romero spoke directly to Mowgley. 'We have seen this film several times, but show it again in case you might recognise any of the people in it?'

As the translator continued to speak rapidly into the ear of the uniformed officer, Mowgley replied: 'Only Michael Finlayson, Andrew Wheatcroft and Detective Inspector Hopkirk. None of the others.'

'Ah.' Romero smoothed his moustache thoughtfully as if Mowgley had said something of significance, then continued. 'As I know you now understand, inspector, we –' he nodded across the table to the uniformed officer and then the man in the tan suit '-we are working in close cooperation with senior officers in your specialist law enforcement departments.' With this he nodded in the general direction of Jane Stanton and Iain Gentley, then said, 'As you will also know, our operation is centred on the activities in the United Kingdom and Spain of Mr Finlayson, and it has been in train for several years. Within the last year, Mr Wheatcroft has appeared on the scene, and brought a new dimension to the situation.' He waited until the translator had caught up, then looked at the man in the lightweight suit. The man nodded curtly, and Romero continued. 'Without, I hope, going into too much detail and covering ground already familiar to the others here, I think it is no secret that there has been a great deal of illegal behaviour in and around Marbella over the years.'

'From outside have come drug traffickers who find the town a convenient and pleasant place to do their business.

They also found they could buy privilege and even immunity by paying the right people.' He paused for the translation and again looked at the man in the suit as if to check how he was doing. Then he went on: 'I think you will understand if I say corruption was endémico at all levels of administration and local government, and, in some cases, the forces of law. As I said, I will not go into detail, but to say that our mayor was convicted of the misuse of public funds last year. There are now serious allegations against his replacement. At the heart of it all are the vast amounts of illegal money coming in to the town to be, as you would say, laundered. It comes largely from illegal activity on a grand scale by no more than a handful of foreign individuals, of whom your Mr Finlayson is one. Now, the situation has been compounded and worsened, as it seems Mr Finlayson and his new colleague are moving into trafficking more than illegal drugs.'

The Lieutenant-Colonel paused again, wiped his brow with a paper napkin, then took a packet of small cigars from his jacket pocket. He lit one, blew smoke at the ceiling, and went on: 'As you know, Mr Wheatcroft is a member of the armed forces, and has been using his connections to acquire and offer for sale a range of weaponry.' Again he paused for the translator, and while doing so asked Mowgley if all was clear to that point.

'Yes, I understand,' said the detective. 'I believe he is organising raids on military armouries.'

'It's moved on a bit since then.' Jane Stanton leaned forward and tapped her cigarette against an ashtray. 'We now know he is setting up deals with former terrorist groups in Ireland.'

Mowgley puffed out his cheeks. 'Blimey. You mean the Boyos?'

She nodded. 'And the Prods. It was comfortable to think that the arms caches were all surrendered or weapons decommissioned as part of the follow-on from the Good Friday Agreement in 1998. In reality, there's still enough undeclared armament out around the six counties and over the border to equip a fair-sized army.'

'And Wheatcroft has been dealing with the dissidents while he's still in the Army?'

'He used his Special Services contacts to find out where to go and who to speak to, then set up meetings with Finlayson to talk money and the nuts and bolts of getting the merchandise here. Having invested so much money and time in setting up his drug routes and systems, he plans to adapt them to handle arms.'

Mowgley shook his head. 'Like a sort of one-stop shop for Armalites and Class 'A' drugs?'

'That is exactly right,' Romero stood up and stretched, puffed at his cigar then sat down again. He nodded at Jane Stanton as if in acknowledgement of her contribution, then continued: 'Some of the people in those pictures were colleagues of yours from different police forces arriving at the Granja Dinero to take advantage of Mr Finlayson's hospitality. Others were government officials or people of influence. The man on the boat was a well-known sympathiser with ETA, the Basque terrorist organisation.'

'And the man behind the camera?' Mowgley asked. 'He is one of yours?'

Romero nodded solemnly. 'He was one of our men, posing as someone with an interest in broking weapons.'

'You say 'was'?'

Romero nodded again. 'He passed on the latest of those pictures, then disappeared. We have not heard from him for three months. So, as you can see, inspector, we are in effect fighting a small war here. As allies for once –' he smiled and nodded at Jane Stanton and Iain Gentley '-we are working together to put an end to Mr Finlayson and his friend's ambitions.'

Mowgley took a pull at his roll-up, then, just to see the reaction, asked: 'Wouldn't it be easier and much cheaper to just knock off Mr Finlayson and his friend?'

He waited and watched as the translator explained what he had said. The man in the uniform looked at Mowgley as if to see how serious he was, then almost smiled. Across the table, the man in the suit made no reaction.

Romero gave a wintry smile. 'Of course it would be much cheaper and a lot quicker, but it would also be highly illegal...even in Spain. As well as that, to cut off the head would at first appear to be effective, but would leave the rest of Mr Finlayson and Mr Wheatcroft's network free to carry on when, as I think you say, the dust had settled. We would like to get them all in the same bag and make a clean sweep.'

Again, Romero fell silent, sitting back and obviously watching to see how the translator would handle his last sentence. Then nodded in approval and continued. 'Can I ask if all is clear so far, inspector, or are there any questions you wish to ask before we go on?'

'Only one, really,' said Mowgley. 'Why are you bringing me in on this? I'm flattered, but you could have kept me out - or even disposed of me. I would surely not have been as much as a problem as Mr Finlayson.' He watched for the reaction of the Spaniards; the man in the uniform made no reaction, but the man in suit looked thoughtfully along the table as if it were or had been a reasonable suggestion.

After another small smile. Romero said; 'I don't know what you have heard about our various law enforcement agencies, inspector, but we haven't made a practice of eradicating inquisitive foreigners for some time. Or at least while I have been with the Guardia Civil.'

twenty seven

Jack Mowgley, Jane Stanton and Iain Gentley were sitting in a bar just along the road from the Guardia Civil building.

'Cheers,' Mowgley lifted his beer glass. 'Well, that was interesting, was it not?'

'I hope it was for you,' said Jane Stanton. 'As Juan said, we'd seen and heard it all before.'

'I'm sure you have, but I still never got a proper answer from your chum Juan as to why they hauled me in to go through it all.'

Jane Stanton exchanged glances with Iain Gentley, then said: 'To be honest with you, and whatever was said in the meeting, I think it was either bring you in or think of another way of getting rid of you.'

Mowgley paused with his glass half way to his mouth. 'Are you saying they would have knocked me off for being in the way? Come on, surely not even in southern Spain?'

Stanton shrugged. 'Well, I'm sure it would never cross Juan's mind, but I'm not so sure about the scary bloke.'

'Which one? The one who looked like Goebbels with indigestion or the rent-a-thug in the smart suit? Personally, I found them both a bit scary and it would have been nice to know who they are and what they do.'

DCI Gentley looked at Jane Stanton as if for permission, then said 'The Goebbels chap with the crossed swords on his shoulders is no less than a Brigadier General. He is about as far up the ladder as you can go in the Guardia Civil and is said to be representing the Minister of Foreign Affairs and Co-operation with regard to the project.

Mowgley sniffed. 'But he can't speak English for all his rank, can he?'

'Don't be so sure,' said Jane Stanton. 'I heard he likes to pretend he doesn't so he can listen in to our private asides.'

'Okay; so what about the other mystery man?'

'The thug in a suit as you call him really is scary. We don't know his name and I don't even know if Juan Romero does. He told me the guy is something in the CNI – the Centro Nacional de Inteligencia. They're a bit like MI5, MI6 and my lot rolled into one. Officially and on paper, their mandate is to prevent any risk or menace to the independence and integrity of Spain, its national interest, rule of law and institutions.'

'Oh well,' said Mowgley, looking out of the window and frowning. 'I suppose that about covers all contingencies.'

'Exactly.'

'If I'd have known he was a sort of Spanish James Bond I would have been nicer to him. So apart from thinking about who to knock off next, he was sitting in as a representative of the whatchermacallit?'

'The National Centre for Intelligence. The thing is that Finlayson's activities had reached a level beyond shipping a few million quid's worth of drugs through the country a year and bribing a few relatively minor officials. The silly boy is moving into altogether different territory now he and Andy Wheatcroft are going into arms trafficking. When the surveillance shots showed the ETA guy, it went upstairs to the CNI and the mierda really hit the ventilador.

Mowgley frowned into his empty glass. 'You know, what gets me is why people like Finlayson don't know when to stop. He must be worth millions already. Why risk it all by going for more?'

Jane Stanton smiled at him and patted the hand holding his glass. 'That's what makes you what you are, Mog. People like you never understand people like him. That's why you haven't got any money and he's got so much. The Mike Finlayson's can never have enough.'

'Anyway, that's where we are with it. We've now got the bloody Spanish Secret Service involved, and despite all Juan's gags, I wouldn't put it past them to knock Mickey Finn off and add Andy Wheatcroft for good measure.'

'But you reckon I'm okay?'

She patted his hand again before taking the glass from it. 'I think and hope so. That's why I suggested bringing you in on the act. All the time you were blundering around you were upsetting all the wrong people, and coming over here to find out more about your mate's death on a thin excuse made things worse. Telling you what was afoot short-circuited things. Now you know what's going on you're not going to tread on any toes or upset the apple cart with a runaway bird in the bush, as Juan would probably say.'

Mowgley nodded at his glass. 'Same again, please. And what do I do now to keep everyone happy?'

'Bugger off home, basically and forget everything you heard today. Leave it to us and I or Iain will keep you up to speed. You can be sure that Hoppy's death will be avenged when Mr Mickey Finn gets his comeuppance. But before that, Iain can go and pick your bag carrier up and you can buy me a really expensive lunch. 'Are we all clear and in accord now?'

As she waved at the bar with his empty glass, Mowgley stood up, looking through the big front window of the bar.

'It's over there, where the sign with the arrows says hombres,' said Iain Gentley.

'Ah,' said Mowgley, beginning to button his jacket up 'thanks, but I just need to nip out for a packet of baccy. I saw a shop down the road.'

Outside the bar, Mowgley waved as if saying goodbye to his colleagues and set off down the road. He passed several junctions before arriving at a pedestrian alleyway, then walked briskly into it. As soon as he had left the road, he stopped and stood with his back to the wall.

It was no more than a minute before the ponytailed small man in a bomber jacket, jeans and scuffed trainers turned into the alley and found Inspector Mowgley blocking his path.

'Hola, cocker,' said the detective, 'do you speak English?'

'No,' said the man in accented but good English.

'Ah, shame,' said Mowgley, 'that means we'll have to rely on sign language.'

Taking hold of the lapels of the man's jacket, he swung him round and held him against the whitewashed wall. The man looked displeased but unafraid and made no effort to resist.

'That's better,' Mowgley said. 'Now, will you kindly tell me why you've been following me around for the past two days? Do you fancy me or do I remind you of your mother?'

The man looked up at Mowgley, then said 'I told you once, I

do not speak English. But you do remind me of my mother, who was said to be the ugliest woman in all Madrid.'

Mowgley groaned. 'All this way and I have to meet a comedian. Shall we start again?'

'Not really,' the man replied, 'I have run out of jokes.'

He shrugged despite Mowgley's grip, then reached towards the inside of his jacket. Mowgley let go of one lapel and grabbed the man's right wrist, pushing it back against his chest. The man grunted, then brought his other hand up, hitting Mowgley under the chin with the heel of his hand. It was not a savage blow, but hard enough to rock the bigger man back on his heels.

Keeping his grip on the man's wrist, Mowgley grabbed his left arm and forced it back against the wall. They stood looking at each other, Mowgley panting and the other man looking unperturbed. 'Are you going to let me go?' he asked. 'I have something in my pocket to show you.'

'Not a chance, matey.'

'Ah, well then...'

As he smiled pleasantly at the detective, the man brought his knee up into the soft tissue of Mowgley's groin area.

Giving a heartfelt moan, the detective let go of the man's arms and instinctively reached for the damaged area.

It was now the man's turn to push Mowgley against the wall. As the detective straightened up, the smaller man kept his left hand on Mowgley's chest as he reached again for an inside pocket.

Before he got there, Mowgley pulled his head back and butted him in the face. It was a mistimed and misdirected blow, catching the man no more than a glancing blow on his forehead. But it was enough to cause him to let go of the detective and fall to the ground.

After getting his breath back, Mowgley took his foot off the man's chest, knelt down and reached into his jacket.

In the inside breast pocket he found no weapon, but what felt like a wallet. He pulled it out, and keeping one hand on the man's chest, he flipped the leather holder open. Inside was an oval badge with a shield at its centre, surmounted by a crown. Inscribed beneath the shield in capital letters were the words POLICIA LOCAL.

'Oh shit,' Mowgley groaned. He looked around and then

down, then shook his head and said to the unconscious figure: 'You could have told me you were one of us.'

twenty eight

Inspector Mowgley watched from his office window as a bulky figure in a high-visibility jacket put on a surprising turn of speed and rugby-tackled a man who had taken to his heels after crawling out from beneath a lorry. The man's dash for freedom took him across the link span and technically on to British soil before he was apprehended. The ferry boat carrying the lorry and the lorry itself were both owned by French companies, and had just arrived at the port from Cherbourg.

'I wonder why they do that,' Mowgley said to no-one in particular.

'What?' asked DS McCarthy, arriving at his side and following his gaze towards the lorry, 'bring cheese from France to here? I think quite a lot of Brits like French cheese, especially the twenty seven varieties found in Normandy-'

'Har-de-har.' Mowgley took the proffered cup of coffee and stole DS McCarthy's cigarette before continuing: 'As you well know I was making reference to that poor sod they're carting off to the Customs Detention Centre. Why would they risk their lives to get over here when they're already safely in France?'

DS McCarthy considered the question, then asked: 'Would you rather live in Britain or France?'

'True. But that's not the point. What I mean is they've come hundreds or thousands of miles from some place where it's not very nice to live, so why don't they stop when they get to France? It's a fairly civilised country even if they don't do proper chips.'

'Well, the illegals do stop at the Channel if they're from some part of North Africa or anywhere where they speak French. But I think you'll find most of those trying to get in here come from a country where English is at least a second language. I suppose we shouldn't have colonised and taken over so many countries in the days when the sun never set on the British Empire.'

'No,' said Mowgley, 'I suppose not.' He watched as the man was marched away in the direction of the Customs shed, 'Poor sod.'

The inspector was generally sympathetic towards those who tried to gain entry through his port, and no less so today because of his recent experiences of being unwanted in a foreign country.

He had arrived back in Britain the previous day with DS McCarthy; unlike her, he had been more or less repatriated.

When a resident of Calle Maestro Armado had seen the exchange between Mowgley and the undercover member of the local police force, she had phoned his colleagues. They had arrived in some number, and despite the unruffled equanimity of the downed officer, had handcuffed and taken Mowgley in a none-too-gentle manner to a cell in their town headquarters.

As the inspector was to learn, the Policia Locale is a fairly autonomous law enforcement body, operating in towns with a population of more than 20,000 and recruited, funded and controlled by the local town hall.

Understandably, miscommunications and even strained relationships between the different police forces were not uncommon. Given the situation in Marbella concerning the ongoing investigation into the mayor and city fathers, it was not surprising that the Guardia Civil had not shared with the Policia Local the news of their joint operation with the British police service.

Inevitably, leaks and garbled rumours had made the senior officers of the Marbella division of the Policia Locale aware that something worth knowing about was going on. Subsequently, undercover officers had been assigned to follow and report on the movements of the British officers whilst they were in the town. Unfortunately for Inspector José Pérez Abrigo, he had been detailed to tail Inspector Mowgley.

It had taken the personal intervention of Teniente Coronel Juan Antonio Romero to secure the release of the Englishman. Taking the advice of Lt-Col Romero, Mowgley had left Spain on an early flight. As the officer had said, drawing attention to the presence of British police officers on covert duty in Marbella was not a good idea. Especially if it gave the Spanish Secret Service reason to even consider alternative methods of getting rid of the troublesome English detective.

*

By noon, Inspector Mowgley was already at his table in the Ship Leopard. It was his first full day back on the job and so it was to be a working lunch. He, DC Mundy and DS McCarthy had been given a tour of the newly refurbished Gents before getting down to business. Landlord Two-Shits was particularly proud of the hand dryer and toilet cubicle door, as it was the first time both had been in place and working at the same time for a number of years.

Lunch was served, and the meeting began with a briefing from Stephen Mundy on relevant ferry port events and incidents during the past week.

Arrests of note included a 71-year-old Dorset man found to have thirty kilograms of cannabis powder hidden in inner tubes in the spare tyre compartment of his car. He had arrived from Caen after travelling across Spain and France from his winter retreat in Morocco. When stopped, he had said that the powder was for his personal use as it gave relief from his arthritic pains.

Another pensioner probably heading for prison was a 68-year-old Portsmouth woman found to have fifty thousand pounds in Euro notes concealed about her person while attempting to board the overnight boat for Bilbao.

'Another oldie mule', said Mowgley through a mouthful of pasty and chips, 'I suppose she was poor old Mr Wheatcroft's replacement?'

'I do hope so if it cost Mickey Finn a week's wages,' said DS McCarthy. 'Was she wearing a money belt, Stephen?'

'No, sergeant. Some of the notes were found in her tights and knickers, but most were in her brassiere.'

'Good God,' said Mowgley, 'she must have had a massive pair of knockers.'

'The Customs estimate her weight at more than 20 stones sir, and she was only a little over five feet tall. My contact said she was probably chosen because, as he put it, she had a lot of stowage room.'

Mowgley paused with the fork halfway to his mouth as he strove to dismiss an image of a Customs officer interfering with a twenty-stone pensioner's underwear in search of contraband. After a moment he shook his head as if to clear it, put the forkful of food back on his plate and reached for his tobacco pouch. 'So is that it this week from our friends guarding the borders?'

'Yes, sir, apart from a number of confiscations of tobacco and alcohol. There was also the arrest and holding of an alleged double bigamist.'

'A what?'

'A double bigamist, sir.'

Mowgley looked perplexed. 'Isn't that a-' he looked at DS McCarthy for help.

She obliged: 'A tautology.'

The inspector looked relieved. 'Yep, that's it. Bigamists are bigamists because they have two wives, aren't they?'

Mundy nodded. 'Yes, sir, but the man being held is accused of going through four marriage ceremonies. Apparently he had families in Scotland, East Anglia Wales and Basingstoke.'

'Blimey. What does he do for a living?'

'I believe he is a long-distance lorry driver, sir. The wife in Basingstoke found out about the other three and called the police. He tried to catch an early boat to Caen, in disguise.'

DS McCarthy looked puzzled. 'And what was he disguised as?'

Mundy looked slightly embarrassed: 'Erm, a lorry driver, sergeant.'

She frowned. 'But he is a lorry driver.'

'He was disguised as a female lorry driver, sergeant. He had taken his Southampton wife's passport. Apparently they were similar in size and colouring, but she was much taller and less hairy than him.'

Mowgley shook his head as if to clear it. 'Okay, I think I get it. But why would any bloke want to have more than one wife on the go at the same time? You never hear of female bigamists, do you?'

'I wonder why,' said DS McCarthy dryly.

'So is that finally it, Young Stephen?'

'Yes, sir, apart from the arrest of an alleged illegal immigrant earlier today.'

'Yes,' said Mowgley, 'we saw that. So any other business?'

'A couple of things, sir. I followed up the coded number found on the mobile phone with the photo of you and DS McCarthy.'

Catherine McCarthy looked bemused. 'You're not going to tell us that the Albanian yo-yo actually registered the security number?'

'It was registered, sergeant, but by the original owner.' Mundy consulted the notepad that lay open on the table. 'A Mr Darren Savage.'

'And was he?' asked Mowgley.

'Was he what, sir?'

'Savage?'

'Not really sir. He just appeared to be a little unhappy. He's a schoolteacher, working and living in Southampton.'

'Well, I suppose that's enough to make anyone a bit shirty. So how did you upset him?'

'I don't think he was too happy to hear he would be getting his phone back when Forensics are done with it, sir. He'd already bought a new and better one with the insurance money.'

'Tough chunky,' said DS McCarthy. 'So what was his story?'

'He said he left it in on a table in a pub while he went to the toilet and when he came back it had gone.'

Mowgley pursed his lips. 'And do we believe him? The insurance company clearly did.'

'I think so sir. He's got nothing against him and seemed genuine.'

DS McCarthy nodded, then asked: 'And he didn't see any suspicious-looking characters in the pub he could describe?'

'No, sergeant.'

'Have a heart,' said Mowgley. 'If it was a pub in Scummerville it would have been shoulder-to-shoulder with suspicious-looking characters.' He puffed out his cheeks and looked at his glass reflectively. 'I suppose we can assume Mr Savage did not take the photo, and that is was an identification guide to Mr Yo-Yo so he would know who to beat up at the crematorium. But who would want to have me roughed-up?'

DS McCarthy raised an eyebrow. 'Is that a serious question?'

Mowgley nodded. 'Fair play. I suppose the mystery will have to pertain for the while, then.' He turned back to DC Mundy. 'So is that it, then? Nothing further?'

'As you will know from the messages on your desk, sir, Superintendent Brand left several messages requiring you to report to him on your return from Spain, and DS Ross called several times earlier today.'

'Ah yes.' Mowgley exchanged looks with DS McCarthy. He was not too concerned about Brand's summons. He guessed it would be about his justification for the Spanish jaunt, and was confident he could use Jane Stanton and DCI Gentley to confirm the necessity of his presence for the briefing by the Guardia Civil. He was, though, feeling guilty about Karen Ross. He had not spoken to her since the discovery of Dave's body.

'Bland can wait, but I'll give Karen a call when we get back to the office.'

'Why not do it now?' asked DS McCarthy.

Mowgley made a show of patting his jacket pockets. 'It's gone missing again. I think I may have left it in Spain.'

Catherine McCarthy opened her handbag and dipped into it. 'You did, but I saw you.' She handed the inspector his phone. 'And it's fully charged for a change.'

'Oh, right-o.' Mowgley weighed the phone in his hand for a moment, then finished his pint and stood up. 'I need to go to test the new toilets and I'll give her a call from there. The signal's better.'

'No it's not. But just make sure you call - and not until after you've finished whatever you've got to do. I don't want to have to send poor Stephen fishing in the urinal again - no matter how clean and new it is.'

In the Gents, Mowgley did what he had to do, then selected DS Ross's name from the list Catherine McCarthy had inputted. He listened to the ringing tone for a moment, and was about to press the red button when she answered. He thought she sounded vague, her voice flat and listless.

Mowgley frowned. 'Are you alright, mate?'

'Yeah, why?'

'You sound a bit... woozy.'

'The doc's got me on a load of stuff to cheer me up.'

'It don't sound like it's working very well.'

'No.'

'Look, K...' Mowgley rubbed his chin with his free hand, then continued. 'I don't need to say how bad I feel about Hoppy. I meant to call you before I went to Spain, but- '

'It's alright Mog. I know. I only called because I need to see you.'

'Of course. I can fill you in on Spain and about...Dave, and...'

'No. I don't want to talk about Dave. It's about something else.' There was a brief silence, then: 'I didn't tell you everything when we met before. I've got some names for you.'

'Some names?'

'Yeah. Names and numbers.'

'You mean from Dave's contact list?'

'Yeah, a contact list, but this one was...off the record.'

'You mean snitches and stuff like that?'

Again the short silence, then 'Sort of. But mostly cops in other areas. And some Customs people he was doing unofficial business with. You know, the Spanish thing and that.'

'Ah.' Mowgley grimaced. Now he was beginning to understand. She had probably been more than just a spectator. But did she just want revenge for Dave's death, or to get out of jail free? He thought quickly, then said: 'So how do you want to handle this? What do you want me to do? Wouldn't it be best to take it to your boss?'

'No, I've had enough...and I don't want to be involved in it. It might come back and bite me. I met some of these people.'

Mowgley did not need to ask her why she did not send the names in anonymously. She wanted it to come from internally, and from him. As Hoppy's best friend, it would make a sort of sense that he would have been given or sent the list before the drug squad detective headed for Spain.

He thought quickly about the implications, then said: 'Okay, K, so you want me to pass it on?'

'I know you're mates with that SU woman. If you gave it to her and didn't say it came from me...'

'Okay. I know where you're coming from. Shall I come to you?'

'No. I'll meet you. How soon can you make it?'

'Straightaway if you want. Where?'

'You know the burger van on the Hill, where you and Dave

and me used to go sometimes after a night on the lash when even the Indians were shut?'

'Of course. How about half an hour? I need to get a car.'

'Okay. Half an hour.' He shook his head and looked at the phone. She sounded even worse than when they had begun the conversation. 'Okay. But are you sure you want to do this now? I can come to your place later.'

A final pause, and then her voice seemed to gain strength. 'No. For fuck's sake, just do what I fuckin' ask, will you? Dave was your best mate, wasn't he?'

twenty nine

Despite a driving technique and pace that infuriated other drivers, it took Mowgley less than twenty minutes to reach the crest of Portsdown Hill.

He had requisitioned Stephen Mundy's car and left him and DS McCarthy to walk back to the Fun Factory. When she had asked why he did not want her along, Mowgley had said it was something he had to do on his own. She knew he had been speaking to Karen Ross, and looked troubled when they parted outside the Ship Leopard.

Turning off the road, he left the car on a sloping area of tarmac in the corner of the car park, then returned to check he had put the hand brake on.

For a number of Portmuthians, Mick's Monster Burger Bar was an institution. It was common custom to visit the big red van when in the mood for a meaty challenge. Mowgley knew that some young men would take their girlfriends for an evening out at Mick's. It made a cheap date and the views across the city were great.

Patrons could choose from more than twenty varieties on a theme, and it was a rite of passage for many young males to take on the 1lb Jawbreaker or Gutbuster burger specials. They came adorned with eggs, bacon, sausage and mushrooms. Chips were also available for those who did not think the platter would be filling enough, or wanted to show off to their companions. In all, Mick's was a home-grown and thriving business of which it was generally agreed Pompey could be proud. It was also probably the only burger van in the county which took all major credit and debit cards.

Although lunch was only an hour old, Mowgley found the smell of frying onions irresistible. He limited himself to a hot dog and full garnish, and took it and his polystyrene cup of tea to one of the bench tables overlooking the city and, beyond the ribbon of the Solent Waters, the Isle of Wight. It was hardly Tennyson's dim, rich city, but Mowgley felt very much at home in Pompey.

He was taking his penultimate bite of the hot dog when a car drew up close to the table and a man got out of the passenger side. Mowgley did not recognise him, but the man clearly knew who he was looking for and made directly for the detective.

As Mowgley began to rise, the man held his hand out and asked: 'Jack Mowgley?'

The inspector could see no harm in nodding to confirm his identity, but did not take the proffered hand; instead he stood up and moved away from the table and the man.

He was of a height with Mowgley, but younger and slimmer. He was wearing a well-tailored black overcoat over what looked like a dark grey suit. The wearer was probably in his mid-thirties, and had a short, neat hairstyle with a side parting not unlike the one adopted by Dave Hopkirk. He looked very confident and as if he did not really care what Mowgley or anyone else thought of him. Mowgley had seen that look before.

The inspector maintained the distance between them and asked in level tones: 'What do you want?'

The man abandoned the attempted handshake but gave an easy smile before saying: 'DI Mick Jenner. I'm Dave Hopkirk's replacement.'

Mowgley continued to look unimpressed. 'So where's Karen?'

'She didn't feel up to it. I guess you know she's on compassionate leave and full of tabs. She phoned and asked me to make the meet and give you this-'

He reached into his overcoat and Mowgley instinctively took a small step away. The man noticed and the smile reappeared along with a sealed buff envelope. He held it out, but Mowgley made no move to take it, so the man laid it carefully on the table top.

They stood looking at each other, then Mowgley said: 'I don't suppose you've got your warrant card with you?'

The smile stayed in place as the man held his hand out

again, and again had it refused. He used it instead to pat his breast pocket, then said. 'I must have left it in the office.'

Still smiling but with no humour, the man turned and quickly walked to the car. He got in without looking at the detective again, and the car backed up, did a U-turn and left the car park.

Mowgley looked down at the packet, then reached for his phone.

DS McCarthy answered after one ring. 'Hello, you. How was the man and the dog you had to see?'

'Not sure. Can you check-out this licence plate?' He held up his left hand, made a fist and read out the letters and numbers written there.

'Okay. Got that. Anything else?'

'Yeah. Could you phone Drugs and ask if they've got a new DI called Jenner taking over from Dave Hopkirk.'

'Yup. Any special reason for your request that I should know about?'

'Nope. Just need to check something out.'

'Okay. I'll call back so just remember to keep your phone on. Where are you, by the way?'

'Mick's Burger Bar.'

'Surely even you can't be peckish this soon after lunch?' Without waiting for an answer, she asked: 'So what's next? Are you bringing Stephen's car back or have you pranged it already? Do you want me to come and pick you up or keep you company? What's afoot?'

'Don't know yet,' said Inspector Mowgley, looking thoughtfully at the envelope on the table. 'I'll keep the phone on, but I've got to go and see someone a bit rapid.'

'Not another man about a dog?'

'No, not another man, and not about a dog.'

*

DS McCarthy called before Mowgley reached the traffic lights at the bottom of the Hill. He picked the phone up from the passenger seat, where it lay on top of the buff envelope.

'Well?'

'Well, there is a DI Jenner taking over from Hoppy.'

'Did you get a description?'

'I didn't ask, but it wouldn't have been much good anyway.'
'Why's that?'
'Tracey Telephones said he's coming down from the Met - but not till next week. So what's to do?'
'Just curious, that's all. A bloke calling himself DI Jenner just gave me an envelope stuffed with money.'

*

Mowgley left the car on yellow lines and walked past the faded splendour of the Queen's Hotel.

Karen Ross's basement flat was in one of the roads leading from Southsea Common. This was a seaside stretch of ancient land where Richard the Lionheart and his fellow Crusaders had gathered before embarking en route to the Holy Land. More recently, the leaders of four great nations had met at the giant memorial overlooking the sea to mark the fiftieth anniversary of the ending of World War II and the part the city and its people had played in it.

The dwelling places facing the common were a mix of stolid Edwardian villas and tall, mid-Victorian terraced houses. They had once been home to well-to-do members of the city's bourgeoisie community. Now they were an awkward mix of swanky residences, desirable apartments, cheerful if not cheap B&B establishments and blocks of what the locals called Benefit bedsits.

DS Ross's garden flat was one of three apartments in the same building, each worth fifty times what the house would have cost to build when Edward VIII finally got his bottom onto the throne.

The bell in the middle of the front door worked, but earned no response. Through the heavy oak panelling, Mowgley could hear the rhythmic thudding of a bass beat. He bent down to the letter box and the volume of the music increased as he pushed open the flap. There was nothing to see and no reaction to his shout. The vertical blinds on the bay windows either side of the door were closed, and no answer came to his heavy knocking on the glass. He had called DS Ross's number as he walked down the basement steps, but it had rung only once before the answer phone cut in.

Mowgley considered the mock-Gothic door at the end of

the basement area. He knew it opened on to a passageway to the rear of the house and small courtyard.

After squeezing past a row of wheelie bins, he steadied himself and gave a heavy flat-footed kick at a spot just below the keyhole. The heavy door shuddered, then regained its composure as he fell backwards into the bins. He swore softly and repeatedly till the pain in his ankle receded, then stood up. After two attempts at shoulder-charging his way through, he adjusted his clothing and limped off towards the nearby shopping centre.

Half an hour later, and the edge of the one-inch wood chisel was beyond redemption. Mowgley had once watched an allegedly reformed burglar open a similarly mortice-locked door in less than a minute. The man had used a wafer- thin sheet of very springy silicate to follow the contours of the lock and push back the latch. It seemed frighteningly easy until Mowgley had tried his hand. But now and after his direct action, the door to the rear of the house lay open.

Keeping the hammer and chisel to hand, Mowgley entered the passageway to the yard.

After knocking on the kitchen door and windows, Mowgley was about to use the hammer and chisel again when he noticed that the heavy terracotta planter to one side of the door was at a slight angle. Reflecting on how police officers were usually even more sloppy than the general public when it came to home security, he tilted the planter further out of the horizontal and pulled out a plastic cash bag containing a key.

In the kitchen, he slipped the chisel into his coat pocket but kept hold of the hammer as he opened the door into the hallway. The insistent thump of the bass guitar led him to the living room, where he found and turned off the music centre. He listened to the silence for a moment, then walked across to the nearest door.

It opened to a bedroom which had become a home office. A work station of wood and grey metal stood against one wall, with a swivel chair in front of it. On the top level of the work station was a printing machine and a framed photograph of Dave Hopkirk. The work surface at waist level was bare except for a mouse pad and a laptop computer power lead. The other door leading off the sitting room opened on to a bigger bedroom. It was fully furnished and ready for occupation but had the unused air of a guest room.

He found the master bedroom off the passageway to the front door, and thought it was probably created from the original butler's pantry and private quarters. It was dark in the room, and as he did not want to disturb the blinds in the bay window he held the door to the passageway open with one of a pair of trainers lying beside the big double bed. In the gloom, he could see a line of light coming from beneath a door on the other side of the bed. He could also hear a faint trickling. Moving round the bed, he approached the door, then stopped as his shoes became reluctant to leave the carpet. Bending down, he felt the wetness. When he lifted his hand, he saw was that the tips of his fingers were tinged pink.

Standing up, he took a firmer grip on the hammer and opened the bathroom door.

thirty

In a grim echo of how Elizabeth Sidall had posed for the Millais painting, Karen Ross lay on her back in the bath, eyes and mouth slightly open. Coils of auburn hair framed her bone-white face as they floated in the pink water.

Also as in the painting, her hands were raised above the water level, palms upwards in the manner of a priest making a gesture of expiation.

Unlike those of Dante Rossetti's wife, DS Ross's wrists had been crudely opened. The deep cuts had obviously been made by the pair of bloodied kitchen scissors on the floor alongside the bath. At the foot of the bath, the brass mixer tap had been left running, and the red-tinged water was overflowing on to the white floor tiles.

In unseemly contrast to the scene, the bathroom was imbued with a fragrant odour. It was coming, Mowgley realised, from the row of stubby candles lined along a shelf between the edge of the bath and the tiled wall. They were all lit, and provided the only illumination in the room.

He stood looking down at the empty body and thought about death and how all Karen Ross and Dave Hopkirk had been and done was now gone as if it had never been.

Resisting the temptation to turn the tap off or touch the body in farewell, he backed away and closed the door on the fragrant, peaceful room.

*

At the top of the basement steps, Mowgley looked around then walked rapidly away from the house.

He had spent almost an hour searching the apartment

before remembering that the wheelie bin he had knocked over had contained a heavy, green garden sack. The bin had Karen Ross's apartment number daubed on its side, and the others were empty.

At the nearest telephone box, Mowgley put the sack holding the laptop on the floor before calling 999. Refusing the operator's repeated requests for his name and location, he passed on Karen Ross's address and used the words 'dead body' to ensure the information would be acted upon. Then he picked up the sack, walked back to the car and drove away, careless of the busy road.

*

'So, you're telling me that a total stranger approached you in a car park and gave you an envelope full of money?'

'That's about the size of it, sir.'

Mowgley had arrived at the Fun Factory to find two officers from the city crime squad waiting in his office. He could tell by the atmosphere that they had not come on a social call. It was also obvious they had not been made welcome.

DCI Moss had told him that his presence was required immediately by Superintendent Brand, and that they had come to see he got there. By their manner and address, Mowgley knew that Brand wanted to see him with regard to a more serious matter than his absence without leave in Spain. Or even the fight with a member of one of that country's law enforcement agencies.

Given that no more than ten minutes had elapsed since his treble nine call, it was unlikely that the summons was in connection with the death of Karen Ross. Even had the news got back to Brand, it was far too soon for the investigating officer to have checked out her recent phone calls.

When he had handed the envelope containing the money to one of the officers, Mowgley had reprimanded DS McCarthy for leaving police property in her car, given her the laptop, winked reassuringly and gone quietly.

'So, take me through this remarkable scenario again,' Brand spoke in an almost openly contemptuous tone. Mowgley knew that the superintendent had not forgotten any of the details, but was hoping that he would get his story wrong in the re-telling.

Mowgley cleared his throat and looked across at the bulky man sitting in the corner. The presence of the Police Federation Representative had confirmed the seriousness of the situation, and the man nodded as if in support before Mowgley repeated his version of recent events.

Before starting, he gave a smile to the uniformed woman officer sitting with her back to the wall behind Brand's desk. In a replay of his last appearance in this office, DI Geraldine Prosser was taking notes of the exchange; and also as with his last appearance, she would not meet his eye.

Looking at a point a foot above the head of the seated Brand, Mowgley began again: 'After a working lunch with two colleagues-'

'"A working lunch"- in a pub?' Brand sneered and shook his head, exchanging glances with the Chief Inspector who had escorted Mowgley to the Crime Squad building. It was clear that Brand liked to outnumber the opposition when on home ground. 'Alright, go on.'

'After a working lunch,' Mowgley repeated to further rile his inquisitor, 'I drove to a car park on Portsdown Hill to meet an informant.'

'Ah yes. This mysterious informant. Remind me again of his name and relevance.'

'It's Dave, sir. Dodgy Dave as he is known around the port. I only know his first name, and he's not in my contacts file or expenses claims because I only began using him a couple of weeks ago.'

It was thin stuff, Mowgley knew, but he could hardly tell the chief superintendent that his appointment had actually been with a drugs squad officer now laying dead in her bath.

'And what did you say was the purpose of the meeting with...Dodgy Dave?'

'It was to do with the pensioner who died of a heart attack at the ferry port last month and was found to be wearing a money belt containing a large amount of money.'

'Ah yes.' Brand looked down at some notes he had made during the first telling of the tale. 'That would be Mr Wheatcroft. Not making much progress there, are you? Even after your flit to Spain.'

'That's why I was meeting Dave, sir.' Mowgley spoke slowly

and deliberately as if explaining an obvious fact to a slow child.

Brand gave him a sharp look. 'Don't be insolent, inspector. Just tell me why this informant would know more about the case than you.'

'Dave works the ferry port...'

'"Works"?'

'He makes a living ducking and diving - bringing in and buying and selling tobacco and alcohol from Belgium and generally doing deals.'

Brand frowned. 'And you let him get away with illegal activities like that?'

'It's very low level stuff, and he is more use to me on the ground and passing on information about more serious criminality taking place in the port.'

'Hmm.' Brand grunted to indicate his reluctant acceptance of a common arrangement. 'So why would you meet him on top of Portsdown Hill? Fancy some fresh air, did you?'

Mowgley gave a half-sigh to show his contempt for the heaviness of the Superintendent's attempt at wit. 'We met on the Hill because (believe it or not, tosspot) Dave does not think it's a good idea to be seen chatting with the police officer in charge of the ferry port. Especially in a pub which is used by many port workers and other interested parties.'

Brand affected not to hear the sarcasm in Mowgley's voice. 'So there'll be a record of your phone call or calls to set the meeting up?' He spoke like a man delivering a killer blow, but Mowgley was ready. 'No, we made the arrangement in the toilets of the pub, sir.'

'How convenient. He just happened to be there, then?'

Mowgley gave another barely disguised sigh. 'No sir, He's a regular at the Ship Leopard. When he's got anything for me, he gives the signal and we meet in the Gents.'

Brand looked disappointed at the plausibility of the story. 'And what did he say while you were communing in the toilets? What was the content of his information?'

'He didn't say (for what should be very obvious reasons, numbnuts). It would be too risky for him. Again as I said, that's why we made the arrangement to meet at the car park.'

Superintendent Brand made no comment but again looked down at his notes. Mowgley suppressed the urge to run a hand over his brow or give a loud and genuine sigh. It was not a bad story, he thought, given the short time he had been given to concoct it. The officer investigating Karen's death would be asking him about their exchanges by phone, but he could explain them away by saying he was telling her about his findings in Spain with regard to Hoppy's death.

'Alright.' Brand looked up from the desk. 'Now tell me - us - about this fake policeman. He just arrived and gave you the envelope?'

'No, sir. As I said, he said he was DI Hopkirk's replacement and he had some information for me.'

'And didn't you wonder where this Dodgy Dave had got to and how the so-called DI Jenner knew where to find you?'

'Not really, sir. He said he had called my office and been told by DS McCarthy where I was meeting my informant. I suspect that Dodgy Dave turned up, saw me with someone else and did a runner.'

'So you had given the information about your meeting to your DS?'

'Of course, sir.' Mowgley spoke confidently, hoping he would have time to talk Catherine through the story before she was questioned. If not, he knew from experience she was a Class 'A' bluffer.

There was a moment's silence as Superintendent Brand shuffled through the selection of photographs spread out on his desk. They had arrived attached to an e-mail an hour earlier, and appeared to have been taken by a camera with a zoom lens. Although some were out of focus, the clearer ones showed Mowgley talking with the man in the Crombie overcoat. One showed the man laying the envelope on the bench table and another was taken as Mowgley picked it up. As he had been told, the e-mail address from which they had been sent had already proved untraceable, and the photograph of the man was being run through the system.

'So you have no idea who or why someone would bother to set you up for photographs of you apparently taking money from a stranger?'

'Not a clue sir,' said Mowgley mildly, '... unless of course it was somebody who thought you would be stupid enough to fall for such an obvious set-up.'

Brand had looked increasingly irritated as Mowgley trotted out the excuses he had invented in the car on the way to the

Crime Squad building. After the second tale-telling, he stood and looked across his desk and down at Mowgley, as if trying to use his height to intimidate the truth from the inspector. 'So you're claiming that whoever it was who went to all this trouble to try and incriminate you was trying to get you out of the way and off their backs?

'Erm, no sir. As I said, I don't know who it was or why they did it. We also don't know yet who took the photographs of myself and DS McCarthy in the phone of the man found hanging at Fort Widley.'

Brand had another stab at sarcastic wit. 'Yes. It does seem that you have a secret admirer or even a stalker, following you round just to capture candid snaps.'

'Actually sir, I'm okay about it, but I know that DS McCarthy has been extremely worried about being photographed and the possible reasons for the photographs being taken.'

A cloud passed over Brand's face and Mowgley knew he had scored a hit. Any appearance of unconcern about the safety of a woman officer could lose him points with his modernising and very PC female boss.

'I can understand that. The safety of our female officers is paramount'. Brand spoke hurriedly, glancing towards DI Prosser as if for approval. Then he continued: 'So you are of the opinion that it is this Michael Finlayson who is behind the killing of DI Hopkirk, and he is constructing some sort of plot against you? If what you have been saying is true, wouldn't it be simpler just to have you removed from the scene?'

There was an audible silence in the room, as both DI Prosser, the Federation Representative and DCI Moss looked at the Chief Superintendent in surprise.

Mowgley took the opportunity to look reproachful and almost shocked: 'Yes sir,' he said, 'that thought had occurred to me...'

thirty one

'I still can't believe it. It's just not the sort of thing Karen would do.'

Catherine McCarthy and DI Mowgley were in his office, looking at the laptop.

'I'm not going to argue with that,' said Mowgley, 'but that's what their friends nearly always say about people who kill themselves.'

It was a little more than 24 hours since Karen Ross's body had been found. The unit responding to Mowgley's call had arrived within nine minutes of the message being relayed through the control centre. The two officers had found their way into the apartment through the garden and kitchen doors, both of which Mowgley had deliberately left open.

Following procedure for an apparent suicide, a potential crime locus had immediately been established and protected. At the same time, one of the attending officers had called the situation in and set the procedure in motion to summon a police surgeon, a Scenes of Crime unit and a suitable CID officer.

Within an hour, Karen Ross's apartment was filled with people, and arrangements were being made to transfer her body to the hospital mortuary. When the investigating officer had realised whose body it was, he had contacted the drug squad. From there the information had been passed on to the duty officer at the crime squad building in Kingston Crescent. Superintendent Brand had been informed shortly after he had completed his interview with Inspector Mowgley.

Another hour on, and efforts were being made to locate and notify next-of-kin. At the same time, house-to-house enquiries were being made in the immediate area. So far, it seemed that the only possible witness to anything suspicious at the relevant place and time was an elderly widow living in the upper ground floor of a block facing Karen Ross's apartment.

It was, she told the young WPC who knocked at the door, her daily custom to sit in the bay window and watch the world go by. It was the only contact she had with the outside world except for when the health visitor, the cleaning lady and the nice woman from the Meals on Wheels arrived.

Mrs Dorothy Norcross said that she had seen a figure going down the basement steps earlier that day, then leaving after a short interval. He or a similar figure had returned a short time later, and then left again. The figure had reappeared, then emerged from the basement and walked up the road carrying a bag of some sort.

The problem with giving a clear description was that her distance glasses were at the opticians having a hinge repaired. All she could say was that the figure or figures appeared to be male because of their size and way of moving.

After further questioning, Mrs Norcross admitted that the activity she witnessed may have taken place at one of the basements on either side of number 29 or even further along the road. She could also have been mistaken as to the time or even day of the event. As she explained to the woman police constable, the figure might also have been one of the ghosts in period dress regularly passing down the road on their way to Southsea Common.

As expected, Mowgley had already been recalled to Superintendent Brand's office and asked to account for the nature of his recent telephone exchanges with her. As he pointed out, it was natural that she would want to know of any additional information he had uncovered relating to the death of her colleague and lover. He confirmed that he had spoken to her by mobile phone to this regard a number of times, but had not seen or met with her for some months. So far, it appeared that Brand reluctantly accepted Mowgley's story, but enquiries would obviously be ongoing.

'But what do you think?' asked DS McCarthy. 'Do you really believe Karen would do herself in because her long-time boyfriend had been killed?'

'No I don't.' Mowgley blew a cloud of smoke upwards and studied one of the foil darts festooning the ceiling and which appeared to be on the brink of coming unstuck. 'But if she had been in with Hoppy in all the bad stuff and thought it was going to come out, that could have tipped her over the edge. At least, I think that's what the Coroner will think.'

McCarthy looked steadily at him. 'But you haven't mentioned the other possibility, have you?'

'What other possibility?'

'That the suicide could have been staged, and she could have been killed by Finlayson.'

Mowgley frowned. 'Why would he do that?'

'Well, obviously because, if Karen was involved with Hoppy's dirty business, she would know where the bodies were buried, as it were.'

Mowgley examined the smouldering end of his roll-up and tossed it into the ashtray, from where DS McCarthy picked it up and stubbed it out. 'That's true, but to use your phrase, there is another possibility.'

'And what's that?'

'That she wasn't killed by Finlayson, but by one or more of Hoppy's fellow feeders at Finlayson's trough. That's why we need to get a look into that bloody computer.

*

By mid-afternoon it had been announced that the Inquest into the death of DS Karen Ross would open on the first day of the next week. Given the circumstances, it was possible that her body would lay unburied for several weeks.

This was because a funeral may not take place until a Certificate of Death has been released. An inquest may not begin until the Coroner has received the post mortem report, and the Registrar of Deaths cannot record a death until the Coroner has announced the verdict. In the case of Karen Ross, circumstances surrounding the discovery of her body suggested the inquest might be a lengthy one.

On the first day, the Coroner would receive written identification evidence and then adjourn the inquest to a later date. At resumption, general and expert witnesses would be called to help the Coroner and (if there were one) his jury to reach a decision. Juries are formed when the circumstances are not straightforward, and because of the broken outer door and the open kitchen door, this was the case with the circumstances surrounding the death of DS Ross.

As probably the last person to speak to her, Detective Inspector Mowgley would be making an appearance. He would not be appearing as a police officer, but as a 'person of proper interest'.

At the conclusion of any inquest and contrary to popular belief, the Coroner may bring in any one of a dozen verdicts. These include Death through Natural Causes, Accident or Misadventure, Unlawful Killing, Neglect or Suicide. There is also the option of an Open verdict, which is brought in when the Coroner believes that there is insufficient evidence to decide how the death came about. The verdict is given this name as the case will remain open until further material and conclusive evidence can be found and presented.

thirty two

In the hope of finding material evidence relating to the death of Karen Ross, Inspector Mowgley and Detective Sergeant McCarthy were on their way to an address on the outskirts of the city.

Here, between Fratton and North End, thousands of tiny and mostly identical houses lined a network of narrow, straight streets. To cope with the ever-more rapacious demands of the motor car, the City Council was in the process of establishing what had been called a co-ordinated series of restrictions to ease traffic flow and simplify the navigation of the streets. One-Way and No-Entry signs had sprouted on posts throughout the grid, and some restrictions had been enforced by simply blocking one end of a street off.

The ongoing programme had, most residents agreed, made the situation worse. Infrequent visitors and even long-term residents often became lost in the labyrinth, and it was said that a journey from one street to the next could now involve a detour of several miles. For these reasons, it took all DS McCarthy's skills to locate and find her way to number 36 Stanley Street.

The house was easily distinguishable from other homes in the street as it was by far the most decrepit and neglected. It was also the most colourful. The resident had painted the narrow, flat frontage a virulent red as far as he could reach by standing on a kitchen chair. As the resident was very tall, this brought the tidemark to just beneath the sill of the single first floor window. Above the wavy line, what remained of the cracked plaster had been left the same hue it had been painted eighty-seven years previously.

Another remarkable feature of the house was that both the

upper and lower windows were protected by heavy metal grills, and a sheet of steel obscured most of the wooden front door. It was not, as the rare visitors knew, that the residents had anything much of material value to protect. It was just that they were both extremely paranoid.

According to official records, the owner of the premises was one Roland James Jackson. To his customers and few friends, Mr Jackson went by the handle of Captcha.

As DS McCarthy had tried to explain to Inspector Mowgley, this was the name of a challenge-response test used to determine whether a visitor to a web site is human or an automated 'bot' trying to gain access for its master. Mowgley had stopped listening when DS McCarthy had reached the words 'web' and 'site' in near proximity, but he got the point.

Captcha was a gangling individual with a narrow forehead and a long, convex face and chin, hardly disturbed by small features. With the yellowish pallor brought about by a damaged liver, a life spent mostly indoors and a diet which remained untouched by any vegetable but chipped potatoes, his head from certain angles put Mowgley in mind of a banana.

His long-term partner Julie also had a computer-related sobriquet. Hers was Gigaflops, and as she was very short with a body-mass index in the high 30s, even Mowgley got the gag.

The couple were known to the inspector and his sergeant because of their occasional brushes with the law. Mowgley had once been instrumental in preventing their being charged with a minor drug possession offence, and they returned the favour when asked. The only conditions were that the work they did would not impact on fellow hackers and that they would be paid a fee sufficient to maintain their modest lifestyle.

There were internal agencies which specialised in solving computer-linked problems, but Mowgley and his team preferred the services of Captcha and Gigaflop. They were not only more discreet, but much better at what they did. There was also the point that Mowgley had not declared his possession of Karen Ross's laptop.

Had the pair been interested in material possessions, they could have sold their skills and sometimes dark arts to a major software-producing company for a small fortune. Had they used those skills for criminal gain, they could have acquired a very large fortune. But Captcha and Gigaflop were perfectly content in Stanley Street. As they said, there were three hamburger outlets, two kebab houses and five pubs within walking distance, and their supplier of cannabis sativa in its various forms lived just around the corner.

Apart from the occasional commission, the duo spent their days taking delight in breaking down firewalls, penetrating fortresses and visiting virtual places others could not reach. To them, the superhighway of communication was merely their setting-off point. They were generally not concerned with the level and potential value of the treasures held in the strongholds they broke into. They did what they did to prove they could.

After shouting through the letterbox and using the current combinations of knocks upon the door, Mowgley and McCarthy were admitted.

Inside, the house smelled of cats, skunk cannabis and blocked toilets. It would also have smelled of unwashed bodies and rotting food had the power of the first three not overwhelmed the less pungent odours.

Mowgley thought about tucking his trousers into his socks but reasoned there were probably so many experienced fleas on the premises they would not be deterred by such a simple preventative measure. The last time they had been to consult with Captcha, Mowgley had counted eleven cats either living at or visiting the house. That was not counting the dead one in the kitchen.

DS McCarthy was visibly relieved when Gigaflop said they could not offer their guests coffee as they had run out. The detectives followed their hosts into the tiny front room, which was pristine in comparison with elsewhere, and filled with electronic equipment which made it look to Mowgley like the bridge of the Starship Enterprise.

'Are you telling me you just want me to get into that?' Captcha looked at the laptop and then at Mowgley as if regarding someone who had asked him to do up their shoelaces. He was, as the detective knew, one of those people who thought anyone not having a similar level of competence in their field of interest to be stupid rather than simply unversed.

'It needs a user password for starters,' said DS McCarthy in a placatory manner, 'but there's probably more. I reckon what we're looking for won't be on show when you've got in. It may have been encrypted.' She turned to Mowgley, and explained: 'There may be documents and other stuff hidden behind what appears on the screen.'

Somewhat mollified by the prospect of a reasonable challenge, Captcha took the laptop, regarding the logo disparagingly. 'Do you mean just a simple triple DES, or something more interesting?'

'I don't know,' said DS McCarthy sweetly, 'that's why we've come to you, Catchie.'

Catherine McCarthy had spent over an hour trying to deduce the password with which Karen Ross had protected her laptop. Captcha found and keyed it in in less than four minutes. Unfortunately, DS McCarthy then asked him how he had done it. Captcha was also one of those people who like to demonstrate how clever they are even when they know you won't know what they are talking about.

After several minutes, Mowgley stepped back and did a passable impression of a traffic policeman stopping oncoming traffic.

'Do me a favour, mate. Can you just do it and not tell us how you did it?'

Looking bemused that anyone should not want to know the technical details, Captcha turned back to the laptop screen. As he did so, DS McCarthy opened and looked at her phone, then held it up towards the ceiling.

'That won't do any good, love,' said Gigaflop, 'there's no signal here.'

'That's strange, isn't it?' said DS McCarthy, 'a rotten signal right in the middle of the city...and how do you get on?'

'It's not a bad signal.' Captcha looked over his shoulder at her without his flashing fingers missing a beat. 'We put a virtual wall round the house and we've got the only door. You'll have to go outside and up the street a bit.'

'That must please the neighbours,' observed Mowgley as DS McCarthy left the room.

'They don't know it's us,' said Gigaflop unconcernedly. 'the woman next door has changed networks three times in the last month.'

*

'So who were you calling?'

They were on their way back to the Fun Factory. When he had cracked the code, Captcha had taken them swiftly through the folders and files on display. They were a typical selection of household bills, other domestic affairs and general correspondence. There was also a picture galley containing photographs of Karen Ross at various ages. One showed her standing stiffly to attention but unable to suppress a proud smile as she posed in her brand new uniform. Others showed her with Dave Hopkirk on holiday in various exotic locations.

Following his quick inspection, Captcha was of the opinion that if there were any hidden files they would take some finding, even by him. It could take an hour or even longer if the encrypter was any good.

Seeing that her superior officer was in a condition approaching terminal boredom, DS McCarthy had given Gigaflop a fifty pound note and said they would call later for a progress report.

Receiving no immediate answer, Mowgley repeated his question.

'Oh, just Iain,' said Catherine McCarthy in an attempt at unconcern. 'He said he'd be around from today.'

'Ah. I wondered why you were looking so starry-eyed. And did you tell him about the computer?'

She looked at him quizzically. 'I mentioned it; why?'

'No reason. Just asking.'

They sat in silence as DS McCarthy concentrated on escaping from the labyrinth, then she said. 'That's a point...'

'Is it?' said Mowgley, looking at where a youth was swaggering along the pavement with a dog wearing a heavily studded collar at his heels. 'I thought it was an American Pit Bull.'

Undeterred, DS McCarthy continued: 'I forgot to ask you about Karen's phone.'

'What about it?'

'Well, where is it? I would have thought you'd be interested in what was in it.'

'I would,' said Mowgley,' but it wasn't at the flat. Or if it was I didn't find it.'

'So that could prove someone had been in the place at the time she died?'

He nodded soberly. 'I reckon it could indeed.'

*

'Have you ever wondered how that pub got its name?'

'The Admiral Nelson? I should have thought that was a no-brainer.'

'No, dopey. Not that one. The Air Balloon.' DS McCarthy nodded towards the mock-Gothic monstrosity they were passing.

'Not really, it's just a name isn't it?'

'Far from it. I was reading on a local site the other day that they launched an air balloon from here in the 18th Century, with a bull in it.'

'Dare one ask why?'

'I suppose it was like that dog they sent into space. You know—'

'Laika.'

'Yes, funny how everyone your age remembers her name isn't it? Anyway, I suppose they thought it was too risky for a man, and sending the bull up seemed a good idea at the time.'

'Not to the bull I reckon. Do we know what happened to it?'

'No. But that's where Flying Bull Lane comes from. And the school of the same name.'

'Gedaway. In that case we'd better drop in and see if the landlord knows the history of his boozer.'

*

'I suppose this is where they would have put poor Karen a couple of hundred years ago.'

They had finally been allowed by the landlord to leave The Air Balloon. He had known about the origins of the name of his pub, and was also able to tell them it was built on the site of an ancient crossroads which would have lain outside the town in the 18th century. As he said, suicides and executed criminals were not permitted a final resting place on consecrated ground, and the tradition was to bury their bodies at crossroads.

One school of thought was that the cross was a gesture towards giving the dead a decent Christian burial.

Other historians said it was a tradition that a crossroads was chosen because the multiple choice of routes would confuse the shades of the departed, making it harder for them to find their way back to haunt the town where they had perished.

They had reached the car when Catherine McCarthy's mobile rang.

She answered, listened, and then said 'You have got to be fucking joking.'

It was so rare to hear her swear that Mowgley knew that the call was of some significance. He waited as she exchanged a few words and then snapped the phone lid shut.

'What is it - your bloke can't make it today?'

'No, that was Gigaflop.'

'What did she want - have they found some hidden stuff?'

'No. And they never will.'

'Why not?'

'The computer's been nicked. They went down the road for a kebab and to stock up on Mars bars and some fresh skunk with the fifty we gave them. When they got back the laptop was gone.'

Mowgley groaned. 'But that place is like Fort Knox. How could anyone have got through that steel-plated door?'

'They didn't. She said they always leave the back door open for the cats...'

thirty three

The old man smiled impishly, revealing gums untroubled by teeth or dentures.

Sitting back, he pushed his greasy flat cap on to the back of his head and used the other hand to knock over the row of dominoes lined up on the table in front of him.

Making a show of draining his pint pot, he slid it across the table at his opponent and wiped his mouth with the back of a hand in triumphant anticipation.

Mowgley smiled approvingly. Although he liked the familiar surroundings of his local, a rural hostelry made a pleasant change. Providing that the local toffery didn't look down their long noses at him for drinking cold, clear lager and not some flat, muddy concoction with a silly name.

A couple of candidates for squiredom stood at the bar, each wearing the inevitable uniform of Barbour jacket, green Wellington boots and flat cap. Their clothes were pristine, and the caps looked as out-of-place on them as the old man's looked right and proper. Even the way the pair lifted their elbows when taking a sip from their jugs of ale annoyed him. He would have had a big bet they had never got their hands properly dirty, worked in an office during the day and played at being countrified in the evenings and at weekends.

It had been raining, and a steaming spaniel lay contentedly on the flag floor, hogging the wood-burning stove. Dogs had it right, he reckoned, as long as they had the right master.

Inspector Mowgley looked at Iain Gentley and Catherine McCarthy and nodded at the bar. He lifted his narrow sleeved glass and inspected it for clarity in mockery of the Barbours, then asked in a loud, braying voice: 'How's your Parson's Fart, old boy?'

The object of his mockery decided not to notice, and his companions looked satisfactorily embarrassed.

At DCI Gentley's suggestion, they had come to a pub sufficiently far from Portsmouth to avoid the chance of running into anyone who might know them. 'The beer's very good, actually,' responded DCI Gentley, pretending ignorance of Mowgley's jibe at the two men at the bar, 'or are you only asking because it's my round again?'

'No, just making polite conversation until you decide to tell us why we're here.'

'I thought you liked doing business in pubs?'

'You know what I mean. Why all this cloak and dagger stuff?'

Gentley raised an eyebrow. 'Not exactly cloak and dagger. I just thought it might be a good idea to meet somewhere different and where we're not likely to be overheard.'

Catherine McCarthy looked around the busy bar. 'You say that as if you think someone might want to listen in?'

Gentley shrugged. 'I don't want to be overly dramatic, but given recent developments I can't help feeling someone's keeping an eye on us in Portsmouth.'

'Any ideas who...and why?' DS McCarthy asked.

Gentley frowned and shook his head. 'Not really, it's just a gut feeling. Don't forget about you starring on the Hanging Man's camera phone, and other mysterious events.'

'You mean like you popping up and befriending me and...' Mowgley did not finish the obvious sentence but instead looked at Catherine McCarthy and then back at Iain Gentley.

The DCI held up a large hand in protest. 'Steady on, mate, that's a bit below the belt. Sometimes things just happen. I'm not going to apologise for being bowled over by Catherine. Or even finding myself liking you in spite of all my instincts and my position and your reputation.'

Mowgley gave a wintry smile. 'Point taken. But do you mean we're being spied on by the mutual enemy or supposed friends and colleagues?'

Gentley shrugged. 'I honestly don't know.'

Mowgley thoughtfully fingered the spot where he had been shot by a fellow officer. 'On that note, what news of Jane Stanton and the combined operation to nail our local drug baron?'

'As I said on the phone, things are coming along with the forensic sweep of Finlayson's villa. Although someone had given it a fairly professional clean-up, they've still got plenty of prints and other stuff. And, of course, there's the film record. So far they reckon they've got the goods on no less a personage than the Mayor of Marbella and a number of his officials and pals. Then there's some senior police officers and very rich people who have got even richer by doing under-the-table stuff with the town hall. The word is that the Guardia Civil and the Intelligence Service are going to scoop up the lot in a big net and put them all on trial. We - and I mean the British part of the operation - are waiting until they've got the big Spanish fishes lined up before we use the evidence to move in on Mr Finlayson and Co.'

'What about the undercover guy who took the movies,' asked Catherine McCarthy. 'Did he turn up?'

'Yes, I'm afraid he did,' said Gentley. 'His head was sent in a box to the Teniente Coronel at Ronda HQ.'

'My God.'

'Yes. Whoever did it clearly wanted to send a message, but it may have backfired on them.'

'In what way?' Mowgley asked.

'Romero is now taking it very personally. I get the idea that he is a slow-burning type, but if you mess with his men, he won't give up till he's got you.' Gentley emptied his glass. 'The big news from our end is that there's been some interesting developments into the death of DI Hopkirk and that Andrew Wheatcroft is out of the game.'

Mowgley pushed his empty glass across the table. 'You mean Wheatcroft's been nabbed?'

'A bit more final than that,' said DCI Gentley, 'He's turned up dead.' He picked up the two pint glasses, stood and looked enquiringly at DS McCarthy: 'Ready for another?'

*

'So can you run that past me again just so I can get my head round it properly?' asked Mowgley. 'Andy Wheatcroft is probably definitely dead, and Dave Hopkirk may not be?

DCI Gentley made a 'maybe' rocking motion with his right hand. 'Well, there's not much doubt that Mr Wheatcroft has gone to his reward. Last week a goat keeper in the hills outside Marbella was minding his flock or whatever the collective noun for goats is when he smelled what he thought was a barbecue on the go. He went to investigate and found a burned-out Range Rover on its back in a gully about 20 metres below the nearest road. Inside the motor and still strapped in was a body. It was badly burned, but there's not much doubt it was Andy Wheatcroft. Even the Spanish forensics and pathology people couldn't cock this one up.'

Catherine McCarthy grimaced. 'So he was recognisable?'

Gentley nodded. 'Just about. The thing that held up identification for a while was that the car was on hire to someone using the name Michael Finn, and what was left of the passport in the glove box was in the same name.'

Mowgley reached for his tobacco pouch. 'Blimey. That's interesting isn't it? Was Wheatcroft having a dig at Finlayson or what?'

'I suspect we'll never know. But the body was Wheatcroft's for sure. Romero made sure they did a proper job on this one, and the dental and army DNA records tallied.'

'Any idea who did the dirty...or could it just have been a genuine accident?'

Gentley scratched the side of his face and looked perplexed. 'That's the rub. What we know for sure is that Wheatcroft deserted a week ago. He simply disappeared from his barracks, leaving no forwarding address.'

'So why wasn't I asked for help in case he came to see his mum?'

'Keep your shirt on, Mog,' said Iain Gentley mildly. 'The desertion was followed up by the same military guys you met in Brand's office. I don't think they wanted you involved or at least couldn't see that it was any of your business.'

'Charming. So what else do you know?'

'Obviously, Wheatcroft thought it a good idea to make himself scarce. But we don't know if he did so with or without Mickey Finn's connivance. Or even if he was on the run from his partner in crime.'

DS McCarthy frowned. 'It would be a bit silly to do a runner to Marbella if he was trying to keep out of Finlayson's way, wouldn't it?'

'Very much so. But he may, like DI Hopkirk, have been on a

flying visit to pick up a stash of money. Anyway, the upshot is we don't know if it was murder, and probably never will.'

Mowgley lit his roll-up and returned the lighter to DS McCarthy. 'Just supposing he was knocked-off, who's in the frame?'

Gentley shrugged. 'It would be quicker to list who isn't. It could have been Finlayson if they had fallen out big time. We know there was some friction between them as Wheatcroft was pushing for more and more of the action and the profits from the drug-running. Then there was his side of the business, which was supplying arms to the highest bidder.'

'I suppose,' asked DS McCarthy, 'that going into arms trafficking adds to the list of people who would like to see you dead?'

'Absolutely. It might be other people in the same game not wanting him muscling in. It might even have been some dissident IRA people who didn't like the idea of their former mates flogging off their undeclared and un-decommissioned stockpile. Just to further complicate matters, it could even have been our menacing-looking friend from the meeting in the Guardia Civil HQ at Marbella. It's a lot quicker and cheaper to simply knock someone off who's likely to be supplying Basque terrorists with some heavy firepower and explosives than do things the proper way. Of course, it might just be that Mr Wheatcroft's luck ran out when he blew a tyre or tried to take a corner too quickly.'

'Is there a definite cause of death yet?' Mowgley asked.

Gentley nodded. 'There is. With the smoke in his lungs and how he was obviously trying to get out of his safety belt and the door, it's pretty certain he burned to death.'

DS McCarthy shuddered. 'But I thought that the car bursting into flames after leaving the road and rolling down into a ravine only happened in movies?'

DCI Gentley shook his head. 'It's rare in real life, but can happen if a fuel line or the petrol tank ruptures and it's a hot day and the air mixes with the petrol fumes and is set off with a spark from a torn battery cable end. As I say, it's not exactly common, but it does happen.'

'But surely it would be much easier and sure to kill him some other way and disguise it as an accident?'

Gentley gave a shrug. 'True, but we don't know all the

circumstances. If it was murder, they could have stopped him on the road, pushed the car over with him inside then set fire to it at the bottom.'

It was Mowgley's turn to shudder. 'Urgh. Just imagine being trapped inside a motor and watching someone getting the matches out.'

'Quite. We'll know more when a really in-depth examination of the vehicle is done. But whatever the cause of his death, Andy Wheatcroft is just as dead.'

Mowgley grunted assent and thought how Wheatcroft's mother and sister must have taken the news. He drained his glass and put it on the table. 'But now, what about Hoppy? I thought the DNA and stuff had made it conclusive?'

'It should have done. Then someone made an anonymous call and said that big money had changed hands to fiddle with the evidence.'

'But how could they do that?' asked Catherine McCarthy.

'Quite easily. Someone would just have to give the right people some samples which would turn out to be DI Hopkirk's when they went to the test lab.'

Mowgley raised his eyebrows. 'By 'someone', I guess you mean Hoppy?'

'Probably, but not necessarily.'

'So you mean the anonymous call was phoney and it was Hoppy's remains, or the call was genuine and it wasn't Hoppy's body on the track?'

Gentley nodded. 'Something like that.' He reached for Mowgley's glass. 'As you should know, Inspector, real-life crime usually leaves more questions than answers.'

thirty four

'Remind me why we're doing this.'

Mowgley looked at DCI Gentley over the top of his glass and winked. 'Male bonding, lad. A few beers, a club and then a red-hot curry at the Midnight Tindaloo without a female around to get in the way.'

'Why would you say a female would get in the way?'

'You know.'

'Not really. Tell me.'

Mowgley shrugged. 'You have to think about what you're saying and if they're happy or not.' He paused, then shrugged again. 'You know what I mean. It just makes things...different.'

'Do you feel that way about Catherine?'

'Of course not; she's not like a woman, is she?'

DCI Gentley decided to pursue the subject would be fruitless and reached for his glass.

Mowgley had persuaded Gentley that he should accompany him on what he had called a boy's night out. He had used the term just to antagonise DS McCarthy. Surprisingly, she had not only agreed to but approved of the proposal, though neither Mowgley nor the Internal Affairs officer had yet worked out why.

'Anyway,' said Gentley, what I meant was why are we really doing this?'

Mowgley looked appraisingly at his companion, and smiled. 'No fooling you, is there, sunshine?'

Their attempted pub crawl in the heart of the city had not so far been a success. In the days when Portsmouth had more pubs than lampposts, it was said that no naval rating could survive the standing challenge of sinking a pint in each of the dozens of pubs lining the Old Commercial Road. All had tales told of them, and the names of the most infamous were known wherever in the world Royal Naval ratings met.

As the ships and men had been winnowed away since the war years, so had the Portsmouth pubs that served them.

In his varied pre-police career, Mowgley had worked briefly as a drayman for the local brewery. His job had been to deliver and replenish stocks of the deadly scrumpy cider which rotted cellar and bar floors and stomachs without compunction. He would take seventy, five-gallon tubs to the biggest ale house on the Commercial Road run on a Monday, then return each Friday with another fifty to see the customers through the weekend. At six old pence a pint, it was a very quick and very cheap way to get very drunk.

Nowadays students, stag and hen parties and general revellers visiting the city centre had more sophisticated tastes. They got just as drunk, but it cost them much more. And there was generally less mayhem than in the good old days when local youths and matelots fought pitched battles as part of a long-established tradition. Although it could get quite hairy at weekends, the pub route was much shorter and with fewer stops and was no longer known as Blood Alley.

Gentley watched idly as a young woman dressed as a nurse looked blearily at a giant dildo. It was covered in glitter dust and had just been presented to her by her hen night companions. Along the bar, a group of young men were calling for her to try it out. She regarded it and then them, then switched the device on and plunged it into her cocktail to a chorus of cheers and disappointed jeers.

'So,' said DCI Gentley, 'what's next in our tour of the city's more sophisticated haunts?'

'I thought we'd go clubbing. There's a lap top place around the corner.'

'I think you mean lap dancing. And are you serious?'

'Why not? With any luck we might meet the boss.'

Gentley regarded Mowgley thoughtfully. 'Why do I get the feeling that you have a not-so-hidden agenda? And what sort of trouble exactly are you trying to get me in to?'

Mowgley smiled encouragement at the girl with the dildo.

'Surely you know who owns Twirlers?'

'You know that my investigations will have revealed that the proprietor on paper is one Adi Gulshan, but the real owner is your and my bonny chum, Michael James Finlayson. So what?'

'I just fancied dropping in to say hello. After all these years, we've never met. And I'd like to at least establish a nodding acquaintance with a bloke who killed one of my oldest friends. Or perhaps did.'

'Are you kidding?' Gentley leaned forward and scrutinised Mowgley's face to see how serious he was, then answered his own question. 'No, you're not, are you? Quite apart from the eighty-two reasons I could come up with that being a very bad idea, what makes you think he'll be there now? He doesn't mind the door or serve drinks, does he?'

'Haven't you seen The Sopranos? It's his Bada Bing! club. He's there every Wednesday when he's in the country. He likes to summon all his minions and acolytes so he can play the Godfather. Remember why he works so hard to be the number one supplier in the South and spread fear and obedience along with the Class 'A' stuff. It's not about money, if it ever was. He has to be the centre of attention, the biggest fish in the biggest pond. That's why he's getting in to arms as well as dope.'

'Okay, okay, I get the point.' Gentley rubbed his chin and frowned. 'But what good is it going to do to go and stick your face into his? You don't really think he'll conveniently clock you so you can pull him for assaulting a police officer not in the execution of his duty, do you?'

'No. I just think it's time we met. Indulge me.'

Gentley did some more rubbing, then said: 'Ah. I see. As a senior officer and working with Jane Stanton on Operation Mickey Finn, I'll cover your arse with your boss if it comes out we stopped by to see him. It'll also be my arse if it goes wrong. Short of arresting you, I take it there's no way I can persuade you not to do this?'

'Nope.'

Gentley sighed. 'Okay, then I suppose I'd better come along to keep you out of trouble. Just promise me you won't start anything.'

'Moi?' said Mowgley, getting to his feet and holding a hand out. 'Time for one before we go?'

*

Like many social innovations, lap dancing clubs was a gift to Britain from the United States of America. The renaming and re-branding of thousands of tired and common-or-garden strip clubs started in 1999.

The only real change was that, in a lap dancing club, the performers could now get very close to the audience. Depending on local canons and club rules, the dancer and patron might even make tactile exchanges. After the dance, the customer would be expected to reward the dancer. In some clubs, the dancer and dancee might retire to a darkened booth somewhere on the premises to discuss the fine points of her (or sometimes his) performance.

Compared to many lap dancing clubs, though, Twirlers was almost a paragon of respectability. A team of highly-skilled door stewards ensured no likely causes of trouble gained admittance, and those inside made sure order was maintained.

Ironically, given the owner's main occupation, there was a zero tolerance policy to the presence or use of even technically legal drugs on the premises. Clearly, Finlayson did not want this insignificant part of his business empire causing any ripples. Twirlers was there for his amusement.

On his behalf, then, the management was very fussy about who entered and how they behaved. This policy made it an exclusive and so inevitably popular venue.

The club was situated down a narrow passage-way leading from the Old Commercial Road. The still-cobbled and dead-end street once held a variety of small warehouses, workshops and other commercial premises. Former sweatshops were now design studios or other centres of trendy endeavour, and a multi-storey car park occupied the site of a once-thriving corset factory. Although not generally known even by the leaseholders, most of the buildings on the street were owned by the proprietor of Twirlers.

Being a Wednesday, the entertainment was provided by male artists and only female members were admitted. Reflecting the changes in societal norms, this was the busiest night of the week and the one most likely to give problems to the door stewards. To a minor degree, trouble could be caused by men who were turned away. But the most violent behaviour generally came from those women deemed unsuitable for admittance.

DI Mowgley and DCI Gentley arrived to find themselves at the end of a mostly orderly queue of young, middle-aged and sometimes surprisingly mature women. All were in groups, and many were in hen-night regalia.

As Mowgley stared in fascination at a pensioner brandishing a riding crop and dressed in a basque and black stockings which did little to disguise her prominent varicose veins, one of the stewards left the entrance to the club and strolled towards them.

Standing in standard bouncer pose with ham-like hands folded across his crotch he looked down on the two men, smiled and said; 'Sorry gents, ladies only tonight. It's all male strippers, so not your scene...' he paused, then smirked. 'Well, probably not your scene.'

'That's a bit sexist of you, cocker. Have you never heard of the Gay Association of Police Officers?' Ignoring Gentley's warning look, Mowgley flashed his warrant card. 'Anyway, It's not the Wedgewoods we've come to see. We just want a word with the guv'nor.'

Looking much more unsure of himself, the man said 'Mr Gulshan is not in tonight-'

'It's the owner not the manager we want to see, son,' said Mowgley, putting his card away. 'I know he's in 'cos I saw one of you minions parking his motor as we arrived. You do know what 'minions' means, do you?'

A flash of anger crossed the man's blunt features, then he stepped back a pace, turned and walked back to the entrance. Leaning forward, he spoke to an even larger man who was wearing the sort of headset and miniature microphone favoured by pop stars on concert tours. The man put a finger to the right side of his head and spoke rapidly. He waited for a moment, then nodded. Looking towards the two detectives, he beckoned with a raised hand. Accompanied by a selection of coarse remarks and the odd wolf-whistle which Mowgley assumed must be aimed at his companion, the men walked past the queue and into the entrance.

*

It was the first lap dancing club Mowgley had been to, but it was more or less what he had expected. Twirlers was decorated and furnished loosely along the lines of the Union Jack bar in Marbella, and the music was even louder. For all Mowgley knew, one place might have inspired the other, and both might belong to Mickey Finn. Perhaps, thought Mowgley, Finlayson's bar in his big house on top of Portsdown Hill followed the chrome and black leather theme.

They were met at the top of the wide stairs by a large, tuxedo-wearing, shaven-headed man who could have been a brother to any of the three they had encountered at the entrance to the club. He waved a heavily-tattooed and be-ringed paw at a bar at the top of another set of stairs, then cleared a way for them across the packed dance floor.

Mowgley felt his forehead grow damp, and realised his unease was not so much in anticipation of meeting the drug lord of the city, but passing through a writhing mass of female bodies. It was strange, he thought, how women would dance as happily and with as much abandon with each other, but most males would not even consider taking to a dance floor with another man. Unless it was in an all-male pub or club, of course.

At the top of the stairs, the steward summoned a barman, then left to carve his way back to his station at the top of the main staircase.

'It's Chippendales, by the way.' Gentley reached for his Scotch and shouted above the wall of sound.

'Who is?' Mowgley shouted back.

'The male strip group. You said Wedgewoods.'

'Ah. Okay.'

Mowgley gave up trying to make conversation and walked over to lean on a rail overlooking the dance floor.

At least a hundred women were gyrating around a raised area from which three metal poles rose to the domed ceiling. Like the Union Jack bar in Marbella, the representation of the night sky was dotted with a host of twinkling lights. At the centre of the dome, a mirror ball reflected the beams of a dozen spotlights, each pulsing to the bass rhythm of the deafening music.

In alcoves ringing the dance floor, cowgirls sat alongside nurses and St Trinian schoolgirls, and one table was occupied by five Shirley Temples, with little-girl gingham check dresses, bunched plaits and giant lollipops. Amazingly to Mowgley, they all seemed to be talking animatedly despite the thunderous music. Perhaps, he thought, they had learned to lip-read after years of clubbing.

As he was thinking how strange it was that normal women could enjoy themselves so much without a man around, Mowgley felt a hand on his shoulder. He looked around to see another identikit steward.

After leaving the bar area and passing through a mostly unoccupied cluster of tables and chairs, the detectives arrived at a door guarded by another heavy in a dinner jacket. This one had a full head of hair, though it was cropped very short. Without any acknowledgement, he opened the door and ushered them through with a nod.

Almost as soon as the door closed, the pulsating sound stopped. After the noise, it was almost eerily quiet. They were in a lofty-ceilinged passageway with deep white carpet underfoot, and the starkly white walls were lined with a number of modernist paintings. Mowgley did not recognise any of them, but they had the look of being original and as expensive as they were childish.

At the end of the alleyway of paintings, yet another big man in a black suit waited to usher them through to what was probably the inner sanctum.

Although he had never seen Michael Finlayson in person, Mowgley knew what to expect. Had he stood up, Mowgley knew he would be an inch under six feet, and the latest information on record was that he weighed around 14 stones. According to his dossier he was in fairly good shape, despite his fondness for rich food, nicotine, alcohol and the high end of some of the products he traded in. He stayed in trim with the help a personal trainer and a comprehensively equipped gymnasium next to the covered swimming pool at his house on the hill. From other indications, it looked as if he stayed in shape for other reasons than vanity.

Unlike most of his security staff, Finlayson wore no visible tattoos or jewellery. He was prematurely balding, but made no attempt to conceal the loss of hair. What was left was combed back, leaving a patchy, moth-eaten widow's peak. He was clean-shaven, with a puffy face. There was a livid horizontal scar on his forehead, and his cheeks were pitted with the evidence of severe acne in his youth. His most prominent feature was his nose, which was large and lumpy, like a badly modelled piece of clay.

But for Mowgley, the most significant aspect of Mickey Finn's features were his eyes. They were not cold or dead as those of gangsters and psychopaths are supposed to be. In fact, they were full of movement. They were small and bright and in constant motion as their owner evaluated the changing situation and what was in it for him. They were the sort of eyes you saw in the face a school bully or anyone who would inflict fear and pain just because they could. But they were dangerous eyes. Mowgley had seen their like before, but thankfully rarely. It was as if the owner did not harbour any degree of the normal constraints of fear or compassion.

But for all his power, ill-gotten gains and pretentions to sophistication, to the detective Mickey Finn was still a cheap thug in an expensive suit.

The calculating eyes appraised Mowgley for a moment, then he said: 'I saw you looking at the Modrians. I've got more than the Tate.'

'Ah.' Mowgley glanced at the bank of monitors alongside the desk. 'Good for you. I wouldn't give 'em house room, myself. It's all bullshit, really I reckon. A con game for people with loads of money but fuck-all sense. And you'll find it's Mondrian, not Modrian. And if you think you've got more of 'em than the Tate, one of you has bought some knock-offs. Wonder who that's most likely to be?'

Finlayson did not speak, but his face flushed with anger. He fumbled with the coat on the back of his chair and took out a packet of American cigarettes. If he had known or cared anything about fashion, Mowgley would have recognised the jacket as being by Prada. At Finlayson's shoulder stood another member of his army of shaven-headed warriors, and he leaned forward with a lighter. Mowgley saw that the curved wall behind the desk appeared to be of smoked, one-way glass. Through it came no sound, but he could see the tops of the three chromium poles rising from the dance area. He wondered how often Finlayson stood at the glass wall and looked down at the people far below, and what he thought of them.

Finlayson took a long pull on his cigarette, then stubbed it out in a heavy onyx ashtray. Mowgley saw that his hand was shaking. Clearly, he was not used to being spoken to in the way the detective had chosen.

At his side, Gentley turned slightly and shot Mowgley a warning look. He knew what the detective was up to, but did not think it a good idea to push the gangster beyond the bounds of his self-control. He was not used to being spoken to in that way by anyone, including policemen.

Finlayson took a deep breath as if to master his rage, looked at Mowgley with his small glittering eyes, then said: 'So what the fuck do you want?'

'I just wanted to stop by and say hello while you were in town. Nice club, by the way. Suits your personality. And I wanted to tell you what a cunt you are.

My boss here came along to see fair play and that I didn't upset you too much. But he says you're a dinlow and a right wanker, to use a technical expression...'

Finlayson's face had become white. He stood up. With a shaking voice, he said 'I know who he is, and you're both a fuckin' pair of two bob losers. I've bought and sold a hundred fucking Old Bill cunts like you – and much higher up the fuckin' ladder.'

'Would you like to make a statement to that effect?' Gentley spoke in a soft, pleasant burr, as if he were asking Finlayson how he took his tea.

'I don't reckon he can write, do you?' said Mowgley in an even milder tone.

Finlayson looked as if he was about to lose control and abandon himself to a towering rage. The man at his side moved slightly forward as if to prevent him from coming round the desk to get at the detectives.

'Tell you what,' Finlayson said, obviously controlling his voice with some effort. 'I may not be too good with fuckin' painters' names or spellin', but I bring in more in a day than you two cunts make in a year between you. Now why don't you fuck off before I forget myself?'

'No problem', said Mowgley smoothly. 'I just wanted to say hello.'

As he turned away, he paused and looked back as if with an afterthought. 'Oh yeah. I hope your accountant is keeping your books a bit more carefully than when we last looked. I suppose you know he's had his hand in the pot and is getting very scared. That's what they got Al Capone for, you know. Tax evasion. Don't matter how many Spics you pay off, you just can't beat the taxman back home. Anyway, thanks for your time, Mickey. We'll catch you later.'

*

Outside on the pavement, two of the bouncers were busy with the hen night group from the pub. The bride-to-be was waving her spangled dildo in the face of the biggest steward while insisting she and her friends were sober and in good order.

Her argument was weakened by the obvious condition of one of the party, who was leaning against a nearby wall trying to stop a torrent of vomit landing on her glittery red shoes. Another squatted in a darkened doorway, watching a stream of urine run down the pavement into the gutter.

'Just another night in old Portsmouth Town,' observed Gentley. 'I might as well be in Glasgow.'

It began to rain, and they stepped back beneath the awning as a sleek black car drew up outside. It was, as Gentley had explained earlier, a Bentley Continental GT. Mowgley looked back up the stairs and saw Mike Finlayson had appeared through the double doors leading into the dance area.

Like a pop star, he was hemmed in by a gaggle of stewards, admirers and employees. Like Elvis, the star of the show was preparing to leave the building.

'Say goodnight, Gracie.' Seeing where Mowgley was looking and at whom, Gentley took a firm grip on his arm and started to hustle him across the street and away from a possible confrontation.

'Steady on, mate.' Mowgley disentangled himself, and turned to face the club entrance from the other side of the street. 'I just wanted to wave him off.'

'I think you've done enough to get his back up already. And what was that all about? Al Capone and tax evasion and criticising his art collection? I thought he was going to stick one on you.'

Mowgley shrugged. 'I think that's what his minder was there for. To keep his boss from going laitz and getting himself into trouble. I just wanted to stir the pot and leave him with something to think about.'

'You did that alright.'

The two men watched as Finlayson and his entourage came down the stairs.

Reaching the bottom step, he stopped and looked back up to where a steward was holding a mobile phone aloft. The rest of the group stayed where they were as Finlayson made his way back up the stairs. The driver of the Bentley re-started the engine, then got out of the car and moved towards the back door. The head steward held up a cautionary hand and moved towards the door. As he reached for the handle, Gentley again took hold of Mowgley's arm. 'Come on then, old feller, let's go for that curry. The show's over.'

But it was not.

As he allowed himself to be led across the street, Mowgley felt a giant hand at his back. It threw him forward on to his knees as the darkness of night became the brightest of days. A roar of angry gods rolled over him, then all sound disappeared. He lay, face down, in a world of silence and smoke and fire and bewilderment.

Something flopped on to the pavement, and he almost detachedly registered that it was an arm. The hand bore a large gold ring and a tattoo he had seen earlier. He looked at the arm for a while and thought about trying to get up, but decided he would be more comfortable staying where he was.

thirty five

It was a cold, clear morning with a promise of spring and new life.

Inspector Mowgley, DCI Gentley and DS McCarthy were sitting on a bench in the shadow of the cemetery chapel. A squirrel was regarding them mournfully from a branch of a nearby oak.

'That poor thing,' said McCarthy, 'we've got nothing for him.'

'Eh?' Mowgley cupped a hand to his right ear. 'What did you say? I wish you wouldn't mumble.'

'I said the squirrel looks really...' DS McCarthy stopped shouting when she saw Mowgley and Gentley smiling.

In the week since the explosion outside the night club, Mowgley's hearing had returned almost to normal. Apart from the constant buzzing in his ears, the only injuries he had suffered were a lump on the back of his head, a badly twisted right knee and terminal damage to his favourite overcoat and pair of trousers. The heels of his hands had also been grazed as he instinctively tried to prevent a collision between his face and the pavement.

DCI Gentley had been between Mowgley and the Bentley Continental, and taken more of the force of the burst of pressurised air generated by the explosion. He had suffered no loss of hearing but had a mass of shallow lacerations on his back, thought to be from glass fragments. He also had a gash on his forehead, the bruise around which was now an interesting hue of blue, yellow and purple. One of his eyes was closed, and his left ankle had been fractured by a flying piece of metal. His nose had also been broken when making contact with the back of Mowgley's head.

Although the two detectives had been lucky, the people in closer proximity to the car had not fared so well.

The driver was dead and the head steward had lost an arm, but had got off relatively lightly. He had been mostly shielded from the blast by the back door, which had directed the explosion directly towards the driver. The bride-to-be had lost both her legs below the knees and her friends had received a variety of non life-threatening injuries. A number of his acolytes had been hospitalised, but the intended target of the bomb had suffered not a scratch.

After taking the call at the top of the stairs, Michael Finlayson had been halfway down them when the head steward had opened the back door. This had triggered an explosion which was thought to have come from a shaped charge. More would be known after a complete examination of the wreck of the car.

As the explosives expert leading the investigation had told Mowgley, it would have been a waste of time wiring up the charge to the ignition in the way they always did in gangster movies. All that would have achieved would have been the blowing up of the driver when he went to pick up the car.

Whoever did the job was aware that Finlayson always sat in the back, and -because of where the car was always parked - that he would invariably enter through the nearside door.

The expert estimated that the charge and battery and wiring would have taken no more than half an hour to set in the privacy of the car park. But, as he said, car bombs were notoriously unreliable and ineffectual. They either did not go off, went off at the wrong time or for some other reason did not take care of the intended target. It was nearly always, he said, other people who got it in the neck.

The city police investigation into the incident was underway and the local media was working itself into a frenzy of speculation. Mowgley and Gentley had already been interviewed by several senior officers and asked what they had been doing in the proximity of Finlayson's lap dancing club at the time. Gentley's explanation that they had been working together with the Special Project Unit had been grudgingly accepted when confirmed by Superintendent Jane Stanton.

While getting their story straight, the two detectives had rightly assumed that Finlayson was not likely to divulge details of their meeting.

*

The interment of Karen Ross had taken place a little earlier, and her pitifully bewildered mother and father had been escorted back to Preston. The three detectives were sitting on the bench to rest Gentley's ankle after walking the short distance from the graveside.

The inquest had come to an end three days before, and the Coroner had, as expected, recorded an Open Verdict. In his summing-up, he had explained that the verdict did not mean he believed Karen Ross to have been murdered. It meant that too much doubt surrounded the circumstances of her death for him to record a verdict of Suicide. The Open verdict indicated that the evidence was inconclusive.

It could be that the young woman, deeply depressed by the death of her long-term partner, had decided to end her life. But the fact that her partner had been brutally murdered and involved in a major drug-smuggling operation was bound to give an extra dimension to the tragic event. Even the open kitchen door and the forced outer door could have completely opposing interpretations.

It could be that someone had gained entry and killed Ms Ross and made her death appear to be a suicide. Equally, it could be that Ms Ross had forgotten or mislaid her keys and forced the door to the yard herself. The fact that a hidden key had been used to open the back door could add weight to that possibility. A set of keys to the apartment were found hanging on a hook in the kitchen, but they could have been a spare set.

Then there was the evidence of the elderly lady living across the road. She was the only person to have noticed anything possibly significant happening in the road outside Ms Ross's apartment on the morning of her death. Mrs Norcross had said that she thought she saw two separate male figures entering and leaving the basement area at around or before the estimated time of death. But she had been without her spectacles, and also believed she regularly saw ghosts from the past using the road.

As to the forensic evidence, the pathologist had stated that, although she had lost a great deal of blood from the cuts to her wrists, Ms Ross had died from drowning. This was irrefutable as her lungs had contained water. Ms Ross must have drowned after her wrists were slashed by the pair of scissors found beneath the bath, or the heart would not have pumped out so much of her blood. This could indicate a passing into unconsciousness and Ms Ross's face slipping beneath the water. But it could also indicate that someone had cut her wrists and then forced her head beneath the water so she would drown. The killer could then leave with the surety that his victim was dead.

There were no marks on the body to suggest this had happened, but it had been demonstrated that the weakened woman could have been pushed beneath the surface by the top of her head, and if there were two assailants, one could have raised her feet, causing her face to sink below the surface. The position in which the body was found neither confirmed or rejected either of the theories. Ms Ross having drowned, her face could have become exposed by a partial floating action caused by the inflow of water, or the lowering of the water level as it overflowed. On that note, tests demonstrated that the capacity of the overflow system could be overcome by the rate of entry of water into the bathtub when both taps were turned fully on.

Another small but perhaps significant mystery the coroner had taken into account was the presence of a computer power lead and workstation, but no computer. Detective Sergeant Ross's mobile telephone was also missing. Then there was the question of who had made the anonymous call to the emergency services.

Because of all these uncertainties, he had concluded, he had no choice but to register an Open verdict. He finished by extending sympathies to the parents, relatives and colleagues of DS Ross, and hoping that the ongoing investigations would bring enough additional evidence to light to enable closure to be brought to the sad event.

'Would you say they're dead?' Mowgley nodded towards the rows of headstones.

DS McCarthy gave him a bemused look: 'I sincerely hope so. Did you know, in Victorian times some people used to have a bell put beside their graves with a rope going into the coffin so they could raise the alarm if they'd been buried alive, as it were?'

'No, I didn't mean that. What I mean is that we use the verb 'to be' when we talk about dead people.'

'So?'

Mowgley screwed up his face as if he were confusing himself. 'We say someone is dead. But if they no longer exist, they can't 'be' dead, can they? They can be no longer alive, but...'

To Catherine McCarthy's obvious relief, her phone interrupted her colleague's peroration. She flipped open the lid, punched a button, identified herself, listened for a moment and then handed the phone to her colleague. 'It's for you - your scary lady friend calling from Spain.'

Mowgley unconsciously ran a hand through his hair before putting the phone to his ear. 'Hello.'

'Hello you. Where are you?'

'On a bench in Milton cemetery.'

'Oh, of course. DS Ross. How did it go?'

'Same as funerals usually go. We pretended to listen to the preacher, then stood looking down a hole wondering what it's all about, and promising ourselves to make the most of what we have left and not get upset over small things. Now it's back to normal'

'So you're off to the wake?'

'Just a couple at the Leo I reckon. Mum and dad have gone. There's nothing laid on and as it didn't happen in the course of duty and there's no TV cameras, the big shots all kept away.'

'Sounds about right. Anyway, I've got some news that may well cheer you up.'

Mowgley frowned. 'Go on then.'

'As we speak, your mate Mickey Finn is sitting in a stuffy cell in Marbella.'

Mowgley looked up at the sky. 'There is a God. What did they get him for, non-payment of parking fines?'

'No, a bit better than that. He was nicked for the Spanish equivalent of GBH.'

'Blimey. Who was the recipient?'

'His book-keeper.'

'You don't say.'

'I do. All will be revealed, but it looks as if Finlayson got the idea that his accountant was stitching him up.'

'And was he?'

'We don't think so, but Finn clearly did for some reason. By the way, he sends his regards.'

'Oh? That's nice. I think.'

'Yes. I went to see him and he said to let you know he was looking forward to meeting you again when he gets back to the UK.'

Mowgley smiled a grim smile. 'Me too; I can't wait as long as he's on his own. Any other good news?'

'I think so. I've done here but got a few days left. Why don't you come over and buy me dinner? Don't panic - I've found a Brit pub that does Cornish pasties.'

'You certainly know how to tempt a man...'

They said their goodbyes and Mowgley handed the phone back to DS McCarthy, who asked. 'What did she want, apart from your body?'

'Tell you in the pub. After you've booked me a flight to Malaga.'

Mowgley stood and, together with DS McCarthy, helped Iain Gentley back to the car.

As his sergeant fired the engine, Mowgley looked across the rows of headstones to where they had watched Karen Ross's body committed to the earth. He saw that a figure, head bowed, was standing beside the mound of earth.

It was too far to make out many details and the man had his back towards the car, but he seemed to be around middle height with closely-cut hair. He was wearing a dark-coloured overcoat which stopped short of his knees. Even at this distance it was obvious that the man was very fussy about his appearance.

'What's up?'

Mowgley turned in his seat to find Catherine McCarthy looking at him with a quizzical smile. He returned the smile and shook his head and she turned back to the wheel. When he looked again at the graveside, the figure had gone.

'It's nothing,' he said. 'Just thought I saw someone I used to know.'

Epilogue

At time of writing there have been no charges laid in connection with the murders of Detective Inspector David Hopkirk, Colin Chapman (the man found drowned beneath South parade Pier) or Baksim Bushani (the Hanging Man). After the Coroner had considered the Spanish police report, a verdict of Accidental Death was brought in after the inquest into the death of Andrew Keir Wheatcroft.

The Open verdict brought in on the death of Detective Sergeant Karen Ross remains in place. The identity of the person or persons responsible for setting the car bomb which caused the death of Mikael Andrzejewski (the driver of Michael Finlayson's car) and claimed the limbs of the club steward and the hen night hostess remains unknown.

After two weeks in custody in Marbella, Michael Alexander Finlayson was charged with causing severe injuries to his Spanish accountant, Javier Miguel Allende. With charges pending concerning money laundering and drug-trafficking, there was outrage when the presiding judge granted Finlayson unconditional bail set at 50,000 Euros. Finlayson disappeared after leaving the courtroom and has not been seen since.

After long-term undercover investigations began in 2002, the unprecedented dissolution of Marbella council in 2006 was followed by the biggest corruption trial ever seen in Spain. Proceedings began in September 2010, and two former mayors and fifteen former town councillors were amongst the 95 people packed into the dock. Amongst them was the judge who had granted bail to Michael Finlayson.

Together with a number of other charges, the defendants stood accused of taking 670m Euros (£569m) in bribes and from municipal funds. Those in the dock also included a German aristocrat, a former football club chairman and other defendants accused of money laundering.

After a two-year hearing, 53 of the accused were found guilty. It took the judge more than forty minutes to read out the sentences, most of which were considerably shorter than demanded by the prosecution.

One man who escaped sentence was Jesus Gil, mayor of Marbella from 1991 to 2002. He faced numerous charges and was said to be at the heart of the culture of corruption. He thwarted justice by dying at the age of 71 before the trial began.

George East gained his early knowledge of police procedure and culture as a result of a number of arrests for violent behaviour in his very early youth. In the 1980s, he gained more of an understanding of and affection for plain clothes policemen while running an inner-city pub which acted as a local (and once as a murder room) for a whole police station's-worth of CID officers.

Deadly Tide

If you enjoyed Dead Money, here's a taste of the previous Inspector Mowgley novel:

The gunshot echoed flatly across the open waters.

With no more than a surprised grunt, the body rolled over and slipped beneath the surface, leaving only a spreading stain of red to mark its passing.

On shore, the man straightened up, took off his headphones and looked out to where a fishing boat chugged towards a reluctantly rising winter sun. He had heard that some of the local fishermen shot seals. There was a colony on the other side of the harbour entrance, and he had read that each one could eat up to ten percent of its body weight in fish every day. It didn't seem a lot, but an adult seal can weigh in at more than five hundred pounds. Whichever way you did the sums, that was a lot of fish. You couldn't blame the fishermen for protecting their livelihoods, but the animal rights brigade would be up in arms if they found out. He reached down and patted Alfie's head and thought how sentimental humans could be. It was fine for the boat's crew to catch and kill thousands of fish every day because people liked to eat them. But even quite logical people would be horrified at the idea of shooting an inedible - unless you were an Eskimo - seal.

The man put his headphones back on and started the next sweep. He had been over this stretch of the beach every day for the past week and this would be his last trawl. It was unlikely at this time of year that he would find any recently mislaid money or valuables, but more historic shallow-buried and detectable coins, jewellery and other items worth picking up might lie in wait. This was because they were constantly on the move as a result of heavy seas or even modest tidal changes. The incoming tide also brought small and non-floating objects lost at sea on to or towards the shore.

So far he had not won enough from sand, sea or stones to do more than cover the cost of his detector, petrol for journeys to and from the beach and the odd pint at the Legion. But he was convinced that some really good stuff was down there, and it would make all his efforts a waste of time if he chucked it in and stopped looking. He had been hunting on this beach and coastline for more than a decade, and, was convinced something really worthwhile was waiting for him. Of course, all beach combers and hunters thought that, or they would not do what they did in all weathers and times of day and tide. But it was true there were some very rich pickings for the lucky ones.

Finds along this part of the coast over the years included ancient coins and rings and other ornamental pieces which were sometimes made of gold. Once, a beach hunter had literally stumbled upon what had been reported as a priceless Celtic figurine. When it had been declared Treasure, the finder had made £49000, and something along those lines would do him nicely. If, or rather when it happened, he would buy a state-of-the-art machine and take a long break in some suitably exotic location where pirates had done their best business. The experts said that there never had been any such thing as buried treasure, but the odd mislaid doubloon or piece of booty would be quite enough to keep him going. Somewhere in the Caribbean would be nice, but until then, life was a beach on the rarely sunny and often shitty south coast.

The man half-smiled at his much-used pun, then frowned as a middle-aged woman walked past with her cocker spaniel on a lead. The annoying thing for any hunter was that most of the really good stuff was found by people walking their dogs or taking an early-morning stroll. But it was about time his luck changed, and the start of a new century was a very suitable time for him to strike gold. Or anything else worth a good few bob. He breathed deeply of the sharp air like a sportsman or warrior preparing for the fray, checked his settings and switched on the finder.

Almost immediately, a strong signal came through his headphones.

He took them off again, pulled the mini-trowel from his belt, sank to his knees and began to probe the shingle.

Unsurprisingly, his search turned up nothing more exciting

than a strip of metal foil and half a dozen ring-pulls. Beer or soft drink can ring-pulls were the most common cause of a signal, but if you discriminated against them, you were also discriminating what could be much more valuable items, including gold. He sighed, put the handful of junk into his gash bag so he would not find it again, and stood up. Perhaps now the tide was right he would try a bit of wet sand sounding. It looked really strange, but people did not understand that you could use a detector in water as long as it did not reach up to the box, and shallow waters could be the happiest of hunting grounds.

After lighting a cigarette and having a good cough, he was on his way down the beach when he saw something floating in the water. It was black and bulky and seemed about the right size, so at first he thought it was the body of the seal. Then he put on his distance glasses and felt his heart quicken. It was not a dead seal, but some sort of bag. Not a bin liner, but a proper bag. It was floating high on the gently moving surface, but showed no sign of coming in to shore.

He looked round to where Alfie was worrying a strand of seaweed encrusted with slipper limpets and whistled. When the brindle Staffie arrived at his side, he pointed at the bag, threw a stone at it and made encouraging noises. As he had suspected, Alfie regarded the bag coolly, then put his head on one side and looked at his master as if doubting his reason. Some dogs loved the water; others like Alfie did not. In fact he clearly thought it undignified to go chasing off anywhere after something uninteresting and inedible just because his master thought it was a good idea.

Keeping his eye on the bag, the man switched the detector off and laid it carefully down on the dry sand beyond the reach of the incoming tide. He thought for a moment about taking his shoes and socks off and rolling his trousers up, then saw that the bag appeared to be moving slowly away from the shore in spite of the tidal movement. Its height and square shape was probably giving it the properties of a sail, with the action of the wind helped by the slight undertow. So, without bothering about his state of dress he splashed into the shallows and made directly for the possibly rewarding piece of flotsam or jetsam.

As he got closer, his heart rate upped again and his heavy

breathing was caused by more than the effort of wading through the icy water. From this distance, he could see that it was no ordinary bag. It was black and roughly the shape and size of a small cricket bag, with large, looped handles. The top flap was secured by two strips of leather, their stylised brass ends held in place by an ostentatiously ornate brass padlock. The bag had a crocodile skin texture, and given its overall quality, he would bet it was real skin. He was no follower of fashion, but knew that this sort of giant handbag - if genuine - could cost a fortune. Also, people who owned bags like this one did not usually use them to keep their sandwiches in. If genuine and empty it could be the best find for many a month. If not empty, it might contain something worth even more than what it would make at the weekly boot sale.

He stopped, drew deeply on his roll-up, dropped it in the water and breathed deeply to try and calm his racing pulse. The reason his heart was trying to get out of his chest was that he had fantasised about a situation very like this for years. Some people dreamed of winning the lottery or having sex with a supermodel. He dreamed of being presented with a valuable gift from the gods of the sea. Apart from the excitement of the find, his increased heart rate and shortness of breath was also caused by the knowledge that he would soon have to make a decision about what to do with the bag and what might be inside it.

He was waist deep now and within arm's length of the prize. Reaching down and taking hold of the handles, he realised it was not empty, and that whatever was in it was quite heavy. Rather than try and heft it from the sea, he turned and waded back to the shore, towing the bag by one handle.

On the shore and completely unaware of the keen wind on his wet legs, the man pulled the bag from the sea and placed it on the sand. He looked for a moment at the small golden lock, then reached for his belt and the screwdriver he used to fine tune his detector.

*

A little more than a mile away, a yacht was heading for the shore on the other side of the harbour entrance. Enthusiasts would have recognised it as a Westerly Centaur, and real yachting anoraks would know it was a little over twenty-one feet in length and eight foot five inches in the beam. The Centaur was a popular and enduring model which had been designed and launched with a suitable fanfare at the 1969 London Boat Show, and this one had obviously been well looked after. The sails were furled neatly and it was running under the power of its MD2B 25HP Volvo diesel engine at a cruising rate of around five knots. In the cockpit, the large chromed wheel was unattended and moved slightly from side to side as the vessel came in at almost a right angle to the shoreline of the deserted beach.

The keel hit bottom as the water depth dropped to less than half a fathom, but the impetus of the boat and the continuing thrust of its propeller pushed it on for another yard before the Daydream juddered to a stop. It sat upright in the shallows for a few moments, then gently fell to one side. The engine laboured on for a few moments, then coughed and stalled, and the lapping of the small waves against the hull was the only sound breaking the calm of the day and place.

*

The padlock was obviously more for show than protection, and surrendered meekly to his screwdriver. Turning the swivel catch, he separated the strips of leather and lifted the flap. It was full light now, and he could see a layer of oblong, plastic-wrapped packages close to the top of the bag. The plastic was opaque, so he could not see what it was covering, but when he took one out, it seemed solid and quite heavy. He gently lifted another block out, and then another, and continued till there were nineteen packets ranged neatly on the sand. Their removal revealed another layer of packages. These were narrower than those in the top layer, and the shape and size was immediately familiar. The plastic was also fairly translucent, and what he saw through it caused him to sit down on the sand. He had never owned a Euro note, but he had seen them featured on the wall of his local post office since it had become a Bureau de Change as well as issuer of stamps and tax discs. The sandwich board outside showed a selection of notes, and one of them had the same type of number 50 that he could see through the plastic wrapping. At a very rough guess, there would be around a hundred more notes in the packet, and there was a whole layer of packets.

As he began removing them, he realised that Alfie seemed as interested as he was in the bag's contents. The dog had begun to scrabble at the side of the bag, and was making a low, primal keening sound his owner had not heard before. As he continued to empty the bag, the man became aware of faint but distinctive odour. He thought for a moment what it reminded him of, then remembered. His regular drinking partner at the working man's club was a butcher, and though apparently quite fastidious in his dress and matters of personal hygiene he gave off the same faint, almost sweet smell.

The odour grew stronger as he removed the last of the packets and the layer of plastic which he found beneath them. Alfie was now so anxious to get his nose into the bag that the man had to grab and hold his collar.

With what he accepted in the circumstances to be a completely unjustified sense of disappointment, he saw that there appeared to be no more money in the bag. All that remained was another plastic-wrapped package, this time almost as long as the bag and roughly oval in shape. He pulled it out and, holding it up clear of Alfie's frantic scrabbling, peeled off a length of brown duct tape.

As he did so, the sickly smell increased sharply and he instinctively turned his head away. Removing the final strips of tape, he opened the packet and saw what he was holding. Then he gasped, stumbled backwards and felt a rising warm tide in his throat as he dropped the object on to the sand.

Alfie showed no such signs of aversion, and with a somehow triumphant growl he opened his jaws wide, took a firm hold on his prize and scampered away up the beach. He was a mostly obedient dog, but nobody was going to deprive him of several pounds of bone sinew, muscle and slightly decaying but still fairly fresh meat.

*

As the log book would confirm, the triple-nine call from the beach hunter was made at 8.49 a.m. As per procedure, after being taken at Netley Control Room it was transferred to area control for Havant. The nearest patrol car to the beach was despatched on Priority One to locate the caller, detain him and tape off the immediate area of the beach where the bag had been found.

The nearest senior CID officer had been about to enjoy his first breakfast of the new century in the canteen at Cosham, but felt duty-bound to abandon it and was at the scene not long after the patrol car officers had cordoned off the beach at Sandy Point. The Scene of Crime Officers - a middle aged male officer and a younger female civilian specialist - had also come from Cosham, and the man was finishing a bacon sandwich as their car pulled up by the entrance to the narrow concrete strip which led up to the beach. In the next hour, the white-suited pair would carefully examine the bag and its contents, and take a number of photographs of the items where they lay. Using her dual abilities as a forensic officer and fashion-conscious woman, the female half of the SOCO team declared the bag to be a genuine Hermes Birkin Bag, almost new and valued new at around £6,000. Had it been the version with its handles studded with diamonds, she informed her bemused colleague, it would have been priced at around £30,000.

Regardless of its value, the bag would be labelled and packaged and sent for more detailed forensic examination at a central laboratory in Aldermaston. Before a sweep team was called in to conduct a fingertip search of the beach, the packets of banknotes and those containing an unknown substance would also be examined, photographed, tagged and bagged ready for despatch. The same treatment would be given to the human arm which Alfie had been persuaded to release, and the one still in the bag. Both would be taken with all speed to the Pathology laboratory at the Queen Alexandra hospital, some five miles and fourteen minutes away, with the driver of the patrol car relishing the opportunity for once to genuinely use his siren and flashing lights to good effect.

*

The woman parked on yellow lines and walked across the road towards an alleyway which ran alongside an Indian restaurant. All was quiet in spite of the advanced morning hour. It seemed, she thought, almost as if the city had woken up, taken a look at what the new Millennium had to offer, then decided to have a lie-in.

Sidestepping a brownish, lumpy pool of what could be curry sauce, vomit or worse, she shuddered slightly, pushed the unlocked back door open and walked up the stairs, her heels clacking on the uncovered staircase. One of the doors leading off the landing was ajar, and looking through she saw a young Asian man standing by the foot of a bed. He was naked, and their eyes met momentarily before she moved on. As she climbed the steep stairs to the attic, she reflected that he had not looked embarrassed, angry or lustful; rather, his expression had been apprehensive, even fearful. Perhaps, she thought, he was not supposed to be in the building, or perhaps not in the country.

The smell of curry farts, stale rolling tobacco and unwashed socks hit her as she opened the door to the attic room. The curtains on the small dormer window were open but the glass was so filthy that she could only just make out the mound on the bed. But she could hear a rhythmic creaking and panting, so coughed loudly.

"Happy New Year. If you're busy I can come back."

The creaking stopped abruptly and a bedside lamp was switched on, revealing a figure sitting up in bed with a blanket around its shoulders. Detective Inspector John Mowgley held a spoon in one hand, a large foil container in the other.

"It's alright, I was just trying to soften up this lamb bhoona. It's set solid."

Of all people, Sergeant Catherine McCarthy should know her immediate superior and long-time colleague's little ways, but she still winced when confronted with some of his grosser excesses and habits. He saw her expression and paused mid-spoonful. "What's up? Lots of people have breakfast in bed."

"Yes, but not cold curry."

"Are you not being a teeny-bit racist, Sergeant? Millions of people around the world eat curry for breakfast. Anyway, for some reason I was not in a state to eat it last night, and it would have been a waste and an insult to Bombay Billy to chuck it away. He left it on the stairs after closing as a New Year's present." Mowgley laid down the container, stretched, yawned, sucked thoughtfully on and then scratched himself with the spoon in an area thankfully hidden by the blanket, then asked in his best hopeful little boy manner: "Have you come to take me down the pub for a recovery session?"

"Maybe later if you're a good boy. I'm afraid I've come to take you to work. I did try to phone, but a strange man answered."

Mowgley ran a finger around the inside of the foil container, licked it clean, then nodded as he remembered. "Ah yes. That would be King Dong. We had a bet in the khazi at The Leopard and I lost."

Melons shook her head, reached into her handbag and took out Mowgley's phone. "I know, I stopped off at the docks to pick it up on the way here. You owe me twenty quid. I won't even ask what the bet was."

"Good Idea. Not to ask, I mean. Put the money on my account, will you, my good woman?" He reached out and took the phone, looking at it resentfully. "So why have you come to take me to work on a national holiday?"

"Crime never sleeps. They've found something nasty on the boat from St Malo."

"Well, it's a French boat, isn't it? What do you expect? Have they started putting snails and that tripe stuff on the menu again?"

"Not as far as I know. But I don't think Senora Maria Assumpta Sanchez expected to find what she did in the cabin she was about to clean."

"What, a couple having it away? Someone having a poo with the curtain not drawn?

"No, a man's body."

"Oh." Mowgley swung his legs over the side of the bed and got down on all fours to begin a finger tip search of the floor for his clothes. "Well, it happens, doesn't it? I read somewhere that a statistically inordinate number of men die of a heart attack when they're on holiday. Was he getting on a bit?"

"Don't know, there was no passport or any means of identification in the cabin."

Mowgley gave an unconcerned shrug. "So what? Surely a detective of your years and training can tell from a bloke's face roughly what age he is."

Melons reached down, picked up a sock and handed it to her boss. "Not if he doesn't have a face."

"You mean someone had bashed his face in?"

"No, like I said, he didn't have a face, or rather he didn't have a head. Nor any arms or legs."

Printed in Great Britain
by Amazon